The
Muted
Mermaid

The Muted Mermaid

By Del Staecker

CABLE PUBLISHING

Brule, Wisconsin

THE MUTED MERMAID

First Edition
Published by:

      Cable Publishing
      14090 E Keinenen Rd
      Brule, WI 54820
      Website: cablepublishing.com
      E-mail: nan@cablepublishing.com

ISBN 13: 978-0-9799494-6-3
ISBN 10: 0-9799494-6-7

Library of Congress Control Number: 2007940586

Printed in the United States of America

Dedication

For my GG

Acknowledgments

An honest writer will admit that books do not just appear out of the ether. After living in an Idaho cabin with the characters of *The Muted Mermaid*, I came back to "the real world" where I was assisted and befriended by some very wonderful people.

Friends such as: Pat Conroy, Clifton Meador, Lindy Litrides, John Seigenthaler, Nicholas Gage, George Mongon, Jill Muehrcke, Bob Schellman, Bill Byrd, Dale Kubler, Zandy McAllister, John Steiner, Tradd Staecker, Peter Congalton, Stella and Steve Litrides, Helen and Lou Nicozisis, and Wendy and Harry Karopoulos, took part in producing this book. Thank you!

Special thanks goes to Nan Wisherd, who opened her mail and ventured to swim with a mermaid.

Prologue

The sleeve of her new silk blouse snagged a limb, and she didn't care. She made no attempt to free the fabric from its captor.

She was dead.

On the riverbank, several yards above and upstream, two men watched her drift in the river.

"Damn! Now, she'll never sink," muttered the smaller of the two.

His large companion added, "This isn't good. Crap like this usually leads to just more crap."

"We've handled worse problems. This won't be any different."

"So you say! But explaining this won't be easy. Maybe it's time we gave up this kind of work."

Both men turned their backs on the river and retreated.

Downstream the woman and the tree limb traveled with the current, embraced by the river.

The lady had an appointment to keep.

Chapter 1

A sunlit hand slipped over the horizon and groped the water. Fog melted, the hand retreated, and morning began on a tranquil portion of Tennessee's Cumberland River where rolling hills formed a path to guide the river's northwest flow.

At the river's midpoint lay a random collection of trash. The discarded items numbered in the thousands and covered an area the size of a baseball diamond. Waterlogged wood, half-sunken plastic bags, and foam cups formed a colorful mosaic of postmodern life. The mat was centered on the anchor line and bow of the *Awfria*, an aging pleasure craft, home-ported in New Orleans.

The boat had anchored late the previous evening after the first day of its homeward voyage. The Cumberland River was the first leg of a route which would find the craft reversing its earlier journey from New Orleans and the Gulf of Mexico. The *Awfria* was currently headed for the Tennessee River and then on to the Tennessee-Tombigbee canal.

★ ★ ★ ★ ★

The morning sun's growing warmth evaporated the remaining mist to reveal the detail and character of the moored craft. Forty-two feet in length, made of Monel, mahogany, and stainless steel, it was a classic cruiser built in the late forties as a corporate party boat.

Below deck the *Awfria* was compact, but surprisingly comfortable. The forward cabin featured twin crew-type bunks and easy

access to the head and shower which separated the sleeping area from the large functional galley and dining area.

The galley spanned the entire beam of the boat and included a diner-like booth. In the galley's rear area a hatch led to the engine compartment below the salon.

Stairs, with three wide steps, led up to the spacious salon-lounge which offered views to the outside through two large windows and three portholes. Aft of the salon sat the oversized captain's cabin that had been redesigned by the current owner to serve as a combined office, library, and bedroom.

By current boating standards the *Awfria* was lacking, being slow and narrow of beam. The re-powering with twin 120-horsepower Lehman diesels mustered a top speed of only sixteen knots. With its wood hull, the *Awfria* was viewed as an insurance risk, not being considered totally safe in unprotected waters. However, it made no difference to its owner who carried no insurance of any form. His belief was that timid fools were sheltered by policies.

Around seven in the morning, tremors rippled through the floating mat as the boat rocked from the first daily movements of its inhabitant.

The repetitive to and fro increased in frequency and strength, matching the exercise routine performed below deck. When the workout ended, the tremors subsided. The water's calm returned.

The *Awfria's* sole inhabitant opened the main cabin's hatch and peered out to appraise the new day and let the sun evaporate his sweat.

Leaning on the port rail and peering forward, he focused on the

clustered trash. "Terrific!" he spat at the river. "All I need is to drift in front of a barge."

"They must have opened the locks last night," was the reply, followed by, "Jeez, I've got to stop talking to myself."

During the night a lock downriver at Cheatham Dam had been opened. The opening caused the usually placid river, actually an elongated lake, to kick up current and dislodge driftwood along its banks. One of the large pieces, a V-shaped limb, had hung up on the anchor line, stopping other debris and birthing the network that grew around the bow.

★ ★ ★ ★ ★

The size of the floating mat was one thing; its drag another. The accumulation had created enough pull to dislodge the anchor from the soft muddy river bottom. He estimated that the boat had drifted fifty yards from its safe anchorage and was now dangerously close to a channel frequented by barges. Fortunately, traffic was sparse.

He was disappointed. He was a careful man. Everything about him assured the world that he was in charge. It wasn't his appearance as much as it was his approach that defined him.

His looks were slightly above average. A little taller than most, but not imposing, he leaned toward a fair complexion wrapped around an athlete's frame. His eyes were "that color that changes" with the light, and his hair was long-ago blond. When he looked at you his eyes said, "You are the only thing I see," but you knew he saw more. He could see right through you to the edge of forever. Experience

had taught him to be careful. His demeanor attracted good things and good people. That's why he was careful; his goodness made him an attractive target for the not-so-good.

★ ★ ★ ★ ★

The anchorage had been carefully selected. The site, in a small channel behind an island, would have protected the boat from any barge wakes. The anchor had been set firmly.

"Goes to show," he said aloud, "I need to expect the..." He did not finish. His eye caught something amid the trash.

Grabbing the telescopic boat hook he moved forward along the port walkway.

At the bow he knelt on the deck, grasping the bow rail with his left hand, and reaffirmed his grip on the boat hook. He stretched out and pushed the nearest log. It bobbed, causing a Styrofoam cup to dislodge from the floating mass.

The cup drifted downstream.

In a graceful swinging motion, as if reaching for the cup, a hand appeared.

★ ★ ★ ★ ★

It was difficult to free the body from the trash. He poked and pushed. Eventually the tangled debris began to break up. Stubbornly each piece entered the current, yet the body steadfastly remained loyal to the V-shaped limb.

With consistent effort, he hooked the sleeve of a blue silk blouse. *I'm not getting wet for this chore*, he thought.

Slowly and with obvious care he walked aft. His silent visitor followed through the water on the port side.

Reaching the transom, he halted and wedged the handle of the boat hook under the rail, tugging it to be certain it was secure.

Grabbing a dock line, he flipped his wrists in what appeared to be an uncontrolled motion. It was a magician's illusion that brought a smile to his lips and a knot to the line. His father had taught him how to quickly tie a Flying Bowline. With the completed knot he traversed time and thought fondly of the past.

He closed his eyes with hope that the body would not be there when they opened.

"No such luck," he muttered with resignation, looping the line at the spot where the blue silk ended. He secured the line to a stern cleat and went below deck.

Coffee and help were required. Help first.

★ ★ ★ ★ ★

He made his way to the boat's helm. Since the boat was situated in a cell phone dead zone, he used the marine radio. Following a third attempt to raise the operator, he changed channels.

Maybe someone is monitoring the marina's channel, he thought.

"Stone Harbor. Stone Harbor. This is the pleasure craft *Awfria*."

The response came as he was about to speak again.

"*Awfria*, this is Stone Harbor. Go to six-eight."

He adjusted the radio to channel sixty-eight and responded, "*Awfria* on six-eight."

"This is Eddie, Mr. Trabue. I'm sorry I took so long to respond. Barges have been using the marina's usual channel. You're lucky I caught you. Why are you still in range? I'd expected you'd be long gone by now."

The call had been answered by the marina's owner; a young man with Hollywood looks—if you liked side-kicks.

"Eddie, I always call my friends when I find a corpse."

"Say again! Did I hear something about a corpse?"

"You got it," Trabue said. "I've been trying to raise the marine operator to alert the police."

Eddie responded with additional questions, sprinkled with commentary about the attentiveness of the operator on the early shift, and finished with an offer to call the police.

"Before you call, get a chart and check if I'm still in your county. No sense in calling the wrong..."Trabue halted. "Eddie, I'm about two hundred yards upriver from a burned-out house. Does that help?"

"Roger! I know the place. You're still in Davidson County. I'll call for help. You stay put!"

"I'm not going any place. Just tell whoever you raise to get here soon. I'll monitor channel six-eight. Out!"

Trabue hung up the mouthpiece and headed aft.

★ ★ ★ ★ ★

Forty-five minutes after his first call and following two more communications from Eddie, Trabue was informed that a launch was on its way.

Three cheers for the cavalry, was Trabue's thought.

★ ★ ★ ★ ★

A pair of turtles ended their morning bask and slipped into the water as a launch passed. The wake lapped over their perch and cooled the site. Peeking above the river's surface, they eyed the intruder.

The trespassing craft was a twenty-foot Boston Whaler with a forty-five horsepower outboard. The helmsman didn't notice the disrupted turtles.

Great, thought Cal Peters. *My one morning to sleep in and I get the morgue run! At least I am avoiding the weekly excuse session with her.*

Each Sunday, Marnie rose early and prepared to attend The Woodside Baptist Church while Cal played 'possum in their bedroom. This week's routine had just begun when the call came. Marnie was not pleased, yet she could not object. For Cal, the loss of opportunity to sleep in was softened by the thought of overtime pay.

But even the money wouldn't help with Marnie. She was Southern when it came to church.

During the week a man could pretty much do as he pleased. *Just as long as you make an appearance on Sunday morning, you get a pass*, Cal reflected.

It wasn't a religious thing, it was just a Southern fact. Going to

church was not just a moral act, but a Southern duty. "No church, no pass. That's the way it was, twenty-first century or not," he murmured aloud.

★ ★ ★ ★ ★

Cal's attention returned to the river as he neared the targeted spot ten miles downriver from Cleece's Ferry. It was twenty or more miles from downtown Nashville, where most of the local corpses began their trips. This one probably started there and was headed to the spillway at Cheatham Dam.

Something probably snagged it from the current, he thought.

As the Whaler approached the *Awfria*, Cal cut the throttle and drifted. He appreciatively eyed the pleasure craft, admiring its clean, uncluttered look.

Nice, he thought, *Some lucky son of a bitch...* He stopped mid-thought to watch Trabue moving about the deck.

"Your boat is State Fish and Game," were the first words Trabue tossed at Cal. Cal suppressed a flinch. He didn't know if it was meant as a statement, question, or rebuke.

"Yeah, well, I'm the nearest official and it is Sunday morning. No one likes to collect corpses any day, much less on Sunday mornings," Cal replied. "Anyway, for me it beats singing hymns."

Trabue laughed and said, "Perhaps a beer would help. Would you care for one?"

"A little early don't you think?"

"Normally, yes—but not when you consider why you're here."

Cal chuckled and said, "Alright, just don't tell my Mrs. She'd pitch a real mean one if she knew I was drinking on the Sabbath, especially while I was missing church."

"Like I said, at least you've got a solid excuse."

Trabue arched a cold can of beer toward the Whaler and watched Cal's quickness in grabbing the poorly-aimed toss. Cal was a natural athlete, with reflexes well beyond the challenge of Trabue's purposely errant toss.

Cal turned his focus to his assignment and said, "Let's take a look at what you found."

Trabue tossed him a line.

As the church truant secured his end to the Whaler's stern, Trabue tied his end to the *Awfria* amidships. Cal left appropriate slack on the line and pushed gently from the cruiser. Just as the smaller boat reached its furthest point away, Cal dropped a mushroom anchor from the bow. Pulling back on the first line, he brought the Whaler toward the larger craft.

"That should do for now," he said. "I'll set her better once I have a look at your visitor."

He grabbed the rail and in one clean motion pulled himself on board. Trabue was impressed.

On board, Cal's full stature and physical appearance became apparent. He was well over six feet tall, lean, and in top condition.

Trabue could not help but comment. "You're in good shape; not what I'd expect from State Fish and Game."

"Yeah, well, I'm trying not to get flabby by working out regularly. I've been on the river patrolling for three years and all I seem to

do is sit on my butt in that boat."

"Not much of a thrill."

Again, Cal did not know if the statement was just that, or a question. His interest in Trabue increased. It was part curiosity, but even more of his interest stemmed from envy. The *Awfria* was a real diversion from the usual style of craft that he saw.

What sort of guy owned and cruised this type boat? he wondered.

Cal responded to the question-answer. "Not many thrills. I usually just check registrations and fishing licenses. And some bodies."

"Bodies make for a growth industry," came from Trabue.

I don't know if that was a question or a statement, thought Cal. "About two a month," he replied. "Let's see today's."

Trabue motioned toward the stern.

Cal saw the line tied to the cleat and knew what he'd find at the other end. Or so he thought. As he peered over the rail, his surprise was evident to Trabue.

"Anything wrong?" asked Trabue.

"Nothing. It's just not your average bobber."

"Bobber?"

"Yeah, that's what we call them. You know—the winos, street people, derelicts—all the usual types you see in most urban areas. No one is overly concerned about them unless they're causing problems like pissing in doorways or puking on the street. Mostly they get drunk, overdose, or get beat up and end up in the river. They bob along until a fisherman snags one or a boater spots them. Bobbers. But this is no ordinary find. I'd better call for reinforcements."

Trabue thought, *A body was once a person. Finding any type would be disturbing.* He asked, "Are bobbers a particular problem?"

"No. Seldom a concern, but..." was Cal's reply.

"This is a dead spot for cell phones. Mind if I use your radio?" asked Cal. "I'll need to alert the powers that be. We've got what looks to be a respectable corpse here."

"Sure. Follow me." Trabue led Cal down the starboard walkway and opened the salon door. He entered and stepped toward the radio mounted on the salon's bulkhead near the captain's chair.

The spacious windows allowed ample light into the *Awfria's* salon. It was evident to Cal that Trabue ran a tight ship. Spartanly furnished, everything appeared to be in its proper place. Two chairs, a small settee, two lamps, a radio, and no television. Forward through the salon Cal could see part of the galley; also neat and tidy. Nothing appeared out of place.

Trabue handed Cal the radio's mouthpiece and said, "It's set on six-eight. I'll switch it to the marine operator." Trabue made the adjustments. "It's set."

Cal placed his call through the marine operator and was forwarded to the police dispatcher. Trabue wondered if Eddie was correct about the operator's peculiar work habits, or if he had been playing with Trabue earlier that morning.

"This is Cal Peters, State Fish and Game. I need to talk with the Metro Watch Commander."

"One moment," was the reply.

Several minutes later Cal was engaged in conversation with the Watch Commander, handling the delivery of bad news like a diplomat, not a game warden.

At the conclusion of the exchange, Trabue commented, "You've missed your calling, friend. I haven't seen such a performance in years."

"Yeah, well, I'm good because it's Sunday and I have to be on my toes or else Marnie, my wife, will have me singing in the choir."

Trabue laughed. The thought of this particular game warden singing in a choir amused him. He extended his hand and said, "The name's Trabue, Ledge Trabue."

Cal shook Trabue's hand. The grip was firm but not overpowering. Trabue was grateful that Cal was not the type to test his strength through a handshake. Before Cal could speak Trabue continued, "I caught your name while you made the call. I'm pleased to meet you, Cal. I'm glad you came to help. What's next? This is my first bobber."

"Well, based on what I've seen in the past, we'll have a three-ring circus here in less than an hour. She's a possible suicide, maybe even a homicide. She's in her early twenties, decent clothes, jewelry and watch still on. I'd say the medical examiner, the police, and several reporters are looking for their boat keys right now. You'd better decide what you're going to do."

"Going to do? What do you mean, I'd better decide?"

Cal explained what might occur.

"I think that you should get out of here fast. Your boat is by far the largest one available within miles. If you stay here it means that, like it or not, the police will set up shop in your salon."

"You mean they take over."

"You got it," Cal chuckled. "They'll drink your coffee and beer, eat whatever doesn't move, and clog up your head and holding tank, not to mention scuff-up, mark-up, and generally screw-up this nice tidy boat of yours."

"So what's your suggestion?"

"If it was me and my boat, I'd head for the nearest marina. Make your statement for the record and for any nosy reporters on your terms, preferably on the dock."

"Thanks! I'll do it, but what about you?"

"I'll have to wait for the medical examiner, or whoever he sends. They will photograph the body in the water and then I haul it on board and bag it. The detailed work takes place at the morgue. You know, fingerprints, autopsy."

"But this one is different?"

"Yeah, I hardly ever pick up a female, and never a respectable citizen; always derelicts and the like. That's why I said it will be a circus out here. Television news vultures will be all over this one. Very graphic footage will be on the evening news showing the body in the water, then being pulled out, and everything!"

Trabue could tell that Cal objected strongly to the low standards of local television news.

"We'll see it all. If it bleeds, it leads! Good thing she's still got some clothes on."

Abruptly, Cal exited to the port walkway and headed aft. Without comment he untied the line from the stern cleat and walked the body around the stern to the starboard side. Trabue followed, respecting an undeclared boundary that seemed natural when one man allowed another to perform such an unsavory task.

Cal spoke to the body of the unknown woman who had altered his Sunday routine. "What happened to you? You shouldn't be here.

No one like you should be here. You look like you were way too nice
to be dead."

★ ★ ★ ★ ★

The sun evaporated the mist, making the air light. A trace of
breeze eased its way across the deck from the northeast. The humid-
ity was decreasing and there were no clouds.

Trabue tuned his ears to the familiar song of the Lehman diesels.
In a minute they would be warm and ready to take him back to
Stone Harbor Marina. He wanted no part of the three-ring circus
predicted by Cal Peters.

After weighing anchor, the *Awfria* drifted downriver a short distance. Trabue sought to avoid creating a wake near the Boston
Whaler and its ghastly tow. At least that is what he told himself as he
drifted. Yet, he could not fool himself. He just wanted to get away.
Death was not frightening to him. He had seen it before and expected to see it again, but he wanted to distance himself from the
impending circus.

Easing the throttles forward, his craft slowly regained the distance
it had lost to the Whaler. Trabue waved good-bye and the game warden responded in kind. The *Awfria* pushed upriver toward Nashville,
and Trabue wondered if he would ever see Cal Peters again. A hundred yards later, Trabue looked back. Peters had reclined in his boat's
bow to nap, gently rocking to the small wake created by the *Awfria*.
The wake also produced a second, more eerie, effect. Trabue saw the
gentle back-and-forth movement of a hand. Like a mute mermaid,

caught and tied to its captor's vessel, the dead woman waved to Trabue as if beseeching his help.

Chapter 2

Stone Harbor Marina was perfectly named. How it earned its label was a local legend.

Years back, Sy Chambers, the owner of Stone Harbor Marina, had inherited a rock quarry along the banks of the Cumberland River. For most of his working life, Sy labored in the quarry making a modest living. He rose early, worked long, hard hours, and created a reputation based on his diligence and honesty.

Sy's business acumen was limited, yet hard work and honesty served to successfully make ends meet. Sy could have gone on forever in the quarry, and would have, if only the rock had not run out.

His hope was that miraculously he could continue to quarry the high quality product that had been available for years. But as Sy expanded his digging, things only got worse. Gravelly, cracked, and only suitable for road beds and driveways, the rock could not support his needs.

Sy took to drink and would have lost all had Will Daniels not carried that cat into the quarry. God bless that cat!

★ ★ ★ ★ ★

Late one evening, Sy was well into his second bottle of whiskey when Will arrived at the quarry's combination office and tool shop. Will carried a third bottle and a sack. The bottle was nearly empty and contained only a few swigs. The sack was full of cat—a scrawny, gray cat.

Will approached the rear door, knowing Sy would be perched in his usual spot. From his favorite chair, drunk or sober, Sy loved to watch the river flowing past.

Over the years the office had been relocated many times and seemed to hop around the quarry in pursuit of Sy's digging. On this particular night the office was located on a spot it had occupied for more than six months on the north rim of the quarry, about twenty yards from the edge of the bluff overlooking the river. Sy had stopped work not far from that spot and it was assumed the office would move no more. Sy was drunk most of the time and the rock was just too poor.

If his quarry days were over, Sy could still drink and gaze at the river. He saw no alternative. The rock had worn him out. Now, Sy lived only for the two things he loved—drinking and watching.

"Hello, Sy," called a voice approaching the office.

Will Daniels spoke fairly well under the influence. It was walking and other physical movements that failed him when he imbibed.

"Hey, Will. Come sit a spell," answered Sy. "You're just in time."

"Time for what?" responded the wobbly visitor.

"Don't know. But, I'm drunk enough to..." Sy never finished.

As Will neared the small raised porch his well-known lack of coordination caused him to stumble and miss the porch's single step. He fell forward, catapulting his bottle and sack toward his seated friend.

The bottle fell to the porch after grazing Sy's right shoulder. The sack, with its animated contents, landed in Sy's lap.

The frightened animal reacted as a member of its species could

be expected. It clutched the nearest object and clawed for dear life.

With frenzied claws attached to his crotch, Sy also reacted as expected.

"Damn!" Sy howled as he jumped, danced, and swatted at the cat—scaring it even more and causing it to dig its claws deeper into his flesh.

Sy's gyrations became more frantic and bizarre. His screaming was high-pitched, loud, and peppered with language that reflected his pain.

During Sy's dance, Will recovered from his tumble and stood up directly in front of Sy. They collided, and the cat was knocked loose.

The cat, upon relinquishing its grip on Sy's privates, scurried for the bluff's edge.

"I'll get that damn cat if it's the last thing I do!" Sy shouted in outrage as he sprang after the terrified animal.

Primed with close to two quarts of whiskey, Sy was a madman on a mission. Pushing through shrubs and undergrowth he pursued the cat, vigorously swearing and shouting.

Near the bluff's crest, the cat found refuge in a rock crevice only a few inches wide. The terrified animal burrowed in, seeking safety.

Plowing through the vegetation, Sy had caught a glimpse of the cat as it entered its sanctuary.

"Good," yelled Sy, "I've gotcha!"

The crevice was barely large enough for the cat to enter. However, just beyond the entrance was a slightly wider chamber that tapered again to a small continuing crack in the stone formation running along the river's bank. Without hesitation Sy reached in to grab the frightened feline.

Again, the cat instinctively clawed in defense.

Sy howled, "Damn you! You son of a bitch cat! I'll fry your hide for this!" He continued to bellow. "Scratch me? Scratch me?" he went on. "Will! Will! Get your butt over here," he yelled toward the office. "And bring a flashlight."

Several minutes later Will stumbled through the undergrowth, flashlight in hand.

"Now stay here and don't let that cat get out of the hole and run away," ordered Sy. It was good that Sy was drunk. He could not really feel or actually comprehend his wounds and Will preferred not to mention the blood-stained crotch and mauled hand being waved about.

Sy disappeared toward the office, muttering and swearing as he went. Will collapsed near the cat's sanctuary to guard as best he could.

Within five minutes Sy returned. Laden with fuses, black powder, and several sticks of dynamite, he was determined to obtain revenge—even if his actions were beyond all reason.

"Here, hold this!" he ordered Daniels as he shoved the dynamite forward.

"What?"

Will wasn't too drunk to be frightened.

"I said, hold this, dammit!"

Sy reached into his right pocket, extracting a pint bottle of whiskey. He took one long, enormous swig, emptying the bottle and tossing it to the ground.

"Whew! That's the ticket. Now, let's fix a cat!"

He proceeded to pack the crevice with all the explosives.

"There's room for more!" he exclaimed with glee. He made a second trip to the office for additional dynamite. Ten minutes later he lit the fuse for the largest charge ever set in the quarry.

The explosion was tremendous. The scrawny gray cat surrendered all nine lives at once when it was vaporized.

★ ★ ★ ★ ★

Will Daniels was hurled over the bluff's ledge flying more than forty feet into the river. Sy Chambers was tossed in a different direction, landing some yardage from where he lit the fuse.

"Will! Will!" Sy called through the debris-choked air.

Had Will responded, Sy could not have heard through the ringing in his ears from the blast.

Will's focus was devoted to staying afloat in the Cumberland River. He drifted downstream toward Cleece's Ferry where he was picked out of the river by the captain of the ferryboat *Judge Hickman*.

Residents of the greater Nashville community were startled when the immediate shock wave shattered glass and rocked china from shelves. Geologists on duty at Memphis State University, over one-hundred-and-eighty miles to the west, were monitoring the New Madrid fault for earthquake activity and were certain that the next "big one" had occurred.

Sy's dazed attempts to locate Will proved fruitless. The overwhelming and constant ringing in his ears distracted him, making him unable to formulate a search plan. He could only manage to return to the office where several tons of earth, vegetation, and rock had landed, making the structure barely recognizable. After ten minutes of burrowing through debris, Sy admitted defeat and halted his search for a lantern or flashlight. Exhausted and still drunk, he passed out with his back against a tree. He slept until morning when a search party located him.

It has been said that things appear different in the new day's light. How true of the stone quarry. Sy's first thought when he came to was that he had been moved to a new and strangely different location. All he saw was water.

The cat's hiding place was no longer there. The inside of the crevice had been shaped like a large inverted Y with its fork approximately ten feet beneath the point where the cat entered. The twin branches of the Y extended twenty or more feet each, ending below the river's surface.

Rather than creating a standard crater, the explosion had opened a three-foot-wide channel between the river and the quarry. During Sy's alcohol-induced slumber the river had filled the quarry, and as the saying goes, "the rest was history." Word spread fast about the perfect new lagoon.

★ ★ ★ ★ ★

Trabue radioed Stone Harbor Marina one mile downriver from the site of the infamous explosion. Eddie Chambers, grandson of Sy, Dock Master, and current owner of the marina, responded promptly. He directed Trabue to switch to a working channel for instructions and conversation.

"I knew you'd be back. I knew it!" Eddie said to Trabue.

"I didn't. I intended to be at Barkley Lodge Marina by now. I guess a day's delay won't cause me too much trouble."

"Don't plan to be out of here tomorrow. Even if you finish with the police and reports, you'll want to stay awhile."

"Why?"

"Bad weather is coming in tonight. Looks like heavy rain—low pressure with plenty of moisture and wind, too. You won't want to be up in your flybridge traveling any time soon."

"Fine, Eddie, you win. I'll stay 'til the weather clears, but only if you've got a good slip."

"No problem. Same one as before?"

"Sounds perfect, I've got the harbor's entrance in sight and I'll see you in a couple of minutes. I'll stay on channel six-eight. Out!"

Trabue slowed the *Awfria* and headed toward the entrance channel to Stone Harbor Marina.

★ ★ ★ ★ ★

Eddie Chambers watched as the *Awfria* entered the mouth of Daniels' Passage. Grandpa Sy Chambers had named the channel in honor of his loyal friend and had even convinced a long-forgotten bureaucrat with the Army Corps of Engineers to officially label it as such on the Corps' maps.

Eddie delighted in the details concerning the marina's origin and establishment of Stone Harbor Marina. The story always took him back to his childhood growing up around the marina. Grandpa Sy and Will were long gone, but their spirits were vibrantly alive whenever Eddie told listeners about the night of the explosion.

As a youngster Eddie had heard the tale on numerous occasions, both from his grandfather and from Will Daniels. Will and Grandpa Sy would sit on the dock and take turns recalling the various details of their foolish behavior and good fortune. Both of them recognized how close they had been to joining that hapless cat on a trip to the hereafter.

Since the cat's remains were never located, a legend grew concerning the missing feline. Each time a cat's howl was heard anywhere near the marina, people wondered, "Had the cat escaped?" And, although both men continued to enjoy the occasional nip, neither of the pair was ever again observed to be intoxicated. Sy's return to sobriety and hard work converted the flooded quarry into the region's finest harbor. As word spread along the river, the new marina's business steadily grew. The story made it a favorite destination for boat bums, romantics, and cat lovers.

Some boats docked for only a night or two. Others would put in the harbor intending the same but for a variety of reasons, would remain longer. For a time they would join with the twenty or so regulars that filled Eddie's world.

Eddie sensed Trabue would be one of those who stayed more than just briefly. There was something about Trabue that made Eddie wish for it to happen. Now they could resume their easy conversations and regular chess games. While in residence, the *Awfria's* owner had taken Eddie's mind off the things that troubled him so greatly.

Eddie was glad that Trabue had returned.

Chapter 3

Trabue secured the *Awfria* in its familiar slip.

"You missed all the action," Eddie informed Trabue. "The news people were real entertaining."

"Tell me about it. The yahoos looked like a floating disaster headed down river when they came past me. I'm glad they weren't aware of my role in this," Trabue replied.

"They paid Bob Cranston to take all of them in his boat. There were way too many, for an eighteen-footer. Bob wasn't thrilled at the thought of riding with 'em, but the cash they tossed around convinced him."

"I'd pay cash if he'd send a few over the side," said Trabue.

"Some of their equipment already went overboard," Eddie added with a laugh. "A camera and a bag of electronics went off the dock in all the confusion. Channel Six is going to pay a diver two hundred dollars to fish it out. The reporter was pissed. She and the camera man had to scratch the trip."

"You mean they were going to put more people on that boat?" asked Trabue.

"Yeah, crazy fools." Eddie replied.

"Well, I hope they satisfy the morbid curiosity of their viewers. I've seen firsthand what they're headed to film and if I owned a TV, I'd prefer not to watch a dead woman floating in the river. Eddie, do me a favor. I'm going to stretch my legs. If anyone from the police or medical examiner's office asks for me, tell them I'll be around the dock this evening. In the meantime, you don't know where I am.

Can you do that for me?"

"No problem. See you later?"

"I'll be back in a couple of hours."

Trabue headed toward the parking lot, passing boats he recognized from his month-long stay at Stone Harbor Marina. He waved or said hello to each of the owners as they prepared for Sunday boating while socializing along the dock. He did not linger or pause to engage in the dockside banter that was so much a part of the life on the water.

* * * * *

When Trabue returned to the dock he immediately knew the man was waiting for him.

Dressed in a suit and wearing hard-soled shoes, the man was not prepared for the docks. He had to be a cop, and a young one at that.

"Mr. Trabue?" asked the man. Not waiting for a reply he continued, "I'm Officer, no, Detective, Detective Evans, Detective Joel Evans."

"You got a badge?"

The detective's reaction was startled and confused, exposing his lack of confidence.

"Yes, yes I've got one. Here." He reached into his coat pocket and flashed his police badge. It was a regular patrolman's badge.

"Very impressive, Evans. With practice you'll be able to scare kids and senior citizens with the best of them. But why the blue-suit shield? Are you only allowed to play detective on Sundays?"

"Sorry, I'm a Detective—well, I will be. I mean, sorry, I'm..."

"Hold on, hold on. Relax and try to say it slowly." Trabue sensed the embarrassment and anxiety in the young man's voice and no longer saw a point in being difficult.

"I'm officially a detective tomorrow, but the call today put me on duty for the river suicide. I get my detective shield and ID tomorrow, so I pulled my badge off my uniform. I hope you don't mind, I'm..."

"First," Trabue interrupted, "don't say you're sorry unless you've screwed up. Second, I'm impressed you were smart enough to think of taking your patrol badge along. Cops rarely impress me, but maybe there's hope for you. Just relax. What do you need to know?"

"Well, most of it is routine information. For the reports, you know. I need to verify facts." The rookie detective extracted a notebook from his pocket. "Your name?"

"Trabue. Rutledge Campbell Trabue."

"Rutledge? That's a peculiar one. I've never run across a first name like that before."

"Well, I've had it all my life." Trabue was beginning to reverse his appraisal of the detective's intelligence, wanting to conclude the interview. "What does the uniqueness of my name have to do with anything?"

"Didn't you find her? Your name's basic info and it is different and..."

"Then let's get on with the rest of the questions."

"Fine. Your permanent residence?"

"You're standing next to it. The *Awfria*, home port is New

Orleans." Trabue answered.

"You live on the boat?"

"That's what I said." Trabue was annoyed. Evans was proving to be typical, green, and rookie-flavored. Maybe well-intentioned, but slow on the uptake.

"What's your more permanent address? I mean, where do you get your mail?"

"I get it on the boat. I arrange for mail drops along my way."

"Must be difficult."

"Not if you plan for it. If you need a fixed address, use The Colonnade Hotel, Flower Court, New Orleans. That's in Louisiana."

"A hotel?"

"I own it. What else did you want to know?"

"Any telephone number where we can reach you?"

"None. I find it difficult to keep my phone plugged in while I'm cruising. Especially when I cover a hundred or more miles in a day." Trabue's annoyance was obvious. "I often travel where cell phones are useless."

"I'm sorry Mr. Trabue, but the forms?"

"Screw the forms, Evans. Use your head. I live on a boat. Boats move," Trabue added, "and stop apologizing."

"Fine. We'll skip the routine 'Witness Profile Information' and go to your statement."

"Great, let's do that."

"At what time did you find Miss Blaine?"

"Blaine? I wasn't aware of her identity this morning. But it was approximately 7 a.m. when I found the body."

"And where exactly was that?"

"Exactly? I don't know. Approximately, however, it was one hundred yards down river from Chapman's Island, toward the north side of the main channel." Evans was hurriedly writing to keep up with Trabue. "The anchor line was caught in a log jam and I had drifted downstream from where I was anchored the night before." Trabue had eased into describing himself and the *Awfria* as one. "I must have snagged the body during the night with the river trash and logs."

"Is that all?"

"Look, Evans, I was on my way to Land Between the Lakes National Recreation Area. I woke up and found a body. I called in the report and that's it. That's the end of my involvement."

"All right, if you'd just sign the report statement, I'll file it tomorrow morning and that should be the end of it. We appreciate your cooperation and..."

"Cut the speech, Detective," Trabue interrupted. He reached for the report and pen and signed. "I'm glad I could help launch your career. And thanks for not asking a lot of stupid questions about Katrina."

"Hey, you are close, but her name was Karen, Karen Blaine, not Katrina."

"Forget it for now. You'll figure it out later. Maybe."

Evans remained silent.

Trabue waited.

"Oh, oh, yeah! Katrina—the storm. I get it!"

Trabue returned the pen and report to Evans. But before the rookie detective could respond, Trabue had stepped on board the

Awfria, clearly signaling to Evans the end of their exchange. Evans shrugged his shoulders, watching Trabue as he entered the *Awfria's* salon.

Odd duck, Evans thought. *He's an odd duck, with an odd name.*

★ ★ ★ ★ ★

Trabue felt the uninvited stranger's weight shift on the deck and became angry. Boarding a boat without permission was tantamount to breaking-and-entering. Yet, Trabue's curiosity subdued his anger.

Anyone who could stand in the rain for hours watching was worth meeting. Eddie had been correct about the weather. A low pressure front had moved across the region bringing heavy rain, making Monday an inside day. Trabue had spent the first half of the day reading and listening to music in the master's cabin.

Just before noon, Trabue had *that feeling*. It was a non-focused uneasiness pricking the hairs of his neck. He disliked that feeling but had learned to respect its warning. He felt someone was watching, focusing their attention upon him. He looked out and noticed the stranger standing in a recessed spot in the parking lot and watching the *Awfria*. Trabue made no effort to disclose his presence on board. So the observer had remained for three hours, not realizing he was also being observed. Not moving, just watching, Trabue was impressed by the man's tenacity.

Finally Trabue's curiosity prevailed and he made his presence known. The silent observer, convinced that the rocking movement of the craft meant it was occupied, had moved to the dock and stepped

lightly on the deck. He moved toward the salon's port door.

Trabue slid forward to the crew's cabin and unlatched the hatch to the deck. As the intruder opened the salon door and entered, Trabue pulled himself up through the hatch to the deck. The rain made the deck slippery but Trabue was sure-footed as he moved to the still-open port doorway. Entering behind the intruder he said, "Don't move!"

The intruder, ignoring the command, whirled and pointed an automatic at Trabue.

The face showed determination and that its owner was prepared to shoot, but the target had vanished. Trabue was gone.

The intruder moved to the salon's doorway. Left, then right, he looked to find the direction Trabue had moved on deck. Both the forward and aft walk-ways were clear. As he started to move, the intruder was struck from above.

Trabue leapt to the deck from his perch along the flybridge, a heavy flashlight in his grip. He pounced, ready to strike again if required. There was no need.

★ ★ ★ ★ ★

Winton Blaine was unable to touch the lump on the back of his head. His hands were securely tied behind his back with quarter-inch nylon rope. The pain traveling down his neck was as intense as his nausea. He vomited down his chest and into his lap.

"Careful, Pal! Keep it off the carpet, or it's swim-time for you."

Trabue was seated across from his visitor. Blaine made out

Trabue's image through watering eyes. He spit at his captor.

"Easy I said! I'm in no mood to put up with any crap."

"Go fuck yourself!"

"Really. The attempt would be interesting! But not as much fun as bouncing this flashlight off your head."

"Go ahead, you bastard. It'll take more than that to stop me getting even!"

Trabue laughed. It shocked Blaine. The laugh's quality was odd, as if Trabue were both amused and tired.

Trabue laughed again, adding, "Why all the hostility, pal? I was hoping we'd be able to talk. I thought, 'Ledge, you know this guy is persistent, really persistent. First, he stands in the rain for hours. Then he moves in when he's absolutely certain I'm on board. He's definitely interested in a meeting. So. Guess what? He pulls a gun and tries a really cheesy move. All this after he comes on board without an invitation.' Now, you know the saying 'Can we talk?' It goes like this. I ask a question. You answer. Got it?"

Trabue moved closer and revealed the flashlight. Blaine knew that resistance was futile and did not relish a second meeting with the contents of his captor's hand.

"Your move," Blaine said.

"Let's start with a real easy one. Like, what's your name?"

"Blaine, Winton Blaine. My friends call me Win. You can call me Mister Blaine."

"Funny, real funny, Blaine. Now let's try something a little more complex. Like, what in hell do you think you are doing here? Other than puking on yourself and being a generally shitty visitor, you

haven't shown me much."

"I came to check on you. Check you out. Verify you're the one. Then get you for what you did."

"Check me out? Why? Did? Did, what?"

"You were the last one with Karen."

"The bobber?"

"Karen! Karen Blaine was my daughter, you asshole! You found her yesterday and I had to check you out. I don't believe in coincidences!"

"Whoa, Blaine, that's a bit rich. Just because I found your daughter, it doesn't give you the right to spy on me or to come on my boat carrying a gun!"

"You own the boat and the cops said you were an oddball, so I made my move. I wasn't going to let them bumble their way through this. You must be involved. Responsible."

"What's my owning a boat got to do with anything?"

Trabue ignored the reference to his oddity. He'd heard it before.

"Karen told me she had a friend, somebody who owned a boat. She was found in the water and I thought the boat was a connection. It's all I had to go on." His voice revealed his pain and desperation.

"So you think I did it, based on that?"

"The cops think they have it all figured out and it's over as far as they're concerned. They say my daughter killed herself. I don't believe it. Karen wouldn't, couldn't commit suicide. She was killed. You, your boat, it's..." Blaine could not go on. His eyes welled with tears and he sobbed as only a tormented father could sob.

Trabue saw the depth of the man's grief. It was a painful sight.

"Okay now, Blaine." Trabue reached down into the galley, bringing forth a bottle. He liberally poured Jura scotch into a ceramic mug and moved toward Blaine, "Easy, it's going to get better. This stuff will help."

Blaine could not move. Like a frightened animal, frozen before the final moment of life, he sat looking straight ahead. Trabue tilted Blaine's head and placed the cup to his lips, forcing him to sip.

"Thanks," he said. "Thank you, I'm sorry I..."

"Don't," said Trabue. "Your emotions are in charge. No need to apologize. I've been there. Your grief is your excuse."

Trabue leaned over, revealing a knife. One silent move cut Blaine's bonds.

"The head is aft and to your right. Go clean yourself up. We'll talk more when you're finished."

Blaine obeyed.

★ ★ ★ ★ ★

They sat across from one another in the galley. Blaine hugged his mug while he talked and Trabue listened.

"She was a great kid. A really wonderful girl. The kind everyone wants to have as their own." Blaine's voice was full of pride.

"Her mother died when she was seven. We were close, real close. I spent twenty-six years in the army and whenever I could, I came home or had her with me. My mother did the rest. Karen spent the school year in Jamesville with her grandmother and the holidays and summers with me. That is, when she could. I mean, when I could let

35

her. The two years I was in the Mid-East she couldn't visit. But other than that time, she came to stay with me. She was always a really good daughter, really great."

Trabue appraised the intruder-turned guest. Blaine was tall, trim, and had the tell-tale look of an ex-soldier. A real soldier. Trabue was glad that he had been able to surprise Blaine earlier. On even terms, it could have been messy.

"I joined the army when I was seventeen. I had more spunk than brains. I loved it. I never regretted the decision to join. After the Mid-East, I left the Airborne because of my leg. I unwillingly became a home to some cheap Iraqi metal and couldn't stay jump-qualified. I did my last eight years as an MP. Karen called me 'Super Cop' just to tease me. I did the usual MP stuff, nothing special. Two years ago I retired to run a rod and gun shop in Jamesville, Tennessee. It was my retirement dream. That shop and Karen were my dreams. And now she's gone."

"Go on, tell me more about Karen."

"Like I said, she was really a special kid. She was smart, kind, never a problem. She graduated with honors, top of her class at Jamesville High. She received a scholarship to Vanderbilt University. After her first year she moved off campus and began working while she continued in school. She graduated with honors, again. For the past couple of years she's been working and going through graduate school. She was studying anthropology, archaeology, and computers. She's about to finish her PhD." He spoke as if she was alive.

"You said she couldn't commit suicide. Why are you so certain? Life brings troubles, maybe she had too much pressure on her—

work, school—too much, and it got to her."

"No, no! She was way too smart and alive to let things get her down. She was always able to step away and see how things really were. She never met a problem she couldn't lick. No, she would never commit suicide."

Blaine's conviction and belief in his daughter was resolute.

"You can understand why I had to check you out? I couldn't let the police slide and let this end so easily. That snot-nosed kid they have working on the case told me on the phone, *on the phone*, that he already has the paperwork completed and is looking for his next assignment."

"I met Evans," added Trabue. "I agree. He's not much." Trabue recounted his visit with the rookie cop.

"You see," exclaimed Blaine, "he didn't bother to follow up on you; he didn't probe; he didn't even ask if you recognized her or knew her. It's cut and dried, open and closed. I need some help! I don't know what to do, who to ask for help." He looked about the boat and motioned. "You must know somebody. Maybe you could help! Will you help me? After all, you found her." Blaine had a needy look that was aimed sniper-like at Trabue.

"Help? In what way?" Trabue regretted the words as they came out of his lips. Boxed in. Blame yourself, was his thought.

"Help me find who killed her."

"Why? Why me?"

"Because it's you who found her. Maybe you were meant to find her. Maybe she found you."

Karen's beckoning hand flashed through Trabue's brain.

"That is stretching reality!"

"It's all I've got."

Trabue sat in silence. The phantom hand beckoned again.

Trabue heard himself say, "I do have a friend—someone who might at least give you..."

"Us!" Blaine interjected.

"Fine, fine. Us. He might be able to give us a place to start. It's probably not going to do any good, but if you want, I'll see what I can do."

"Thanks, I knew my coming here would do something." Blaine looked relieved.

Trabue reinforced his prior statement. "I can't and won't promise anything. Like I said, it probably won't do any good, but we can try."

Yesterday, Trabue thought, *I found a body, a bobber, a dead girl. Today, the grieving father appears. First he threatens me then he asks for my help. This is nuts and I'm not making it any better by volunteering.* Trabue knew that his long-sought-for and much-cherished solitude was over.

It was time he rejoined the insanity called life.

"I'll ask some questions, make some calls. I'll see what I can do. Anything you can tell me will help, no matter how insignificant. If I'm to be of any good to you I'll need to know more, a lot more. So start wherever you're comfortable."

"Like I said," Blaine began, "Karen was great, an excellent student, never a problem. I was proud, real proud, when she got her scholarship. That was seven years ago. I looked ahead to getting out of the service and being with her, but I knew that I couldn't hold on to her. She was moving up and into a new world. No more being a

Tennessee country girl. I backed her all the way, even if it meant she would leave me behind. She graduated with honors three years ago and ended up with a scholarship for graduate school. Imagine, I've barely been through high school and she was studying to get her doctorate!"

Trabue interrupted. "What was her specialty?"

"Oh yeah, like I said, she was studying in a joint program in anthropology and archaeology. But her expertise was in applying computer analysis to both fields. She was something special. She taught herself computer skills which led her into new areas for both fields." Blaine's pride was evident as his eyes sparkled and misted from thoughts of his beloved daughter.

"She was almost finished with her dissertation when the money dried up. The past six months or so she was working for one of her old professors. She wouldn't take a penny from me. I would send her money or leave it hidden at her apartment after a visit. But she always gave it back. Karen was set on not taking my help. She wouldn't even get one of those easy federal loans. No, she was special. She was going to prove she could do it alone. You know. Succeed on her terms."

Trabue interrupted. "Where was she working? What exactly was she doing?"

"She was working for an ex-professor, Kenneth Forsythe. He works primarily as a consultant for construction projects. Karen explained it all to me and I thought it was pretty easy work. Most states now have laws to protect all sorts of historical sites and even the potential ones. Forsythe left the university several years ago to get in on the business of providing archaeological advice to construction

projects. He would survey a site and then write a report on the potential that there was historical significance to the site. If all went well, that is if nothing was found during the digging of foundations or the grading of roadways, then Forsythe got a sizeable fee without any additional work. If by chance anything was found, a grave, a building site, or the like, then Forsythe made even more."

"How so?" asked Trabue.

"Well, he then went on a daily trip to inspect the site, recommend action and so on. Usually he called in some of his cronies—hand-picked experts—and they all collected their per diems."

"Did Karen get some of this 'daily action?'" queried Trabue.

"Oh no! She wasn't allowed because she wasn't a PhD. She ran his database for the research effort. She was a behind-the-scenes helper. Karen was paid a salary, but not allowed to get into the real money flow even though Kenneth Forsythe made a lot of his fee from her work."

"It sounds like she would be unhappy on being cut out."

"No, she was fine with it. She went into the work arrangement with her eyes open. It was a steady job and she, like I said, was independent. It was good money compared to what she might have normally made around a university. No, the deal was fine with her. She got to run the computers her way and Forsythe got the fame and money."

"Fame?" Trabue's eyebrows lifted.

"Well, not any glitter stuff, but in the world of professor-types, Forsythe was making a name for himself."

"And passing some easy consulting money to his pals probably didn't hurt his reputation," added Trabue.

"Yeah there's some of that. But like I said, Karen had no problem with it."

Trabue stared directly at Blaine and asked bluntly, "What about the men in her life?"

"What? What do you mean? Oh, boyfriends? Karen was not overly interested in guys and dating since high school. She was so focused on getting her degrees. She had several guys hanging around when I visited, but nothing very serious for very long."

"Didn't you find that odd?" Trabue pushed. Blaine wasn't fazed. "No, no, not really. You'd have to know her to understand why. She was, well, it was like she was putting it off until after her doctorate was finished. She loved kids and I'd swear she wanted to have dozens, but not until after she proved to herself and the entire world that she had done what she wanted on her own."

"So she wasn't promiscuous, or lesbian?"

"Of course not!" Blaine almost shouted.

"Easy now, easy! I just need to cover all the bases. If you don't say it, or I don't ask it, then I don't know it. I need stuff to work with."

"You say, work with—but how? I asked for help, and you've said yes, but really, what can you do? Maybe I was off base by asking. What can you do? What can anyone do?"

"Like I said, I'll ask some questions. I'll ask and see where it all goes. If I ask enough of the right ones maybe something will turn up." Trabue responded.

Trabue could see that his guest was spent. The shock of his loss, the frantic misplaced suspicion... The thin hope that Trabue could

help was all he had.

"One more question. Why did you start with me? Why not the professor?"

"I can't say. I mean, I don't know. I felt, I felt..." Blaine stared ahead.

"Come on, Sarge, time to turn in. You're welcome here. Take the forward bunk and tomorrow we can start to find out what really happened to Karen."

Blaine was a like small child reminded of bedtime. He went forward to the bunk, stretched out, closed his eyes and immediately slept.

★ ★ ★ ★ ★

As Winton Blaine entered the world of dreams, his mind embraced a place where Karen still lived. She ran to him, revealing the dandelion she had picked.

Karen blew its silver-crowned rim at Blaine and he caught the small bird it became. The bird grew in his hand and then walked up his arm, growing as it reached his shoulders. Once there, the now-giant bird took flight with him in its claws. Looking down, Blaine saw hooded figures race through a barren field. Above a rock fence line the bird changed into a helicopter and spit fire toward the fleeing figures.

Blaine fell from the bird-copter, and he slowly descended until his feet touched the field that had turned to sand. The sand became wet like at the beach. It was the kind of sand that was perfect for

making castles. Karen appeared as a mermaid and she patted the side of a sand castle and looked at Blaine.

"See Daddy, it's all good now."

His mermaid-daughter pressed her lips with a silencing finger that signaled him to resume sleeping.

In the morning Winton Blaine's recollection of his dream was fragmented. He only remembered seeing Karen as a mermaid swimming in a place that was still wonderful.

Chapter 4

Albert Bryan could not decide what to do next. Should he respond to the less-than-charitable review of his latest book? Or should he finish off the cheesecake sitting on the counter? There it sat, calling his name.

He went for the cheesecake.

Good choice, he thought. *No sense in wasting energy on a reviewer who obviously only skimmed my book. The dolt!*

He had learned his lesson after the publication of his first book. An angry response would do no good. It might even do some harm. In either case, it would not help him to complete his next effort, the sixth of his second career.

As an author, Bryan had a limited audience.

Academics and cops, he thought. *What a strange crowd to write for.*

His latest book, *Frenzied Thoughts - A Serial Killer's Mind,* took six months of intensive interviews with three serial murderers. It was an excellent volume and was received well by everyone except for that lone dissenter.

Let him be, thought Bryan. *Leave him behind. Better to close the door on that book and its gruesome memories. I'm an old beat cop. My foray into the sick criminal mind was interesting. But now I need some old-fashioned chase-the-crooks stuff to sink my teeth into.*

Bryan's sixth book would take him in a new direction. Gangs. He had looked for a topic where the violence was less bizarre, less sickening. He would gladly put number five and its unflattering review out of his mind.

The cheesecake disappeared. Now Bryan could devote a full hour to the outline of the gang book. Classes would be his only disturbance, and it was an hour until the next one.

As a professor he liked the casual work environment, the inquiring minds of his students, and the quiet atmosphere of the southern Florida campus. The routine of his lecture schedule caused only periodic interruptions. His new career was a success. As a full professor with five published books and some consulting contracts, he could support a fine lifestyle. Certainly better than the previous career he had possessed, or that had possessed him, as a police officer.

Professor Bryan was immersed in the book outline when he realized that his phone was ringing.

He grabbed the phone and half-yelled, half-spoke. "Yeah, what?"

"Get your face out of the refrigerator and answer your phone."

Bryan recognized the voice immediately and his annoyance fled.

"Well, well. If it isn't my long-lost pain in the ass. How you been, Ledge? Still on the lam from responsibility? Or was it reality?"

"It's both. And if I recall correctly, you are the reason I'm on this irresponsible trip. How's the diet, Big Guy?"

"Gone. And never coming back!"

"Well, it's good to know that some things never change. The world would be diminished if you were anything less than the plus-sized version of your lovable self."

Trabue's voice, although mouthing insults, was laced with easy-to-recognize love and respect. Bryan's voice was the same.

"My boy! Where are you? I haven't heard anything from you in months and I haven't been insulted with any real charm in the same

length of time."

"I'm in Nashville and I need your help."

"Don't expect any entrees into the music world from me, kiddo. I'm not a fan of the Nashville sound, although there are several artists I can tolerate who label themselves Country and Western."

As a native of The Big Easy, Bryan loved the music born in his home city. Jazz, in all of its forms, was his music. Just the mention of Nashville and its music made the longing for home swell within. University life in Tampa had been good and Ybor City had some fine restaurants. But, he would like it better if his university life was in New Orleans.

God, how I miss the music and the food. Oh! Don't even think about the food or I'll gain weight!

Trabue brought him back. "Well, who do you know in Nashville?"

"What? Oh yes, yes. Nashville, Nashville. Let me check the old rolodex."

Bryan thumbed the huge, stained circle of cards. Well used, some of them ragged beyond belief, with newer crisp, white additions mixed in, Bryan's rolodex was legendary. He made a religion of collecting people for his network.

"Let's see. I was there several years ago for a book promotion."

"How could I have forgotten?" wailed Trabue. "Your face was on TV! Tennessee's children are still in therapy."

Bryan winced at its mention. His reaction was detectable through the phone.

"Now, lay off. It wasn't that bad!"

"Bad? Bad? It was historic! As they say, you have a perfect face for radio. The host—what was his name? Seigenhoffer, John Seigenhoffer. What an actor!"

"He wasn't acting. Actually, he was being polite. He's an intelligent, learned man, and a great interviewer. I was obviously his worst guest, ever. And he graciously nursed me through stage fright. Could we please move on?"

Albert Bryan thumbed the famous card file loud enough for Trabue to hear it in Nashville—without the phone.

"Let me see. Richard Patterson is a possibility. He's a writer-journalist type with *The Nashvillian*. If I remember correctly, he wrote a nice piece for the weekend book section and thoughtfully never mentioned my TV appearance. Only problem in Nashville was that nobody read the book, or at least if they did, they didn't buy it. My sales were terrible there—during the signing party, and even after his article ran. He's smart, or at least smart enough to recognize my brilliance. He liked the book and he liked me. He's a start. So what's the deal?"

"Well, since you're the only famous criminologist I know, I think you'd guess it has something to do with maybe a crime. Oh, yeah, and since you're the largest person I know, you might recommend a good restaurant."

"Hah!" Bryan could not hold back a laugh.

Trabue loved needling his friend about his size. Albert was big, but not obese. It was acceptable for Trabue to joke. No one else would dare insult Bryan, but Trabue's barbs were enjoyed and returned with wit and attitude. It was a game for them. It was Bryan's

and Trabue's game and it was good that Trabue was on the phone and at it again.

"You could try Otis Jackson. He's the Assistant Chief of Police."

"Only an Assistant Chief? I'm sorry, but that will not do; not enough clout."

"Piss off, Trabue. He's just a loose contact. Actually, he'd probably not remember me. Rather, you'd do better talking to Mrs. Jackson." Bryan retorted.

"Mrs. Jackson?"

"Yes, Mrs. Jackson. As in Doctor Jackson. Doctor Amelia Jackson. She's with the Medical Examiner's office as well as Vanderbilt and Meharry Medical Schools. She attended one of my lectures in Atlanta. Her husband, the lowly Assistant Chief of Police stopped by to sit in and be sociable and of course, pay his respects to the eminent Professor Bryan."

"Oh piss off yourself, Fat Boy! The size of your belt is only rivaled by the size of your ego. What's the good in using your name if I have to put up with their reaction to your outlandish, self-absorbed, second-class, washed-up-cop mind?"

Albert knew from the banter that Trabue was back to his regular form. The phone call was long overdue and, although he was pleased that the ribbing was taking place, Albert's curiosity was nagging him to find out more about Trabue's need for help.

"So what type of trouble are you in? Should I be obtaining a lawyer for you, or is it money?"

"No. No trouble. I just found a body and I'd like a few details cleared up before I leave town."

"Hmmm—a body. What type? Any signs of foul play?"

"Can't say as of yet. But, the next of kin has arrived on the scene with enough unanswered questions that I thought I would step in and lend a hand."

"So you think enough questions, or the right questions, haven't been answered?"

"No, they haven't been asked. And the girl..."

"Oh, there's a girl?"

"Yes a girl, or a young woman to be exact. The politically correct types will wag their fingers at the oversight. I'm going to rot in hell. To be correct, the young woman's background doesn't fit with the readily-canned finding of suicide, so I'm asking a few questions on my own."

"Why?" Bryan asked.

"Why?" Trabue countered.

"Yes, why?" repeated the professor. "Why you, and why the need to ask questions?"

"Because I found her, then her father found me, and he needs my help—simple. Are you satisfied?"

"God yes! Good. I'm not only satisfied, I'm pleased. I urged you to take the boat trip. As long as you aren't in a jam and need your old pal to bail your miserable butt out of some intrigue, go ahead and ask. Ask a lot of questions, use my name if it helps. Just don't forget to keep me in the loop. I'll let my answering service and the grad students know that I'm available day or night if you need me. They screen the calls at my office when I'm out. If I'm going out for a long time, I've even been known to remember to take my cellular."

"Great, it's good to know that Big Al is waiting to hear from me."

"Like I said, don't forget to call."

"Yes, yes I'll call, and before you say it, I'll be careful."

"Good, then piss off for real. I've got a class to teach and young minds to inspire."

"Poor kids."

They ended the call without formal good-byes.

Bryan sat back and sighed after placing the phone in its cradle.

"God, it's good to hear from Trabue," he said aloud.

Seven hundred miles away Trabue thought, *God, it's good to needle Albert. I've missed him.*

Trabue made several calls. The first was to the Nashville police. Jackson was unavailable, but after a little soft-spoken banter and name dropping Trabue got what he needed. He wheedled Jackson's secretary and found out that later this morning the Assistant Chief would be at home changing into his "blues" for a luncheon awards meeting. The second call, made to the Jackson home, was hunch-inspired.

★ ★ ★ ★ ★

"Hello, Mrs. Jackson? Oh, excuse me, Dr. Jackson?"

"Yes, this is Dr. Jackson."

"Dr. Jackson, I'm calling on the advice of Albert Bryan, Professor Albert Bryan, from the University of South Florida." He paused, waiting for recognition of his referral.

"Oh, yes, yes. Professor Bryan. He's an excellent and memorable lecturer. How may I help? Mr...?"

"Oh yes, my name is Rutledge Trabue. I'm an old friend and colleague of Albert's. He suggested that I give you a call."

"How nice, Mr. Trabue. It is Mr. Trabue and not professor?" she queried.

"Yes, it's Mr. I'm more of a social acquaintance, although I've worked with Dr. Bryan professionally," Trabue stretched the facts.

"Well Mr. Trabue, what exactly is the purpose of your call?"

"Actually, my need may be more in your husband's area, although you may also be able to provide assistance. If it's not inconvenient I'd prefer discussing it face-to-face. May I impose and suggest a method of our getting together?"

"Why, yes, go ahead." She seemed interested.

"I've spoken with the secretary for the police department's administration and she mentioned that your husband would be at home later this morning. I wonder if I could stop by for just a few moments, say at eleven this morning. I can then introduce myself properly."

"Well, I think that's possible. I can't promise that Otis will be available at any particular time, but eleven should be fine."

"Thank you Dr. Jackson, I really appreciate your willingness to help without much detail or prior notice but..."

She interrupted, "No, don't apologize, Mr. Trabue. If you are a friend and colleague of Albert Bryan I'm pleased and honored to help. I'll be looking forward to seeing you at eleven."

"That's fine. I'll see you then. Good-bye, Dr. Jackson."

★ ★ ★ ★ ★

After hanging up, Amelia Jackson realized that she had not given her caller directions or even an address.

★ ★ ★ ★ ★

Trabue's next call was just as effective.

"Hello!" was shouted in greeting.

"Mr. Patterson, My name is Trabue,"

"Go Ahead!"

"Albert Bryan, Professor Albert Bryan, said you knew Nashville as well as anyone and I should talk to you."

"Albert who?" Trabue held the phone away.

"He's the criminology expert and oversized gourmet," Trabue responded.

"Oh yeah, him, the ex-cop. What do you want?"

"He said you were a good reporter and knew the city. I need to get some background quick and I'm good for a lunch or whatever if we can talk."

"Not today; lunch is out!" Richard Patterson again shouted. "Damned bullshit awards ceremony. If you want to talk quick, get over here before ten. I'm finishing a piece for the next edition. See you then."

The receiver went dead.

"Excellent phone presence," said Trabue to the phone.

Pleased with his morning so far, Trabue headed back to the boat to check on his visitor.

Chapter 5

Win Blaine stepped out of the galley as Trabue entered the salon.

"Sorry for sleeping so late. I'm usually up early, but today I'm moving a bit slow."

"Probably something to do with that egg I raised on your head last night." Trabue patted the back of his own head.

"Oh yeah, how could I forget? You really tapped me."

He turned his head to show the area in question.

"Sorry, but I'm not a good host during armed break-ins." This time Trabue laughed as he patted the back of Blaine's head.

"Ouch! That's still tender territory."

"Yeah, it looks rough; you certain you'll be alright?" Trabue asked.

"No problem, just as long as I don't jog, move, try to touch it, or laugh." Blaine said with a grin, then he changed the subject by asking a question. "Have you had much of a chance to think about helping me out?"

"Haven't thought about it. Been too busy. I've already begun."

"Really? Thanks! Already begun; how so?"

"For starters, I called the one person I know that is certain to link us with a resource in Nashville. As luck would have it, he knew more than one place to start." Trabue recounted his morning.

"What can I do?" asked Blaine. "I want to be part of whatever happens."

Trabue moved toward the salon windows and looked out over the bow rail.

"I want you to go to your daughter's apartment. Go through everything. Try to find some clue about anything—anything that was going on in her life. You are our link to her life. I need that link to be strong and clear. Yes, you need to check out her place while I start the ball rolling as best I can," Trabue instructed.

"And just exactly what are you planning to do? More than just ask questions?"

"Win, if anyone other than Karen is responsible for her death, my plan will work. It's simple. Here's how it goes."

Trabue leaned against the salon's port door, slowly sliding into a seated position on the wood deck.

"People, even the worst, don't kill by nature. Death is not a simple event. Somewhere there is someone thinking about what happened—what they did and the consequences of what they did. Over time they will think of it less and less, hoping that they got away with it. Hoping that it will go away. Their guilt and their fear of exposure will diminish. Today is Tuesday. I found your daughter Sunday morning. From her appearance, most probably she was killed sometime Saturday, probably Saturday night. That act of killing is fresh in someone's mind."

Trabue could see that the mention of Karen's death and potential killers was upsetting Blaine, but he continued.

"If we are going to find out what happened, we have to pierce the killer's sense of impunity. We've got to give the killer, or killers, a real fear that exposure of their act is possible and even imminent. We've got to flush out anyone trying to hide."

"But how? Just by asking questions?"

"Yes, probing questions, and poking into things and areas that are probably insignificant to the casual eye. We will keep asking and probing until we touch an area that is sensitive and ties the killer to the victim. When we do that we will have succeeded."

"At what?"

"Highlighting the possibility of disclosure. We keep the memory of killing fresh. We focus other people's eyes on the deed. Murder is an act that is abhorrent to the civilized. People aren't supposed to kill. It's innately wrong. So, murderers hide. Yes, we'll ask and probe. Maybe you'll be the link. Maybe we stumble on it. But, we ask a lot of questions and then we wait."

"Wait for..." Blaine was interrupted.

"A mistake—a move of some sort. The killer, or killers, will make a move, maybe slight, but a move nonetheless, and we must be alert to see it. The slightest off-beat response to our questions may identify the killer. The response may tell too much or too little. It may be out of place, phony, or just plain stupid. It will come because we will be asking and getting close."

"You sound as if it's something you've done before."

The reply was briefer than Blaine hoped.

"I've got some experience."

Blaine could see for the briefest of moments that Trabue was immersed in the memory of something similar.

"Yeah," said Trabue. "I've got experience."

When he spoke, Trabue's mind replayed the time that his simple questioning led to a Louisiana bayou and a revenge-laden outcome.

Trabue preached internally, *I was right then. We're right this time.*

A single cat-like motion launched Trabue erect. He barked an order to a startled Blaine.

"Let's move! You go through your daughter's place in detail. Go through everything at least twice! I'll take a cab downtown and start with the reporter."

"Cab?" asked Blaine "I'll drive you; don't take a cab."

"No, you get to Karen's. I don't need a chauffeur. I've been cabbing it a long time and like it. You have work to do. You need to examine her things." He sensed that Blaine was trying to avoid the task and the intimate contact it would bring with his dead daughter.

"Okay, I'm just, well, you know. I'm just..."

"Scared at being in her nest," Trabue said bluntly.

"Yeah, well yeah, that's it. I'm not looking forward to being there again—in her apartment. You know, without her being..." Blaine could not finish.

"It's got to be done and you are the only one who can do it."

"Yes, but..."

"No buts, you've got to do it! You do it, because it's got to be done. And if she was murdered, you might uncover whatever will stop her killer from getting away with it."

Blaine needed the push. He headed for the salon's doorway and was off the *Awfria* and halfway down the dock before Trabue could blink.

"I'll ask," shouted Trabue after him. "You dig, and I'll ask."

Blaine waved his hand in recognition but did not stop, slow down, or look back. Trabue had given him a mission and Blaine reacted like the good solider. He was going to follow orders, regardless of how much he dreaded the assigned task.

After calling for a cab, Trabue walked the distance from the phone booth at the end of the dock to the marina parking lot where he would be picked up. Eddie was emptying the trash bin.

"Mornin', Mr. Trabue." chirped Eddie.

"Good morning, Eddie."

"You stayin' beyond the storm is not just a coincidence? You needin' to hang around for the police?"

"Nothing like that. I'm just not ready to go. I'll let you know when it's time to settle my account."

"No problem, no problem. I know you're good for it. Nothin' like that..."

"Sure Eddie," Trabue interrupted, "I'm your best and most colorful customer. Who else has found a body?"

"No, you're better than okay. Heck, with just the amount you spent on supplies and such the month you stayed here, I figure you're good for any bill. That guy, is he a friend?"

Before Trabue could reply, Eddie derailed his own query and looked over Trabue's shoulder at the arriving cab and said, "Looks like your ride's here."

Trabue glanced at the cab.

"So it is, so it is. Catch you later, Eddie." And he was off to the waiting taxi.

Eddie mused to himself, *Ledge Trabue, you could own a car for all the money you spent on cabs—and a basket of cell phones with the coins you've dropped in that booth.*

Chapter 6

Reginald Shavers eased his cab into the parking lot of Stone Harbor Marina. He did not look directly at the man who entered by the right rear door. Rather, he checked the passenger by way of the mirror.

Different type, thought Reggie. *Looks like a hard one, small tipper and not a talker, I'll wager.*

Reggie was usually a good judge of his fares.

You don't drive a cab for forty-odd years and not get a knack at sizing up people, thought Reggie.

The rider told him that the destination would be *The Nashvillian* building.

Reggie tripped the meter and backed the cab around and headed to the exit. Reggie was surprised that he had misjudged this passenger when, before the cab was in motion, the rider spoke.

"Tell me about Nashville, Mr. Shavers." It was half command, half request.

Reggie admired the man's approach. *Mister Shavers,* he mused. *The man read my permit and has the sense and style to call me Mister. I like that. Shows respect.*

"Well," started the driver, "Nashville is a good town. Growin'. Just always growin'. Now, you take the music business. It's big business. It's always in the news and it's always bringin' in tourists." Reggie was giving his Chamber of Commerce speech, the one all the tourists liked.

Before he could go on, the fare interrupted.

"Tell me about the people. Who runs things? What are the leaders, the bosses, the people who decide things really like?"

Reggie definitely knew he had misread this one. The way this fare half asked and half commanded an answer. He wanted to know things, the things that matter. He wanted knowledge. He wanted truth. This was no tourist and he would not settle for the Chamber speech. Reggie liked this one. He was real.

"Well sir, you ask a question that takes a time to tell."

"So, tell me what you can on the way to *The Nashvillian*."

Reggie began to talk about Nashville. What he liked, didn't like, the good, the bad, and the things that could be different. Without knowing how or why, he began to speak about things he normally held inside.

As he spoke, Trabue gazed out the window watching the city blend into Reggie's description. The month at Stone Harbor Marina had been focused on the *Awfria's* repairs and maintenance. He now had a reason to study this city. He both liked and disliked what he saw passing by.

They passed through a blue-collar neighborhood and into an area of greener lawns and bigger homes. As they moved through Nashville, Reggie used the sights and sounds of the trip to prompt his list of topics. By the time they reached the outer ring of the city's business district, Reggie had shared a great deal of information.

Trabue had heard enough to get a sense of how he would frame his work. Trabue placed faith in the accuracy of Reggie's view and opinions. Reggie was not the be-all source of information by any means, but he was an excellent observer. It was a start for the process

that had served Trabue well in learning new places. Soon he would know Nashville, its creases and folds, the stains as well as its bright lights. Trabue was a cat sniffing the landscape, looking for safe spots and trying to find holes.

Trabue had done this before.

Asking open-ended questions of cabdrivers, bartenders, waitresses, and other working folk was one of his methods. The sources were not always right or useful, but collectively they helped Trabue feel the pulse of a city.

Closer to the edge, these working people felt things differently. Sometimes they were remarkable in their ability to articulate truth in bite-sized chunks. Often they possessed a sense of humor that was refreshing and crisp.

Trabue always started with the bottom of the ladder. The top often had the angles, timing, and the inside track. But the bottom had the feel. Feel was good. Better than statistics and printed brochures, feel was the core.

Einstein said, "Intuition is the key." Trabue's world was far less complex than Einstein's, and Trabue believed that if "feel" suited such a genius, it should work for him too.

★ ★ ★ ★ ★

Trabue's thoughts and intake of the city ended when Reggie stopped to announce their arrival. "*Nashvillian* Building; the fare is $10.60," he added as Trabue eyed the meter.

Reggie was reminded again of his error in misreading this fare when Trabue paid with a twenty.

"Keep the change Mr. Shavers. I enjoyed your comments."

Trabue exited the cab and entered *The Nashvillian's* home.

★ ★ ★ ★ ★

As Trabue disappeared inside, Reggie backed his cab to a paid meter he had eyed while arriving with Trabue.

I'll wait this one out, he thought. *He's going to need another cab and I don't expect he'll settle long in this or any other spot. I'll stick with him. I'm surprised I didn't read him better. He's different; good different.*

★ ★ ★ ★ ★

Trabue stepped inside the building and its cavernous, well-lit lobby. Behind a counter sat a uniformed rent-a–cop jointly watching the doorway and several TV monitors. The semi-comatose guard never looked up as Trabue walked over, leaned on the counter and asked, "How do I find Patterson? Richard Patterson?"

"Second floor, all the way to the back," was the languid reply. "Look for the big, messy pile of rubble and you've found him. Dickie may be a good reporter, but he ain't much of a housekeeper," laughed the faux cop.

"You a fan?" asked Trabue.

"No! No way! He's too ugly to have fans." The guard laughed and continued to watch the monitors. He never made eye contact with Trabue.

Trabue ended the exchange by walking toward the elevators across the small lobby. As he approached the opened doors he glanced back at the rent-a-cop. *He's still glued to the tube,* observed Trabue.

The second floor proved to be a maze worthy of any lab rat experiment. Desks, chairs and small tables were filled and overflowing with all manner of personal items. They were placed in no apparent order across the entire floor of the building. The attractive and professional-looking lobby gave no clue to the disorder and chaos found one floor above. The disarray of the area was matched by an atmosphere of disinterest on the part of the floor's occupants. No heed was given to Trabue's presence.

Sensing the "go as you please" style, Trabue cut a nearly straight path across the room. His target was the largest pile at the rear.

In the center of an area that could be described as one of the world's most cluttered work spaces sat a desk, three small tables, four file cabinets, a mini-refrigerator and an indeterminable number of stacked papers and file boxes.

Sitting in the center of the chaos was Richard Patterson, Nashville's most read and also most feared reporter. Peering over the screen of his laptop computer, Patterson eyed Trabue as only the wholly-engrossed can see an intruder.

"Before you utter one word, you had better know that I'm not in the mood to be interrupted. I've got a deadline to meet and I want to screw the mayor real good. So sit down, shut up, and let me work. You can talk when I'm done."

Trabue did just that.

Several minutes passed while Patterson banged the keyboard

with speed and intensity. The clatter of the keys kept a fevered pace and then ended abruptly.

"Mr. Trabue, you got one minute to excite my curiosity or you get the same as our beloved mayor."

Trabue jumped in.

"I found a dead girl."

"Big Deal. People die all the time. Someone has to find them."

"I don't."

"And who are you in this matter?"

"Nobody special, just an interested party who wants to know the truth."

"An interested party who claims to know Big Albert Bryan. Well, the good professor called after you did, to make certain I'd see you. He vouched for you and asked that I not be my usual hard-assed self. He asked that I be helpful to you. So, what is it you want?"

Trabue was impressed with Patterson's respect for Albert.

"I'm pleased Albert called. You seem to think highly of him."

"As high as a jaded cynic like me can. He's a real one—no inflated ego, even though he's got a valid claim to have one. I've seen a lot of phonies and creeps. My job is to make some sense out of how the creeps, dealers, phonies, and plain jerks are running and ruining our lives. I like Bryan. He was a good cop, and now he's a good author and professor."

"I'm glad you like him. I'll pass along your comments. He thought you could assist me. So, I'm asking for your help."

"Go ahead, I'm all ears. I chase stories for a living."

Trabue muscled a space in the rubble and sat across from

Patterson. He recounted his experiences since Sunday. The reporter listened with a trained ear, did not interrupt, took a few notes and really heard what Trabue said and didn't say.

When Trabue finished, Patterson leaned back in his chair and stared at the ceiling.

Trabue had experienced the "deep pondering" situation before. Patterson was a thinker, unaware of all else. Big Albert had the same routine. Listen, really listen, then think. For the spectator, it was wait. Just wait.

Abruptly, Patterson sighed. He would have paced if there was room. Instead he stared out the window. He looked out, sighed again, and spoke.

"You're right. There's probably more to it than a simple suicide. Maybe a complex suicide. Could be a murder. I've heard a lot of tales in my time, but all you've said, when matched with who you are, who you know and, more importantly, who vouches for you—very fondly I might add," he sighed again. "Well, it's either the beginning of a real good story or a dead end. But, I'd bet you're on to something. What you're on to is hard to say. There are some interesting points to consider."

Trabue waited. He knew there would be more.

Patterson returned to his chair and stared at the ceiling. After the briefest of moments his slouching demeanor altered. He leaned forward over the piles of crumpled paper and addressed Trabue.

"Let me tell you what I think."

Trabue nodded.

"When Bryan called, he spoke highly of you. That's why I agreed to see you. He mentioned that you had found a woman's body."

The reporter gestured to the phone on his desk. "One call to one of my contacts and it was easy to find out which woman you found. Nashville is growing, but it's not so 'big city' that we have excess bodies. My source filled me in on who Karen Blaine is, or was. I initially thought that it could go either way. Maybe it's a suicide. Or, there's something worth looking into. Your information pushes me into the 'there's something to it' camp. If I trust your appraisal of the girl's father and his claim that it's not a suicide—and I do—then I'm forced to wonder why anyone would kill this young woman?"

Patterson again gestured to his phone. "Again, my contacts tell me the M.E. has already completed a report. The woman was full of drugs and drowned. For them it's over. She was drugged up and would either have been an overdose, or she fell in the river and drowned prior to the drugs taking full effect. If not a true suicide, then in the eyes of the M.E. it was a self-inflicted death, by accidental drowning."

"Very convenient for the M.E.," stated Trabue. "But so out of character for Karen Blaine."

"Right, my sources mentioned that as an option. And when her father's input is added, you may indeed be on to something."

"And, what?"

"God knows," replied Patterson. "Your bobber, she's clean—maybe too clean."

This time Patterson gestured to his computer. "No record, no nothing on her. She's a nobody as far as I could find. And trust me, I can find a lot and find it fast. I ran her, right after Bryan's call.

Country girl gets an education and works hard, yada yada yada. She's clean. But, like I said, when coupled with your input, it's intriguing. She's probably not a suicide, doesn't fit the profile. It's only Tuesday and the M.E. and police have it all wrapped up. Within everything you've told me there's only one obvious link—Forsythe. Her boss."

"Go on," urged Trabue.

"Well, let's examine him." Patterson started hitting keys on his laptop. "I know he's in here. If my memory serves me it's in my own dear *Nashvillian*, in the business section. Ah! Got it. 'Forsythe and Associates Inks Deal with Fellows' is the title. Here, take a look."

The reporter swung his computer screen around for Trabue to read. Trabue was forced to look through and over more piles. Patterson smiled and got up again to pace before his window and peer into the parking spaces below.

Trabue re-read the headline and then the story. The standard business blurb recounted how Dr. Kenneth Forsythe, CEO of Forsythe and Associates, a locally-based archeological and construction consulting firm, had signed a lengthy contract with Fellows, Inc., a real estate development and construction company. Fellows, Inc. was profiled with several of its most recent and, presumably, most important and impressive ventures being described.

The article ended with a quote from the CEO of each of the involved firms. The quotes were standard fare, obviously written by public relations hacks. They were boiler-plate, enunciating the joy that each firm was experiencing and anticipating in the new joint venture. *Ugh*, thought Trabue. *How lucky I am to have avoided that form of daily life.*

Trabue saw a grip-and-grin photo of the two CEOs.

Dr. Kenneth Forsythe appeared to be in his late forties and very much the professor-type. With longish thinning hair and a crumpled blazer, he looked the part of the brains next to the overwhelming brawn of John Fellows. Fellows looked like the perfect construction man. He was surprisingly young if the accomplishments of his company were truthfully due to his efforts.

"Why the look? You seem pleased for such a slim article," Trabue asked.

"Fellows is the surprise!" The tone told Trabue that a "local" would see the connection.

"Go on. I'm the outsider here, what's so special about Fellows?"

Patterson was silent, hanging on the moment as only a reporter could.

"Maybe it's not him, maybe it's his associates," was all he said.

Trabue wanted more. The reporter's face was aglow. Patterson was holding something out.

"Look," he glanced at his watch, "I'm very late for the Music City Community Awards. You said something about an appointment at eleven, right?"

"Yes, but..." Trabue did not finish.

"I've got to cover this event. It's bullshit, but it's part of keeping contacts fresh. You have things to do, so do them. Follow your instincts. Ask some questions. I'll do the same."

Trabue felt shorted. Patterson had seen something in the Forsythe-Fellows connection and he wasn't sharing.

It wasn't an absolute bum's rush, but Trabue knew he was being

pushed out. Patterson headed for the elevator. Pulling out a card, he handed it to Trabue, exclaiming as he made his exit, "This is my phone and beeper. Call me tomorrow and we'll trade notes."

Trabue took the card. By the time he glanced to see two cell numbers, a home phone, a beeper, and an office number, Patterson had disappeared. Trabue was not pleased.

Trabue knew he was right when he had explained to Blaine that by asking and being "out there" people would act differently. Yet, Trabue was unsettled by how quickly the Forsythe-Fellows connection caused Patterson to bail on him.

At first, Patterson was pleased to help. Abruptly, he couldn't wait to go somewhere else. Patterson's reaction supported Win's belief that Karen was murdered.

★ ★ ★ ★ ★

On his second pass through the lobby, Trabue was hailed by the security guard. Trabue was surprised because he had been certain that the guard was permanently fixed drone-like on the monitors.

"You really spooked Patterson. I haven't seen him move that fast since his last big scoop."

Trabue was glad to have unearthed something. He did not know what. However, he knew the reporter was holding back.

As Trabue passed through the exit he heard the guard muttering, "Yeah, a big scoop! But who gives a crap? Nobody reads the paper anymore, all they do is watch TV!"

In the reflection of the glass doorway, Trabue could see the

guard's eyes fixed on the TV monitors.

Welcome back to the insanity, thought Trabue.

Chapter 7

Reggie was startled when, seemingly out of nowhere, Trabue handed him a slip of paper through the driver's window.

"Can we make it to here by eleven?"

Jeez, thought Reggie, *the man's a ghost!* "Sure, no problem," he replied.

The address was for a new high-rise condo on the most fashionable boulevard west of the university. Reggie was reaching for the meter when Trabue interrupted.

"Never mind that," ordered Trabue as he handed Reggie a wad of bills.

"You're off the meter."

Reggie knew the wait would pay off. This was an exceptional fare on a mission.

Good money, easy money, he thought, *and it may even get interesting. I can feel it. There's something special here!*

★ ★ ★ ★ ★

As the cab traveled west toward the nicest part of town, each man remained silent, slipping into private thoughts. Trabue was replaying the events at *The Nashvillian* and wondered how the information would piece together.

Reggie thought about his family and how good fares such as this can and do change things. The Shavers clan, which Reggie proudly led, was large and doing well, but Reggie was never satisfied with the status quo.

Now somewhere in his mid-years, Reggie still looked ahead. He had served briefly in the U.S. Army prior to Vietnam and returned home to Nashville with the sole aim of owning and driving his own taxi. In a relatively short time, through hard work, saving, and self-control—for Reggie did not indulge in smoking and drinking—the "Shavers Express" was a reality. He had been driving, almost daily, ever since he purchased his first cab.

He was currently driving his sixth version of the Express. There were nine others about town being driven by his children, their spouses, or even some of his grandchildren. Consistent effort and focus, plus some moderation, had produced a good life and a decent little cab company.

He could have, and some say should have, stopped driving and instead run his cab company's office. But he loved to drive. So, drive is what he did.

Yet it wasn't really the driving he loved. It was the people. Reggie loved the constant and varied experience of meeting people. Sure, there were the standard fares. Pick them up here, drop them off there. But there was also the spice. The interesting ones, like the fare pretending to be napping in the back seat.

Reggie glanced at the rear view mirror to confirm that Trabue's eyes were closed. *Yes, he's faking the power nap. This one is up to something. He's thinking, planning. First, it's the newspaper building. Then the day trip cash. Now we're on our way to see somebody important,* thought Shavers as he pulled into the semi-circular driveway of the newest and most expensive luxury residential condominium in the state of

Tennessee.

Half of Music Row's elite passed through this building's lobby each day. It was the in-town haunt for the out-of-town talent. It was also home to the new, young, moneyed crowd—the next generation of movers and shakers.

As Trabue exited the cab and made for the building's entrance, Reggie examined the slip of paper with the address and dialed his cell phone.

"Elvira? This is Reggie. Find who is in Unit 12-D at the Roker Arms Condos and call me back!"

Reggie disconnected fast. He knew she'd be fuming. Elvira hated to be told to do anything. But, he knew she'd find out the requested information—if only to return the call and give her husband a tongue-lashing.

Reggie backed the cab into an available spot and returned to his musings. He guessed it would take Elvira five minutes to cool down, three seconds to figure out which of her friends, relatives, phone pals, etc. would be the most likely source of the requested information, two or three minutes to procure the facts, fill her source in on some useful trade gossip, and then call him back. That would make a total elapsed time of about eight minutes for the return call from the third Mrs. Shavers. He checked his watch to time the effort.

The first Mrs. Shavers had not liked cabs, or cab drivers for that matter. She was gone almost as soon as the wedding ceremony was over. It was a tough but fortunate lesson.

The second Mrs. Shavers, Junie, had been his rock. Junie went through the early years with him. Just when things got good—the kids grown, business expanding—she got the cancer. Poof! She was here one day, gone the next. A bad time. A real bad time.

The next years were tough. No Junie, no rock; that's why Sam, the youngest, wandered and got into trouble. But that was over. Sam's troubles ended when Reggie met Elvira. Junie had been a rock, but Elvira was a wonder.

Elvira was queen and ruler of the house and the cab company's office. She was chief financial officer, dispatcher, head of personnel, and fortune teller. She was plain looking and possessed unlimited energy.

Yes, that was Elvira—a bona fide wonder. She had numerous abilities to match her energy. When provoked, Elvira could use the same few swear words in an uncountable multitude of variations to cover any and all situations. Few attempted to test her will. Those who survived warned others of the experience they would endure. A local badge of courage was to have survived an "Elvira"—the equivalent of a level-five tornado.

But the period of calm following an "Elvira" was as unique as the storm. Due to her strong beliefs about apologies, Elvira would pay her penance and perform acts of kindness bordering on miracles.

Reggie's phone rang, *Three-and-a-half minutes. Wow! Elvira must be burning!*

"Reggie? Reggie, why are you asking about the police?"

Her words drilled his ears. "You better watch yourself, poking around Chief Jackson's home. You better..."

Reggie cut off her off. "Call you back later, gotta run!"

He turned the phone off and placed it on the dashboard.

Damn. I'll pay for that move, he thought. But he did not want to be interrupted. He had to be ready to roll at any time. *Yes, I'll pay for it. But I got a feeling about this, and it's good.*

Having to pay would actually be easy since Reggie was one of the lucky people protected from an "Elvira" by an invisible bubble. The bubble was made of her love.

★ ★ ★ ★ ★

On the ride to the twelfth floor, Trabue considered what approach to use with the Jacksons. He knew that his visit to Patterson meant something.

It could have been better, he thought. *I was caught off guard by his sudden change. He bailed on me, fast. I hope this call is better.*

Trabue's thoughts were interrupted when the elevator doors opened and he caught the view of Nashville's skyline.

Not bad, he observed. *The good Dr. Jackson must be doing well with a side medical practice. No public servant could afford this, not without a trust fund or a lottery ticket.*

Trabue came to a halt several feet before the doorway marked 12-D. Clearly audible through the well-made door came the unmistakable sounds of an argument. Part domestic, part something else, it was raw.

As Trabue allowed the exchange to follow its course, he was lured closer by the growing intensity.

A man's voice, presumably Otis Jackson's, shouted, "I don't care what you think; it's nothing that concerns you! It was my call and I made it!"

"Nothing? Your call? You must be insane! It's beyond anything—everything! I can't believe you did it!" Came the response of a female voice.

"You don't..." He did not finish.

"I don't WHAT? Otis! I do! I do know! I know you're not yourself, and I have had it!! Nothing? *Nothing?* If you want nothing, then you have it!"

A door slammed.

Trabue took a deep breath, slowly exhaled, and stepped the last few feet toward the door. He breathed and exhaled again.

He felt the argument's energy through the door. A miniature sonic boom had occurred. A human bond had been broken and the shock wave had moved outward.

Trabue counted slowly to twenty-five. He repeated the count and rang the bell. The door was opened by Otis Jackson, Assistant Chief of Police, wearing his dress blue uniform.

"Good morning, I'm..."

"Yes, Mr. Trabue. I am aware of who you are." Jackson motioned Trabue to enter. "My office informed me of your call and of one from Dr Bryan. But, I'm running late and can only spare you a few minutes."

Trabue held in a response as Amelia Jackson entered. Her appearance prompted Otis Jackson, "You met my wife on the phone. We discussed it a few moments ago."

Trabue ignored the tension and moved toward the doctor to offer his hand. It was then that Otis Jackson became aware of his omission

and he clumsily extended his hand too.

The scene might have been embarrassing, but Trabue deftly shook Otis Jackson's hand with his own right and offered Dr. Jackson his left.

Trabue said, "I apologize for intruding. It's very kind of you both to see me." Trabue was not the Good Samaritan that visited Patterson, or the soft controller who called Mrs. Jackson. Rather, he was the obliged friend of a friend asking for a favor.

Otis Jackson fell for it, or acted so. His wife had already been exposed to Trabue and suspected a sham. Her eyes revealed the suspicion. They also told Trabue his secret was safe.

Trabue immediately liked and trusted her. Trust is oddly built on such unspoken conspiracies.

"Well then, I guess I should get to the point."

"Please do," said the Assistant Chief. "I really am in a rush."

Trabue sensed a second bum's rush.

"Two days ago I had the misfortune of finding a body in the Cumberland River. I reported it to the appropriate authorities and made an official statement. I thought I'd be on my way from the area. However, the deceased person's family has asked me to help."

"Help? In what way? Do you know the family?" Otis Jackson showed his impatience. Obviously the facts did not interest him. Either he didn't care or he already knew them. He wanted to know why an outsider was involved. It showed.

"I'm not certain why I was picked, it's just that, well her father—did I say the victim was a young woman?" Trabue spoke slowly for effect.

"Yes, yes, go on," Jackson pushed.

Trabue deflected the push and reminded Jackson of professional courtesy.

"Dr. Bryan thought you might be able to assist me."

Jackson kept pushing. "Yes, but please go on."

"It seems the young woman—her name was Karen Blaine—gave no signs of being in trouble or distressed. The father will have no part in believing her death was a suicide. He feels..." Trabue again dragged to see if Jackson's impatience led to some information.

Instead, Jackson swept in to conclude the session.

"Mr. Trabue, young people always hide the truth from parents." He moved toward Trabue and placed his hand upon Trabue's elbow, leading him to the door and away from his wife.

Trabue wondered *Why the rush? I want to talk to her too. Is he preventing that, or just tossing out an annoyance?*

Trabue allowed himself to be led, while keeping an eye on Dr. Jackson. She had stayed quiet and reserved. As Otis Jackson continued talking, Trabue listened to the one Jackson and watched the other.

"It just happens that I am well aware of the incident you've described," the police executive went on. "I was involved in the decision to place one of our most competent investigators on the case."

"Oh, really!" Trabue held back a laugh at the memory of the young detective he had met.

Jackson did not acknowledge the comment and proceeded as if he were speaking before a Neighborhood Watch Committee. Trabue knew it was boiler plate. So did Mrs. Jackson.

"Yes, as an alumnus of the university I was concerned. The school's reputation and name should not be smudged. When the girl was identified as a graduate student I intervened to make certain that the facts would be quickly known. Karen Blaine had a checkered personal history, regardless of her father's view. She was a long-time drug user. Her suicide, although tragic, is a familiar outcome with such lifestyles." He continued to move Trabue toward the door.

"Now, Mr. Trabue, I really must leave. If on our way you think of additional points, we can discuss them in the elevator."

What a hustle, thought Trabue, *He wants me to disappear, fast. He must think I am merely going through the motions of a favor and I'll drop my involvement based on his assurances. He believes I'm just a tourist in over my head, or it's something else. Something is really amiss here!*

As Jackson reached for the door knob, Mrs. Jackson halted him. "Otis!"

He swirled, a bit too quickly to make the movement look natural. Tension shot between husband and wife.

"Yes, what?"

Trabue became very alert.

"Your tie, please fix your tie!"

Jackson shrugged and moved in front of the mirror adjacent to the entryway. As he moved, Trabue glanced toward Mrs. Jackson. Her lips moved but no sound appeared. However, Trabue unmistakably recognized the words, "Call me."

"What do you mean?" inquired Jackson.

Trabue and Mrs. Jackson said nothing.

Again Jackson asked, "What do you mean?"

Trabue and the doctor were frozen, no longer looking at each other.

"It's perfect! My tie is perfect!" stated Otis Jackson.

He went for the door. His attention to the task prevented his noticing the relief sweeping over his wife and Trabue.

Trabue extended his hand, this time directly to Mrs. Jackson, and said, "I'm thankful that you could share your husband and time. I hope to see you again."

With his final word, Trabue applied the slightest additional pressure. Amelia Jackson responded immediately with an equally slight accent of pressure. "You're welcome Mr. Trabue, and thank you!" She pressed again.

★ ★ ★ ★ ★

In the elevator each man was awkwardly silent. Trabue politely nodded his approval for Otis Jackson to peruse the folder of papers which appeared from nowhere.

Jackson murmured, "...notes for my speech." He attended to shuffling the contents of the folder and avoided eye contact.

Trabue took it all in.

As the elevator opened at the lobby floor, Jackson held it and motioned for Trabue to exit. "I'll say my good-bye here, Mr. Trabue. My car is below in the garage."

"Thank you, Chief Jackson." Trabue gave him a promotion in the acknowledgement.

Jackson paid no attention as the door closed.

Trabue left the building.

★ ★ ★ ★ ★

This time Trabue did not surprise Reggie. He was leaning on the cab's fender reading the current edition of *The Nashvillian*.

Trabue was greeted by a question. "Was Assistant Chief Jackson helpful, Mr. Trabue?"

Trabue showed no reaction. He headed for the taxi's rear passenger door and said, "Get in Mr. Shavers, we need to chat."

After Reggie slid behind the wheel, Trabue waited a good long ten seconds. Ten seconds can seem like a lifetime in total silence. Reggie remained cool. Trabue noticed.

Reggie noticed also.

Trabue started out, "Mr. Shavers..."

Reggie interrupted, "It's Reggie, if you like!"

Trabue halted.

Ten more seconds of silence.

The silence ended when both men laughed at precisely the same moment.

With the tension gone Trabue stated, "You first, Reggie. Why and how did you learn who I was visiting? And also, how did you know my name?"

Reggie began, "Well, I like to know what's going on around me. First, we stopped at *The Nashvillian*. You go in and right before you come out, Dick Patterson practically goes through the plate glass door. I read his column every day. He's got a very quick mind but is usually slow on his feet. From my parking spot I could see him inside staring and pacing up in that mess he calls an office. He bolted out of there after something. It all caught my eye."

"How did you know his fast break had anything to do with me?" asked Trabue.

"I didn't, but we came here and I knew something had to be important. Patterson writes about the people who come and go in this neighborhood. The slip you showed me had the unit number on it. So it wasn't difficult to find out who you were visiting. Especially since I am married to a woman with a telephone implanted in her ear who keeps in touch with about half the known universe. If Elvira doesn't know somebody she knows somebody who does."

"Fine. How about my name?"

"No problem. I called Eddie at the dock. I pick up at Stone Harbor Marina from time to time. There aren't many spots with travelers that I don't know somebody. He also told me about why you're still in town. I've been known to take interest in my surroundings."

Reggie continued, "So, you find a body, stop at the paper, make a visit to an ex-college jock who is now a high-level police muckety-muck. It's also news."

Reggie shared his paper with Trabue.

"The story is buried on the inside-back of the city section. Blah, blah it goes, then 'the yet-to-be-identified Caucasian female was found by a transient boater'—that would be you—the dude in the back seat of my cab, paying me a very impressive day rate to drop in on important folks. Like I said, I usually like to know what goes on around me."

"Impressive," said Trabue. "Where do you suggest we go from here?"

"Question is why?" returned the cabbie. "Why you?"

"Simple. The dead girl's father asked me to find the truth. He is stone-cold certain that his daughter was murdered. After he mistakenly thought that I was involved, he asked me to help."

"But still, why you? Why not him out here doing the asking?"

"Call it fate. I'm the one who found her."

"Fair enough. So, like I asked, did Jackson provide any help?" Reggie's voice held a tone of ownership to the task.

Trabue noted the involvement.

"Why the interest on your part, Reggie?"

"Call it fate." They both laughed again.

"Chief Jackson? No, he was a washout. But if you can get me to a phone, there's another Jackson who may be of some help."

"Here, take my cell." Reggie handed his phone to Trabue. "Just be careful not to hit the wrong key! If you connect with Elvira, you'll get a new understanding of radioactivity."

★ ★ ★ ★ ★

Trabue called the Jackson residence.

"Hello, Mrs. Jackson this is..." He was interrupted.

"Yes, yes, Mr. Trabue, I knew it was you. Your voice is very memorable. Thank you so much for calling. And thank you for understanding that, well..." She was hesitant.

"Mrs. Jackson," Trabue became the controller of the phone

encounter with Amelia Jackson. "You asked me to call. Obviously, you wish to communicate with me and I need your help. I suggest you just let go."

"Yes, of course," was her reply. "We need to meet and talk. There is a great deal to share."

Trabue pressed, "I am still in the vicinity; I could return easily." He considered telling her he was at the building's entrance, but decided it would be too intimidating. He wanted to hear what she had to say. Unless he did, the visit to unit 12-D was a bust.

"No, no." She paused. "I wouldn't feel...it wouldn't..."

"Are you uncomfortable meeting alone? Is that it?"

Trabue knew he was applying pressure.

"No, no, it's not that at all, Mr. Trabue. It's, well, I just do not feel that our meeting would be totally..."

"Proper?"

"No. Safe."

Chapter 8

Amelia Jackson suggested that they meet at a neighborhood park. "Palmer Park. It's the site of an old school. Meet me at the south bench on the walking trail. You'll be able to find it easily; it's only a few blocks from here."

She said she'd be there in twenty minutes.

Trabue needed to walk and think. Reggie gave him directions and it was agreed that Reggie would park discreetly near the meeting site.

As Trabue left, Reggie said, "I hope she's helpful. I can't say I care much for her husband, especially since the last time I made any type of wager, I lost at least a mortgage payment on him."

Trabue filed the comment away for future discussion. Reggie was a fortunate find.

★ ★ ★ ★ ★

Amelia Jackson was tall, slim, and athletic. Trabue watched her walk toward him while appearing to pay no notice. She was wearing a baggy inexpensive gray cotton sweat suit, but expensive running shoes. To a casual observer she gave the appearance that she was out for exercise. Trabue saw the worried look she attempted to hide.

She spoke when she neared Trabue, "Mr. Trabue I know this sounds peculiar but..." She halted with a perplexed look.

Trabue opened as if they were life-long friends.

"Mrs. Jackson. Amelia. My friends never call me Mr. So, it's just

Trabue or Ledge; it's short for Rutledge. Perhaps we can be friends and you'll be able to tell me what's obviously troubling you!"

Her shoulders dropped. She sat on the ground, pulled her legs up and wrapped her arms around them. She leaned forward and sighed. "I could use a friend."

In their poses Trabue and Amelia looked like parent and child. Trabue pressed his role, "Go ahead, tell me."

"Well, Ledge," She smiled as said his name. Her voice expressed relief. "I really don't know where or how to start, but here goes."

Trabue leaned forward to express his attention and reinforce her comfort.

"I know Otis was pushing you off and giving false information concerning Karen Blaine. I'm certain of it! I just don't know why. Her death was not drug related, probably not a suicide, and has been handled by the M.E. and police in a very peculiar manner. Especially since it could be a homicide."

"You seem certain," injected Trabue.

"Oh yes! I was the Assistant M.E. on call Sunday when she was brought in. I did a brief exam and had been scheduled to do an autopsy yesterday. That is, until I was pulled off and sent on a court house wild goose chase. This morning, after Otis left for a breakfast meeting, I learned that it was his office that requested my presence at a phony hearing. It's odd that he would get involved in scheduling and assigning an autopsy. Especially when the new Assistant M.E. assigned to replace me is an out-and-out bad choice."

"How so?"

"Triple O! 'Obvious Outcome Osbourne' replaced me. Triple O

barely looks at a body before pronouncing the results based on whatever he last heard in the hallway."

"And you are saying that it would be odd for an Assistant Chief of Police to be involved?"

"Yes, very odd. Extremely odd if you're Otis! He's totally Community Affairs, has no involvement in ongoing cases and no role in assigning anything in my area!" She was clearly upset. "That's why I am certain he lied to you!"

Trabue made no comment or reply.

"I almost burst out, but didn't know whether to laugh or cry, when he referred to Officer, no, it's now *Detective* Evans." Her tone was almost loathsome when she emphasized the word detective.

"Go on," urged Trabue.

"He is incompetent. Every occasion that he has touched any police work associated with the Medical Examiner's office has resulted in disaster. He's ruined more evidence and fouled more cases than the remainder of the police force. He's been all but banned—I mean actually banned—from our offices and the adjacent areas. "Doorstop" has been his current nickname because his assigned place of duty was a chair at the entry way to the *Community Affairs Division*." She placed special and pained emphasis on naming the location.

"They couldn't be serious about anything assigned to Evans; it smells. Somebody pulled big strings to make him a detective. And Otis had to be involved." She looked down and away.

"Amelia," Trabue gently beckoned her back from where her mind had fled.

She went on. "If it had been just the rescheduling and the Evans thing, I would have passed it off as 'things as usual' in a big organization. But when coupled with this case and me being pulled from it, I'm certain that something is going on. I saw her; she had no signs of being a drug user. No signs whatsoever."

She stopped and looked into the distance again. Before Trabue could speak, she turned back to him and said, "The young look so dreadfully dead when they are dead."

This time Trabue looked away. He went back to Sunday and Karen Blaine floating in trash.

"Yes, she shouldn't be dead."

Trabue waited. He wanted to get the image of Karen out of his mind. He shifted the focus to his companion. "Amelia, tell me how and why you became a forensic pathologist?"

"Science, simple science," was her reply. Trabue showed sincere interest and she continued.

"My parents were teachers and I'm an only child. They encouraged my curiosity." She laughed. "It also didn't hurt that I was the tallest and skinniest girl in my class. I was the nerd girl in my neighborhood. By the time my classmates caught up with me in height, I was hooked on biology, then medicine. Pathology is pure science, or nearly so, and I was a lab rat. I looked the part and played it well. It got me into medical school." She glanced at Trabue to gauge his interest. "I like solving puzzles, so forensics was an inevitable match. There's not much else to me; I just love my work."

"How about your husband?" asked Trabue. Her reaction was more sudden and severe than he had anticipated. She gasped.

"You weren't—you didn't over hear us?"

"Yes, Amelia, I heard your argument, or at least the end. I will respect your privacy and..."

She interrupted. "No. No, I want to get it out. I need to tell someone. It's all, well, it's all..." she escaped momentarily, but brought herself back before Trabue could react. "It's all tied together to whatever brought you to my home this morning, I'm afraid."

"Go on."

"Ledge," her tone was one intended for a true friend. "You've seen where we live. We're salaried professionals. We make great money compared to most people in this city, but we can't afford that place!" Frustration tinted her voice.

It was obvious to Trabue that Amelia Jackson, the nerd, the lab rat loner, had few people to count on as friends.

"Six months ago Otis moved us into the condo. I was at a conference. When I came home he picked me up at the airport and surprised me by driving to our new address. It was just one act in a series of things that scare me about Otis. I'm uncertain who he is, what he's become. He's not the man I married. But it's not a cliché. He's changed and not for the better."

"A friend said he'd once lost a bundle betting on Otis. What does that mean?" asked Trabue.

"Oh," she laughed again and Trabue noticed that this remembrance brought a twinkle to her eyes. "That's a local legend by now, but your friend, if he lost money, did not bet on Otis, rather against him. Otis was, and still is, the last great athlete for Vanderbilt's football program. He was the star on their last really competitive team.

They went to a bowl game in Florida and were serious underdogs. Even the locals bet against them. That's what your friend did. But, they beat the odds and went into history as one of the longest long shots ever in college sports! So Otis is certainly well known in this town. I met him years later. I wasn't really aware of who he was when we met. Remember, I was constantly indoors peering into a microscope."

"Did he ever consider continuing his athletic career?"

"No, he was fully aware of his capabilities and the long-term prospects as an athlete. He was good, especially for here, but not an NFL candidate. Not Otis. He was so grounded then, he knew what was real and what was make-believe. I'm not certain that he knows the difference now. He is not Otis anymore."

"How so?"

"Otis rode his celebrity status into law school instead of pro sports. He wanted, or said he wanted, to be an example for the kind of kids he knew best, the ones with skills and talent, the ones who dream of moving up but lack positive role models. He wanted to be a hero, all the time, not just in college and sports, but in the community, too."

"Sounds admirable," injected Trabue. "What happened?

"I don't know how. But the change is recent, in the past year. It may not yet be apparent to others, but I know it. He's changed and it's not good! Somewhere he's learned how to be more than the token."

"African American?" bemused Trabue.

"No. JOCK!" she exclaimed. "He's been the perfect has-been

jock. We met and dated his last year of law school. I was still an undergrad but had secured my med school slot with a prestigious scholarship. That's how I met Otis, or rather how he met me. We were being interviewed by Dick Patterson for his new daily column. We were two young up-and-comers—you know the story. Patterson's angle was to show that Nashville had truly come of age. No racism, and the Old South was in the past. He highlighted all types of non-traditional types—us, Latinos, East Indians, Asians, and minorities of all sorts."

"I met Patterson this morning," commented Trabue.

"What did you think?" she asked.

"I really haven't had much time to reflect on the experience. He bolted when he looked at an old article tying Karen's employer with the Fellows Corporation."

"Fellows? John Fellows?"

"You know him?"

"Yes. Do I! And I wish I didn't. He, or should I say his company, owns our building. For the past year or so, he and Otis have been best friends. But, I can't really say I know him. I just know that whatever has changed Otis is part and parcel to Fellows. Otis keeps me away from John Fellows and even farther from Jan, John's wife. Not that I am complaining. From what I've picked up over the years Jan Hart Fellows and I are light years apart in every conceivable fashion."

"Jealous?" Trabue was probing.

"No. No way!" Amelia Jackson was quick to respond and kept talking. She returned to her original track. Trabue felt she was avoiding discussion of Mr. and Mrs. Fellows. He kept silent. He let her run the conversation away from Jan Fellows.

"Otis never took the bar exam. He made a public announcement that he would attend the police academy and join the force, hoping to be a bridge, an example. You know, the hero I mentioned. But," she paused again, "I think it may have been even then that all this was set in motion."

"What do you mean by 'all this?'"

"Well, the different Otis. He never really served as a police officer. Sure, he graduated from the Academy and was commissioned, but he never really patrolled the streets or served like the other rookies. He was immediately assigned to 'photo ops,' VIP escorts, ribbon cuttings, and the like. And of course, he was at every University athletic event. I don't believe Otis has ever written a ticket or made an arrest. His police career is pure public relations."

"You sound detached from it all."

"Remember, I was in medical school. During those years I saw precious little of Otis. My role was that of the brainy, bookish spouse of the rising community leader. Yes, I'm detached now. I'm detached because I was always excluded. When I did have time and wanted to be involved I felt marginalized."

"By whom?"

"By Otis, and his growing agenda to be whatever it is he is becoming."

"Which is?"

"I think he wants to be mayor, maybe even more. He's into power, money, and running with the smart crowd."

"The John Fellows of the world?"

"Yes, Fellows and more importantly, Fellows' father-in-law. Lawrence Hart is an important man with a very low profile. He's big, but you'd never know it. The Fellows Corporation is actually Hart's, or his daughter's. Who can tell who owns what? They have so much. I expect that John Fellows is, well, in a way just like Otis. Maybe that's why they are friends."

"Like Otis? In what way?"

"All form and no substance," was her blunt reply.

"That's a hard statement." Trabue offered.

"Yes, hard for me to say, especially about Otis. It is easier to say about John Fellows. He's a nice guy when you meet him, but he seems as dumb as the bench you're sitting on. They call him 'John Wayne' behind his back."

"Making fun, because he's macho?"

"Macho? No! No! It's the way he walks."

"Okay, so continue; tell me more about Otis and Fellows."

"Otis can be something other than fluff when he chooses. John would have a hard time spelling it. Next to Otis he's the University's second most recognized ex-jock, but his real claim to fame is that he married Jan."

"Because of her wealth?"

"Yes and no. Money is one thing; Jan is quite another. She's the University's third most recognized ex-jock. She made it to the Olympic swim team. But she's best known because she is involved with practically every charitable event and non-profit in the city. You can't pick up *The Nashvillian* and find three consecutive days without her photo. She's mentioned for her volunteer work, committee memberships, board seats, and so on. People have forgotten her past because of the things she does now."

"Her past, what's in it?" Trabue's interest was roused.

"As I mentioned, she was a swimmer. There was an incident, at the Aquatic Club, when she was eleven or twelve. The club was where all the rich kids trained. Jan Hart and, I forget the other girl's name, were rivals. Both were good, but the other girl was maybe a bit better. Well, no one really saw or knows what happened, but the two girls were alone one day. They were slated for an early practice session. When the next group arrived they found Jan Hart gone and her rival floating face down in the pool. Jan claimed that she never arrived that morning, but her mother dropped her off at the club prior to the incident. Jan never said anything again about it after her first statement. Rumor has it that her father, his money, and their joint influence, halted the interrogation. She taught the hard-boiled police crew what it was like to deal with a real ice queen, even as a pre-teen. She was the coldest and hardest they'd ever encountered. That's when the cute play on her name originated—'more money, less Hart.' I remember because I grew up here. Nashville is changing and growing, so there are fewer people to remember. God, she's everywhere! She is everywhere and with her comes Lawrence Hart's money."

"So, you have reasons not to enjoy your new home?"

"Yes, I don't know how we afford it. Otis isn't very forthcoming with details and I don't like his friends. Frankly, Jan Hart Fellows scares me."

"Scares you?"

"Less heart, as a trend, leads to no heart. The woman, for all her civic front, is heartless."

"How do you know?"

"Remember I said that her mother dropped Jan at the Aquatic club? I'm convinced that Mrs. Hart knew the truth, but she also drowned. She drowned in alcohol."

"Rumors?" asked Trabue.

"No. I saw it first hand. It took years, but Mrs. Hart killed herself, slowly. I'm sure that because of the Hart fortune and influence, the family was able to gloss over the years of self-destructive behavior that ultimately led to the end. Rich drunks are hard to detect. Money buys the cover-up. However, sooner or later it shows. For Mrs. Hart it was a combination of too much alcohol and a staircase. She tumbled head first into the foyer of the Hart mansion. I was an undergrad working in the morgue. Jan's father was away on business and Mrs. Hart was found by a neighbor. So there was the formality of processing her through the system for non-routine deaths."

"Was there an autopsy?"

"No, no need in her case, broken neck, an obvious fall. No signs of struggle, foul play, or anything unusual. Contrary to what popular television would lead you to believe, we do not perform as many autopsies as you might imagine. However, as part of the formalities, someone had to identify Mrs. Hart. That someone was Jan." Amelia Jackson's voice was wooden. A painful look spread across her face.

"It seems like it was a memorable event." Trabue stated.

"I was there. But I was just a nobody as far as Jan was concerned. Today, I believe she could not place me in the room. But I still remember it well, all too well." She paused again. "I caught her eyes after she looked up from viewing her mother; there was no pain, no love, no nothing! I've seen all the emotions possible. Times like that bring truth to the surface. She showed nothing."

Trabue attempted an explanation. "People react in unforeseen ways. I'm certain you've seen delayed responses of grief. It's only natural that..."

She interrupted. "No! No! Ledge, she had nothing! Her eyes were black holes—small collapsed stars sucking everything inward. I will never forget those eyes. That's why I'm afraid of her. I, I..." Amelia froze.

Trabue had never seen such a trance evoked by a memory. He reached forward, touched her clasped hands; she flinched and became aware of her surroundings.

Before she could react, he spoke. "When I started this morning I had no idea what I would find. I'm still not certain where all this is headed, but I need your help. You said you liked to solve puzzles. Help me solve this one. Help explain why Karen Blaine is dead and who is responsible." He hit something in her.

"Yes, I'll help," was the answer. "I feel that I must. But what more can I do? I've told you all I know."

Her response was a plea. Trabue hoped she was open for the assignment.

"Keep a close eye on your husband." He watched her reaction. He was asking her to be disloyal, to spy on her spouse and cross a huge line. Her downcast gaze told him she would. "Do what you must for yourself, but tell me anything that might help my search.

Can you do that?"

"Yes, I can. I will. For quite some time I've known, sensed, the changes in Otis and feared they would lead to something. How and when shall I contact you?"

While writing the marina's number on a card he said, "If you see or find anything you think I should know, call here and then call Dr. Bryan."

She looked perplexed.

"Why would I call him too?"

"If you need to call me, we'll need him! Trust me."

Chapter 9

Trabue said good-bye.

Amelia had literally run away to begin her exercise regimen.

Trabue watched her negotiate the jogging trail and decided that a call on Karen's employer, Dr. Forsythe, was in order. He left the bench and walked toward Reggie and the parked cab.

His thoughts were clear and ordered. Karen Blaine was a good person. She had no bad habits; she was studious, determined, and responsible. Routine events after her death had been altered enough to convince Trabue to stick with his effort.

Karen Blaine had become a wrinkle in someone's fabric. Something had required her removal and a cover-up was being constructed as part of the smoothing process.

Otis Jackson seemed involved. That was probable. Was he a player, or was he just following orders?

Trabue felt progress was being made.

Probe and ask questions. They, whoever "they" are, will make moves. Ye shall know them by their actions, thought Trabue. *Progress is good, but direction is another matter.*

★ ★ ★ ★ ★

Trabue did not hear the gunning of the engine. He was close to the waiting cab and he caught Reggie focused on a spot to his own right rear, the place where Amelia should be jogging.

The screeching of brakes was accented by the squeal of a car

accelerating through a tight corner and speeding away. Trabue whirled to see two vehicles barely avoiding a collision. By the slightest of margins the car had missed a service truck and then a jogger in a gray sweat suit.

Trabue sprinted to Amelia. Reggie reacted likewise and wheeled the cab from the parking space and out the side exit using a roadway course. Trabue's route was cross-country.

Trabue arrived first.

The car, a late model sedan with darkly tinted windows, had actually made contact with Amelia's loose-fitting sweat suit at the knee. It was a close call. Too close to be an accident, which was apparent since the car had not slowed to avoid her and the driver did not hesitate or stop to inspect any injury. The car was long gone by the time Trabue reached Amelia asking, "Are you hurt?"

She was safe, but visibly shaken. "Maybe I shouldn't try to be so healthy," she offered with a weak laugh.

Trabue examined her condition. She was scared. No, she was terrified. The feeble joke was a weak attempt at disguising her distress. Her eyes told all.

"I think it would be best if you rode with us," said Trabue. He nodded toward the cab as it approached. Reggie jumped out, leaving his door open and the cab running. He hurried to them.

Amelia was still dazed. Profession, spouse, home—it all was a fog. Trabue was there. So was another man. They were clear, but she felt fuzzy.

Trabue asked, "Amelia, are you alright?"

She was blank. He asked again. "Amelia! Are you, okay? Please, talk to me!"

She answered, "I'm fine, really! It's just, half the universe is..."

"Is what?"

"Gone. I don't know. I'll go. Yes, I'll go with you!"

"The woman's got sense, knows her mind," said Reggie.

"It was no accident!" snapped Trabue. "That truck saved her."

★ ★ ★ ★ ★

The truck's driver explained, "I was checking a call report. By almost running that stop sign I guess I helped. She missed being hit bad." He pointed up the street. "That car left fast. I didn't get a tag number and I couldn't see inside." He repeated, "Left fast, real fast! You want me to hang around for the police?" His question had the underlying statement of "hope not" in it.

He was relieved when Trabue replied, "No, there's no need; she's shaken, but not hurt."

The truck driver disappeared. Such an event could complicate his life and he wanted no part of reports and police, not to mention his manager asking questions.

Trabue and Reggie, book-ending Amelia, stood on each side and escorted her toward the cab. It was less for protection and more for confidence-building. The intent of the close call was sinking in on her. She nodded agreement when Trabue, in a soft but firm tone, said, "We're calling Albert, now! And you're coming with us."

"No argument from me," she replied.

★ ★ ★ ★ ★

The ride back to the Roker Arms took only a few minutes.

Trabue stepped away from the cab and called Tampa. He found that Albert was in class and would not be available for another thirty minutes.

Trabue said to the grad student, "Tell him T.T. called. The message is: 'Help! I've kidnapped a police chief's wife.'"

★ ★ ★ ★ ★

While Trabue phoned Albert, Reggie escorted Amelia to unit 12-D. He acted as bodyguard and bellhop while Amelia packed enough things for "an undetermined" time. Reggie had insisted on being involved beyond driving, and wholeheartedly joined Trabue's quest.

Trabue had not explained the good guys to Blaine. If you asked, poked, and probed, the good guys would also make moves. Reggie was a good guy.

Trabue borrowed Reggie's phone a second time and attempted to set an appointment at Forsythe & Associates. The answering machine informed him that the office was closed for lunch and would reopen at 2 p.m. He opted not to leave a message and decided to drop in unannounced. Next, he patiently waited to call Albert again. He did not want to rely on someone getting his message to Albert.

Trabue thought about the knot he had agreed to untie. He was certain that bringing Amelia Jackson along after this point was risky, but not bringing her seemed riskier.

She had sensed that her environment was unsafe. Amelia brought up that notion, but may not have believed it. Events proved her feelings correct. She would be safer with Trabue than isolated in her condo. Like it or not, she was part of solving the riddle of Karen Blaine's demise.

In Amelia's case the involvement was personal. For some reason she had also become a wrinkle. It was not lost on Trabue that Amelia had failed to mention any effort, or desire, to contact her husband. She was committed.

Trabue thought, *It appears sides are being drawn, teams are being chosen. Karen on a morgue table and this near miss are proof enough. Bad guys are at work and I'm collecting volunteers faster than answers. Amelia knows that going with strangers is safer than being with her 'charmer' cop husband. I need some professional help. Albert, where are you?*

Chapter 10

When Assistant Chief of Police Otis Jackson felt the vibration of his special cell phone he knew it was not good news. Only two people had the number and it never brought welcomed information. They called in; he never called out. He knew, especially now, that it was bad news. He considered ignoring the buzzing, but there was no escaping either of the callers.

He excused himself from the group of community leaders he was schmoozing and exited the hotel's lobby. The awards luncheon had broken up and the usual jockeying for photo ops and handshakes would proceed without him. Out of earshot he flipped open the phone and barked, "Tell me something good, or stop calling!"

The reply came from a bland voice. "Just thought you would like to hear—the attempt on your wife's life failed."

"What do you mean, the attempt failed?"

"Sorry, can't add any more right now."

"I need more than this if I'm going any further."

There was no reply. Otis Jackson heard the line disconnect.

"Damn!" He exclaimed, visibly upset.

He pushed numbers on the cell phone keypad. He wanted to talk with the other person who knew the number of this special phone.

Things are getting out of hand. I want the dominoes to stop falling. The M.E. shuffle was supposed to be no big deal. But it caused a landslide.

"Yes?" A voice answered on the other end of the connection.

"I want things to stop!" Otis Jackson demanded.

"Calm down. Be careful what you say," the voice warned.

"I want it over!"

"We need to talk when you've got better control of yourself."

"When? When?" Jackson asked.

"Later. Perhaps tonight."

"No, that's too late."

"Sorry. It's tonight." The phone went dead.

Jackson's head began to hurt. Until recently things had been good. His plan had been moving along nicely. Then events began to accelerate. Now this! He reached for his other cell phone, with the police-issued number.

Should I call? If I do, maybe she'll know. If I don't and she thinks, just thinks, I know, then, she will know. I... Oh, damn! This is not good. It's too much, too fast.

Jackson entered the number for his home. The recorder answered. Listening to his wife's recorded voice was strange. Real strange, considering what he had been told.

Pausing after the beep, he drew in a deep breath. *Here goes*, he thought.

"Amelia, this is Otis. Are you alright? After this morning I am worried. Please call!" He exhaled with the end of the last word. *Crap!* Otis thought. *I've blown it! That was the worst message—so fake, so shallow. She'll figure it out!*

Flipping off his phone, Otis reentered the hotel. The swirling activity and the ill-defined chatter washed over him. Amelia and his recent thoughts left his mind. *I'm committed. It is too late to change what is happening.*

He spotted Jan Fellows being interviewed by Patterson of *The*

Nashvillian. Otis moved across the room and cut through the milling herd of wannabes.

"Committed," he muttered to no one in particular. "Committed is better than owned."

As he maneuvered past three nobodies who were timidly waiting to reach Jan, the conversing pair spotted him and broke off the exchange. Patterson blocked Jackson, giving Jan an open escape route. She moved away rapidly and was devoured by the crowd.

"Well Otis," Patterson stated, "Jan has shared some very interesting news, some personal news. I'm always after a good story. You're tight with her clan, so..."

Normally Jackson would have picked up immediately on the personal nature of the greeting, but he was distracted. He muscled the reporter aside and whispering "No comment," and attempted to follow Jan Fellows. However, Patterson's grasp held him back.

"No comment? That's not acceptable."

Jackson easily slipped the man's grasp and reversed the hold. He squeezed back and repeated in a deeper voice, "No comment," adding, "disappear," for emphasis.

"Yeah, sure," Patterson replied. "But I'm headed out of town and before..."

He did not finish.

Jackson had dropped his hold on the reporter and melted into the crowd to search for Jan.

Instead of following the policeman, the reporter scurried out of the hotel in pursuit of the hot lead he had just received from Jan Fellows.

She wasn't upset in the least that I pitched a Karen Blaine-John Fellows love-connection. Karen Blaine may not be a nobody after all, Patterson thought. *She worked for a colleague of John Fellows.* He quickened his pace, still thinking *Young girl. Same office building. In John Fellow's proximity.* Patterson was smiling. He sniffed a sex scandal, maybe more. Sex was still big in Nashville as news, especially with a rich guy like Fellows.

Jan had said, "He's been to Texas and Mexico recently, maybe you should go have a look."

Patterson literally quivered. *Maybe, I will go have a look. There is something big developing around John fellows,* he thought.

It was too big not to check out. Patterson, the ambitious reporter, could see the story. It had his byline.

But why would Jan give me the tip? The thought flittered across his mind for an instant. *Maybe she's ready to dump him?*

The thought of the headlines pushed everything out of Patterson's mind. *My byline!*

His pace quickened.

Chapter 11

Two calls from Trabue in less than a week, was the thought perched in Albert Bryan's mind. It was followed by, *better check the air schedule for the quickest flight to Nashville. He said, it was T.T.; I might even need a charter.*

Albert sat quietly with hands folded across his ample middle. The phone rang. *I hope that's him,* he thought as he answered.

"Yes."

"Need some advice, buddy."

"I'm all ears."

"Are they growing too?" They laughed.

Trabue recounted events since their last conversation. To anyone other than the two, Trabue's cadence, comments, and context of the exchange was code-like. Trabue's use of their verbal shorthand told Albert that Trabue was on to something and was taking precautions.

Bryan listened carefully with his cop's ears. When finished, Trabue kept silent and gave him time to think.

Albert broke the silence. "Patterson smelled a story, can't blame him for bolting, he's a reporter. It's his nature." He drew a breath and sighed. "But Jackson, that's very different. It just smells-bad! You're on to something—exactly what, I won't even guess. But it's not good. I'll be there as soon as possible."

Knowing Trabue's quirk of not liking cell phones, he said, "I'll reach you through the Marina or the cab company. Looks like you found a good ally. Follow up on the girl's employer and the Fellows Corporation. If you can't meet me at the airport, have someone fill in. And I'm sure you thought of it, but don't leave Mrs. Jackson alone."

"Covered; anything else?"

"Yes, but can't think of it now. See you soon. Be careful."

"I'll try not to fall overboard while I'm fishing!"

They hung up together.

Bryan scanned the airline schedule for the best flight to Nashville with one eye while he mentally rearranged his upcoming classes and lectures while eyeing his personal calendar at the same time. *My research assistants will have to fill in*, he thought. *They love and hate it when I travel. The ambitious little bastards.*

But even if something critically important were scheduled at the University, it was second in priority to Trabue. He'd walk to Nashville if necessary. He owed Trabue everything! *I practically forced him to buy that boat. I nagged him into taking the trip. Yes, it's to Nashville—and quick!*

★ ★ ★ ★ ★

With Bryan in motion, Trabue was calmed. He closed his eyes and smiled as an absurd visual played across his mind: Albert Bryan leading the charge as the cavalry came to the rescue. Trabue felt that he owed Bryan so much. It felt good that in a time of need he could call on a friend to be there. He marveled that he and Bryan were so dissimilar, so unlikely to be paired, yet, here he was, in the midst of—what? A mess for certain, and his friend was ready to jump in. He still had a smile on his face when Reggie and Amelia arrived.

No longer visibly shaken, Amelia Jackson reappeared as her hyper-professional self. The analytical scientist-pathologist was eager to know what was next required of her. Even though she had narrowly escaped serious injury and was departing with strangers into a life that would likely not include—maybe even violently oppose— her husband, and his associates. She was ready for instructions.

"Ledge, where do we go from here?" She inquired. Considering the circumstances, she showed no sign of pressure or tension. Trabue was impressed. She was an asset, rather than liability.

He responded by giving directions to Reggie, "Take us to Stone Harbor." Before either could react he continued, "I'll fill you both in as we travel."

"We're on our way," said Reggie.

As they drove, he gave them an abbreviated version of what he had shared with Albert and concluded with, "Albert will be a tremendous help; he'll be with us soon. Amelia, you'll be safe on the *Awfria*. There is a gate and a guard at the dock. I'll ask Eddie to show you the boat and wait with you if Win Blaine isn't back by the time we arrive. Reggie, I'll need you to take me to Forsythe's office and then on to the Fellows corporate headquarters."

"That's easy; they're in the same location. The Fellows Corporation owns an office building near the airport and the address you mentioned for Forsythe is in that building."

"Why doesn't that surprise me?"

As they entered the parking area near the dock, Trabue was glad to see Win Blaine pulling into one of the spaces. *Good, one less person involved if I don't need Eddie,* was his thought.

Blaine appeared worn and used.

The experience of going through Karen's apartment and belongings must have been difficult, thought Trabue.

Blaine waved feebly at the cab when he recognized Trabue as one of its occupants. He walked toward the cab as it eased into a spot directly across from his truck.

"You look played out," observed Trabue. He quickly got out of Reggie's cab to greet Blaine.

"I'm fine, now that I see you're here. I half expected you and the boat to be gone based on the kind of day I've had so far."

He motioned toward Reggie and Amelia, "I see you've brought reinforcements. We'll need them; my day was a bust. Police have the apartment closed. It's an official crime scene. No one can or will tell me why and that idiot detective has been avoiding me. I wasted a lot of time looking for him at the Criminal Justice Building and then back at the apartment. They won't let me in. It makes no sense. If Karen really was a suicide, then why lock down the apartment as a crime scene? Evans was a ghost all day. Someone said he's at an awards ceremony, of all things." He smiled at the newcomers and said, "Hello, I'm Winton Blaine; sorry for rambling on."

Reggie gave Win "the guy nod"—that universal acknowledgement between men that signals, "I'm okay, you're okay."

Win returned the brief gesture and smiled again, this time at Amelia. "I'm Winton Blaine, ma'am. You can call me Win."

"Hello, Win. I'm Amelia," she smiled, and he smiled back.

With introductions complete, Reggie opened the trunk and proceeded to retrieve Amelia's overnight bag.

Amelia's reaction to Blaine was medical. She saw his condition, diagnosed it immediately, and acted. She moved to his side, took his arm and began to guide him toward the dock's entrance. Although she was considerably smaller than the ex-soldier, she was in control, guiding him and speaking in a soft, yet firm, manner. Blaine succumbed to the personal attention. Trabue noted to himself, *Perfect, they will be good for each other while I am gone.*

Amelia continued, "Win, you've been through a lot. Let's get to a place where you can rest and we can all share what we know about this terrible situation." Off they went.

Trabue and Reggie looked at each other, shrugged and followed.

Trabue marveled at the speed with which Amelia acted. When they arrived, Win Blaine had been done in. By the time he was situated in the *Awfria's* salon he was much improved. Better still, she had a patient to take her mind off what she had experienced.

Trabue gave Win the briefest of outlines on the events to date and asked Amelia to fill in the details.

When he left with Reggie, Trabue was immensely relieved that two potential liabilities were cancelled out by each other. They were deep in conversation and barely acknowledged his departure.

Chapter 12

The Shavers Express was about one hundred yards out of the marina's parking lot when Reggie spoke. "I didn't want to alarm the lady. I wasn't so certain, but I am now. We're being followed."

Trabue did not look back.

Good sign, observed Reggie, *the man doesn't rattle easily.*

"What have we got?" asked Trabue.

"Looks like two, in a plain gray four-door. They picked us up at the Roker Arms. Been laying back, but I'm certain it's a tail."

Trabue thought of looping their trail and getting behind them, switching the predator–prey set up. But he was more intent on following the leads on Forsythe and Fellows. He asked Reggie, "Can you shake them?"

He got the answer he expected.

"No problem." Reggie reached for his phone.

Trabue was curious but remained silent. *A street-wise, forty-year cab driver could certainly show me a few tricks.*

"Elvira, no time to talk. Find out who's near the airport and have them call me!" he disconnected before she could reply.

In less than thirty seconds Reggie answered an incoming call. "Yeah, I need you to do a special pick-up at the airport Marriott. Wait in the parking area next to the side door, you know, near the offices. Right! Get there, and stay put. A man will get in. You take him to the Fellows office building. Use the back route under the interstate. He'll be there in ten minutes or less." There was a question. "No, no need to wait for him, I'll do the pick-up at the Fellows

place."

On the way to the Marriott, Reggie explained his plan.

"I'll drop you off at the front entrance. I won't pull over to the cab stand to pick up another fare. Instead, I'll sit like I'm waiting for you. After five minutes, I'll get out and walk over to the valet stand and chat with whoever is on duty. If the tail took the bait they will be sitting and watching. They won't suspect that you bailed out the back door. After I put on my show, I'll move my cab over to the airport line and pick up a quick fare. All of it should take about thirty to forty-five minutes. You'll need more time than that where you're headed, so I'll wait for you in the Fellows building lot when I'm done. Sound good?"

"Sounds perfect, let's do it!"

Trabue added one feature to Reggie's plan: On his way through the hotel Trabue ducked into the gift shop and purchased two items. With a newspaper tucked under his arm and wearing a *Nashville Sounds* baseball cap, he was transformed into a tourist passing through the lobby. He followed Reggie's directions and continued past the elevators, around the corner, and out the side door.

No one paid him the slightest notice. The second Shavers cab was waiting as planned.

Trabue slid into the back seat and the vehicle was rolling before the door was completely closed. The cab exited the hotel grounds, unseen, at high speed.

"Don't worry, we've done this once or twice before," said an effervescent voice.

Trabue looked up and saw the biggest smile in existence.

"Hi! I'm Glory Be! Gloria is my real name, but since I married Sam, Poppa Reggie's son, the youngest, I became Gloria Bea Shavers. You know—Glory Be Forever. That was the joke! So, Glory Be stuck."

She talked as fast as she drove.

Cars, trees, and buildings were one continuous blur. She looked at Trabue as she spoke while keeping only a marginal eye on the road ahead. Nonetheless, Trabue felt safe. Rather than being part of her environment, Glory Be, or more correctly her energy, was the environment.

Trabue absorbed her staccato bursts as only a firing squad victim could. She was capable of conveying more information in a shorter time than anyone he had ever met. She spoke faster than he had ever heard. She was magnificent.

She explained, "As a daughter of an attorney and a fifth generation Fisk University graduate, my family is freaked that I'm hooked up with Sam Shavers and driving a cab. I should be teaching music, which is the family tradition—especially for one whose great-great-grandmother was one of the original Jubilee Singers." She could chirp, talk, sing, chatter, and drive at warp velocity.

In one short breath she shared, "I adore Sam, my husband, Poppa Reggie's youngest child by his first wife—not the short term first one but the real first one—and not Elvira, the current one, who knows everybody and talks on the phone twenty-four-seven, and runs the cab company's office, with Aunty who is not really anyone's aunt, but is Elvira's best friend. They've been friends since, well, forever, and Aunty is always there, you know, like a companion. She

doesn't work or have a job; she just sits in the recliner in the office and watches TV—History Channel, Discovery, CNN, game shows, news—constantly. Never misses all those shows like Jerry, Montel, you know. Oh, and *Oprah!* She won't miss *Oprah* for nothing, and I mean absolutly nothing. Well, she hardly ever talks, just sits, watches TV, works the crosswords and nods and gestures to Elvira as Elvira goes through her phone thing, it's ESP between those two." Glory Be took a gasp for air.

"Well, where was I? Sam, oh yes! Sam, well, I fell for him the first moment I saw him, he's Poppa Reggie all over, that was when I was in school. It was an intern thing with a community group, that's where we were. I was there for school and Sam, well he was there as, well, part of the project from the community group, you see, Sam was always in trouble, not always, but always since his momma died, this is before Elvira jumped on his case so to speak, but she was on him when we met, Sam was out of trouble, but still doing community hours." Another gasp.

"So he was doing his last payback for being a bad boy you know, a real knot head, until Elvira told him the truth and he got it, so he was on the right track when I met him, not like before. He was twelve when his momma died and all the troubles started, some boys got him to tag along when they robbed a convenience store, they gave him a starter pistol from the school's athletic department— blanks. It had blanks, got him in serious trouble, and he kept on once he was tagged as a thug. If it wasn't for Elvira he'd be in jail, or dead, she married Reggie and real quick she turned Sam around, he hated her, now he'd walk through fire for her, she was on him and he hated it, they had a big fight, arguing, yelling, so bad even Aunty got up, turned off the TV and left, it was something, I wasn't there but it's legend."

Another quick breath.

"Sam told her that she didn't know nothin' and she said 'I know one thing' and he yelled, 'yeah, what?' She said, 'I know I love you!' Isn't that just so beautiful? He broke down and cried, hugged on her and wouldn't let go. He's been good and moving on the up-and-up ever since, finished a GED, four years of college in two-and-a-half, working on an MBA at night and weekends all while driving a cab and learning the real things about running a business and he brought me into it all. And he still has the time to keep me happy and in love and, well, that's not your business. My family, like I said, is all against it. Particularly me driving, but Poppa Reggie says no one works in the office, managing and telling drivers what to do, without being a driver. He even made Elvira drive. Imagine her driving and trying to talk on the phone! She scared so many people that Poppa Reggie had to let her work in the office, but she's good there, real good. She keeps in touch with everyone, and I mean *everyone*!"

Glory Be timed it perfectly as she wheeled the vehicle into a private drive heading toward a tall, mirrored-glass building—the Fellows Center.

"We're here."

Trabue got out, more than just slightly shaken.

Normally Trabue observed terrain and topography on all trips, long or short. But he could not remember anything about the route they had just traveled.

Before he could say a thing, she was off again at warp speed, yelling to him "Poppa Reggie said your money's no good, you be careful, he'll pick you up, 'bye!"

She disappeared.

"Glory Be!" exclaimed Trabue.

Chapter 13

The Fellows Center was big, modern, and cold.

Whoever designed this place had no soul, thought Trabue.

The Fellows Corporation had offices from floors five up to twelve at the top. The lowest floors were leased to smaller businesses with a few retail shops situated at ground level to serve the building's occupants. To get to one of the offices, a visitor had to register at the security desk that was located a few paces within the main doorway. Trabue presented himself at the desk and was greeted by a blazer-clad guard sporting an earpiece.

After Trabue signed in and answered a series of questions, the desk attendant busily entered information into a computer. While he waited, Trabue had time to count eight split video screens with a total of sixty-four views. *No soul and paranoid,* was the thought that crossed Trabue's mind.

Trabue was directed to suite 2-C, the location of Forsythe and Associates, by the monotone voice emitted from the robot-like guard.

Pay peanuts, get monkeys, Trabue observed.

Trabue knew that the expense of the video system had to be backed up with some real financial muscle. The up-front drone was fluff. It may have made the unaware tenants and visitors feel secure, but the real security was hidden. *You can count on it,* thought Trabue.

Suite 2-C was accessed by way of a glass-caged elevator or the stainless steel circular stairs on the far side of the lobby. He took the stairs so that he would have the opportunity to inspect the layout of

the lobby. It wasn't inspiring.

The open-to-the-roof area of the lobby was lined on three sides by balconies that recalled cell blocks of the old prison movies. *Talk about retro,* thought Trabue as he climbed the staircase. *Great place to toss a burning mattress, or maybe an inmate.*

The view did not improve with elevation. The Forsythe & Associates suite was at the head of the stairway. Trabue entered the outer office. Noises coming from the rear made it obvious that someone was busy working there. He was greeted by a late-fiftyish-year-old woman wearing a gray business suit.

"You must be Mr. Trabue. The front desk buzzed me and said you were walking up. I'm Emma Jenkins, the office manager."

She smiled and extended her hand, which he grasped.

She looked solid and competent. Trabue bet himself that she was the one who kept the office running. He spotted a tired and worried look about her and decided to take a soft approach. He hoped she might open up a bit before he saw Forsythe. *You never know where help comes from,* thought Trabue.

"Pleased to meet you, Ms. Jenkins. Please call me Ledge; it's short for Rutledge, or if you prefer, just plain Trabue—my friends call me that." His slight pause and the implied offer to join in with his friends caused her to relax.

"Thank you. Sometimes it's so nice not to be formal."

Good! he thought. *Maybe she knows nothing about what happened, so she won't know what to hide.*

She gestured an invitation to accompany her into the inner offices. She spoke as she led.

"It's been a couple of hectic days." They entered a room decorated with photos of archeological sites, excavations, and group shots of diggers. The diggers looked like university-types on summer field excursions.

Emma sat facing him and asked "Now, Trabue, how may I help you? My guess is that you are here due to the recent tragic event."

Maybe I was wrong, he thought. *I better lay it out; be direct.*

Trabue spoke slowly and carefully, "Yes, as a matter of fact. Karen Blaine's father has asked me to assist in his effort to understand what really happened."

"Then you are an investigator?" She started to tense up.

"No, no. If anything, I'm, well, now a friend."

"You were something else?"

It could go either way now. His answer could bring her over entirely to his side, or drive her all the way back to being the competent professional. Trabue leaned a little closer to her, looked straight into her eyes and explained, "Ms. Jenkins, unfortunately, I'm the one who found Karen floating in the river."

"Oh, I see," was her reply as she sat back and almost collapsed. "That must have been very unpleasant."

"Very."

Emma was about to let the dam burst. She tilted her head back, closed her eyes and talked.

Trabue listened.

"I started working at a bank right out of high school. It was a good job. I was an assistant teller. I was there thirty-five years. Moved up, had several good promotions. I ran the administrative department

for Sun Bank, but they went the way of most local banks over the years—buyouts, sellouts, mergers. There are few local ones left. In the end I took an early retirement deal from, what was it, the fourth? No! The fifth corporate entity I worked for—new names on the same company. I'm getting on, but I wasn't ready to really retire so I found this spot here. Professor Forsythe, Kenneth, is my cousin's son. He asked me to be his office manager. I came here when he left the university two years ago. Karen came last year, after her class work was over. She was doing research and writing her dissertation in between projects for Kenneth."

She paused.

"It's hard to believe she's gone. I've worked with a great many people in all these years. She was a good one. Solid. Worked well with Kenneth and his types, you know the professors, the academics. She was one of them, but not really one of them. She was better, very smart, very sharp and very, very honest. Why, the only time she ever disagreed with Kenneth was about an integrity issue. I never knew all the details, but they did disagree—even argued. It was the only time I recall her being upset. I tried not to listen but they were really too loud not to hear part of it. She wanted to be specific about something in a report and he was telling her to be reasonable, that it was sometimes important to be vague. She would have no part of it. No, she was sticking to her guns and said something like 'Seven hundred years plus or minus a century or two is not vague, it's ludicrous!' They fussed some more and since then I guess they never could, now never will, mend fences—with Karen dead and Kenneth gone."

"Gone?"

"I'm so sorry. I've been rambling on—taking your time. And you're here no doubt to see Kenneth and I never told you he's gone. I mean missing."

"Missing?"

"Yes. The last time I saw him was Friday at the end of the day. The police were here early Monday morning. I couldn't find him anywhere. I haven't heard from him and I don't have any idea where he might be. He's not scheduled to go anywhere and he had some out-of-town experts coming in later this week to work with him and Karen on the Fellows project. I've had to cancel those plans. It is so unlike him to just pick up and leave without saying something to me. He is always so good about letting me know his whereabouts."

"You said he and Karen were working on something for the Fellows Corporation. Did it have anything to do with the article I saw which announced a long-term contract? It was in *The Nashvillian*, with a photo of Dr. Forsythe and John Fellows."

"Oh yes! I'm certain it's related to that. That's all we have been focused on for quite some time. I've been doing the general correspondence; you know, appointment letters and itineraries for out-of-towners. Kenneth and Karen have done all the Fellows reports, even the letters, themselves. Yes, it had to be about Fellows; there's precious little else going on in this office other than Fellows work."

"You mean there are only a few other clients?"

"No, I mean there are no other clients. I send one invoice a month upstairs and that's all."

Trabue was hoping for a really good answer when he asked, "Do you know what the nature of the Fellows project is?" Trabue

mentally crossed his fingers, hoping to get something from her that would help him.

"They were always very hush-hush about it. But I believe it has something to do with the development of the Stone Harbor Condominiums and maybe a commercial center. I've never seen anything about it—no letters, no plans, and of course no news articles or the like—but I did hear the name once. But, like I said, there's no such project on paper. At least not that I've ever seen."

"Thank you Emma, it gives me something to start with." Trabue added, "You've been very helpful. Could I rely on you to contact me should Dr. Forsythe return, or call in? By coincidence I'm at Stone Harbor Marina; the dock master's office can always reach me or get a message to me."

"Of course Trabue, I'll let you know the minute I know something. Karen and Kenneth were good to me; I want to be of service. If Karen's father has asked you to be involved in some manner, well, then I'd like to help also. I want to do that for her. She was special. She was such a gifted person."

Trabue rose to leave and Emma Jenkins walked with him to the door. As she shook his hand good-bye, she reassumed her professional, bank-like demeanor, but with a softer, more rested aura.

Trabue felt a tinge of accomplishment in having aided her in such a small way. *That's how people get on. Helping a little here and there.*

★ ★ ★ ★ ★

Outside the office at the top of the staircase Trabue was surprised to be face-to-face with another robot guard.

"Sir, I've been instructed to escort you to the twelfth floor; Mr. Fellows would like to see you. Step this way."

Trabue felt oddly pleased. *Bingo! A move*, he thought.

He followed the drone to the bank of elevators, holding back an urge to smile and wave at the security camera above him.

He had been wondering how best to arrange a meeting with Fellows, but the overabundant security in the corporate enclave solved that. Someone was rattled, enough so to advance a move.

This should be interesting, was Trabue's thought.

At the top floor the elevator door opened and Trabue was immediately greeted by another guard, this one discreetly armed. The exchange was smooth. Drone Number One stayed in the elevator for the trip down. Number Two, with all the personality of a corpse, said, "Follow me." No greeting, no signal that Trabue was another living, breathing human—only an object to move.

Trabue was just a package to be delivered.

Trabue was familiar with the set up. Summoning his appearance was an attempt to show force and gain the upper hand. Trabue was amused that they meant to intimidate him. He was excited at the prospect of finding who was behind the move.

They walked through an area reserved for "Senior Execs." These inner offices were protected by an outer area; populated with gatekeepers disguised as secretaries and administrative assistants.

No one performed any real work. Instead, they mingled, associated, and kept tabs on one another. The head man, or woman, in such arrangements is always found at the end of the hall, in a large corner office.

That's where Trabue was being led.

In this instance the gatekeeper was Ellen—in her thirties, blonde, and very severe.

"Hello, Mr. Trabue, please be seated. Mr. Fellows will be with you shortly."

"Shortly? I prefer to stand because this won't take long."

Trabue knew he had someone rattled. So he decided to push, to be aggressive. Make them make another move, hopefully a dumb one. "Tell your boss that I'm very busy and very annoyed!"

Ellen was not accustomed to such a response. As the gatekeeper she was almost as untouchable as the boss. Trabue caught her off guard. She rebounded quickly and took a different tack.

"I'm sorry Mr. Trabue, you were kind to meet without much notice. I'll see how long he will be." She disappeared into the big office for which she served as guardian. He heard some mumbling. Someone was planning the next step.

Drone Number Two was still loitering in the entryway. Trabue reckoned that their approach would now turn hard. Maybe there was another minion. He had foiled Ellen easily enough.

What's next, a new, bigger drone? I'd better be ready to turn up the heat, thought Trabue.

He was very surprised when the next move came from Fellows himself.

John Fellows stepped from his inner sanctum and strode with a distinct John Wayne gait toward Trabue. He was about to speak when Trabue halted him mid-step in a sharp manner.

"Fellows! I don't appreciate being hijacked for your entertainment.

So, real fast, tell me why!"

Appearing surprised, John Fellows made no response. Fellows waited. When he attempted to regain momentum it was too late. Trabue turned to leave and sent a second burst over his shoulder. "Have your goons step aside; I'm a busy man."

Trabue walked in a careful, measured pace. He reversed the route he had been escorted through earlier. Drone Number Two looked to Fellows for direction. Without specific instructions, the guard merely watched as Trabue approached the elevator and pushed the call button.

God, I hope there's an express headed my way, was Trabue's thought.

The door opened. He stepped aboard and pressed "Lobby" fast and hard.

On the way down Trabue suppressed all outward signs of emotion. He felt the camera focused on him.

Again he was pleased. Events were developing, moves made. He was getting to the "they," whoever "they" really were. From his encounter with John Fellows one thing was certain. *Amelia may be right. John Fellows appears to be fluff. He may photograph well, but in person he isn't impressive. Someone else is pulling the strings,* Trabue thought.

★ ★ ★ ★ ★

John Fellows stood in place for some time after the elevator doors closed. He was deep in thought. His demeanor had changed. He was smiling and seemed at ease.

His pleasure was abruptly interrupted. "Well, that went super!"

came immense sarcasm from the inner office. "I'm so glad I asked Ellen to disappear through the back, or you'd lose all credibility with the staff around here. I'd like to know, Johnny, how do you get by without me here at all times?"

Her voice broke his concentration. He walked toward the sound. It didn't matter to him that the words and tone were derogatory. That was normal.

It was him, that guy, Trabue, he thought. *He was different; nobody talks that way to me, not here in my office. Best to let him have his way.* Fellows was trying to think. She was saying something. *Damn him,* he thought, *Now Jan is mad. When she's mad, she's all over me; it's harder to think when she's like this. She has no idea what I can do—am doing. All she does is bitch at me!*

"Johnny! Whoa! Johnny!" She was bitter. The sarcasm dripped. "Earth to Johnny, Earth to Johnny. Look, we can't have people nosing around our building, chatting up the help. I told you to be your affable self and you couldn't even get him to hang around and see what a nice guy you are and that you care about what's-her-name and all that. You blew it!"

Trabue just lit into me, now her too! He wanted think-time. *I'm better at plotting and planning than doing. One day she'll see. I've learned more than she, or anyone, can imagine. But, when she gets this way, it makes no difference. I'm a fool. In the end I'll win, but not now. Not with her on a rampage.*

He looked at her. She was focused elsewhere. Her gaze was on one of the many security video screens she had installed in "his" office. She was watching Trabue, the guy, move through the lobby toward the building's exit.

"Now what?" she screamed out as she watched Emma Jenkins hand an envelope to Trabue. "Crap! I'm calling Daddy," and she reached for the phone.

★ ★ ★ ★ ★

Twelve floors below in the lobby, Trabue was walking from the elevator and heading for the exit when he noticed Emma Jenkins.

She was seated at one of the courtyard tables in front of the building's coffee shop. A friendly wave and smile told him she was there to see him.

"After you left I had a thought," she said. "Without passwords, the computer is useless. But Karen often kept loose notes in a file. She was an efficient worker and felt that some things were not appropriate for the time it takes for entry and retrieval, you know. I went through those notes." She handed him an envelope.

"These are all the loose items I could find. I hope they are of some use. Good luck, Mr. Trabue."

Trabue could not help but hear the formal tone of her words. As he said "Thank you," she rose and started for the staircase that led to the floor and suite above. Pausing briefly she said, "I won't be much future help. I think it's about time for me to retire. This place has always given me the creeps. All of this is just not for me."

He had seen it before. The good kind-hearted ones concerned about steady jobs, benefits, and security. They knew how to avoid life's unpleasantness. They hid. They hid like small frightened animals.

Del Staecker

They would get scared and hide in what appeared to be a safe place. That's what the cat did. And the cat learned from Old Sy that there are no safe places to hide.

Chapter 14

Trabue stepped out of the building and was greatly refreshed by the natural air. His spirit was likewise refreshed as he saw Reggie in his cab creeping toward the entryway for a pick-up.

"Good to see you!" said Trabue. "I enjoyed the experience, but I believe one trip a day with Glory Be is my limit." He sat up front with Reggie.

Reggie laughed, "Yes, she's a wonder! Talks as fast as she drives, but she's never dented a fender or received a ticket."

"That somehow does not surprise me."

"She's been good to, and good for, my boy Sam. Real good! They're the ones who'll take over the business when I become a full-time fisherman. I plan to catch every type of fish, everywhere, one day. Sam and Glory want to make something more of the business. Sam's into transportation." He emphasized the last word.

"He has all kinds of ideas on moving people and things! Why, last Super Bowl he put together a pizza and sub sandwich delivery system in West Nashville using our cabs and drivers. I thought he was crazy, but he said he'd eat the costs if he was wrong and take only a small bonus if he was right.

"Everyone made good money that day, so instead of a bonus, I told the family—all of 'em—that Sam was going to take over. Nobody said a peep, nobody!"

Reggie was very proud of Sam's transition from troubled youth to future corporate mogul of the transportation industry. "So, how did it go in there?" He switched subjects as fast as Glory Be drove.

"Better than I hoped. I've got something to read on the way back to the marina, but before I start, tell me: Did you see anything at the hotel, after the switch?"

"Well, two of them sat back and waited 'til I did my little act. Then they pulled up to the valet stand and spoke to the guy on duty, but they didn't get out. They asked, or actually told him, to run inside and check on your whereabouts. I got this from the valet after they left. He said they were no nonsense professionals—maybe retired or off-duty cops. Both wore shades, and the sedan had electronic gear in it."

"Was he certain they were pros?"

"Yeah, they never tip!"

Both of them shared a good laugh. Trabue brought them back to the tasks at hand.

"Just keep a sharp eye out for them. I'll wager they switch cars now that they know we know. I need to see what I picked up inside." He opened the envelope from Emma.

There was no note, no identification of where the contents originated. Even the envelope was plain. *No trails*, thought Trabue. Inside was a collection of note slips. Some with phone numbers, mostly area code 202, which Trabue knew to be Washington, D.C.

Nothing appeared extraordinary, and only one item stood out. Karen had highlighted with a yellow read-through marker a Google search of what was her own dissertation.

It read: Karen Blaine, Author, Dissertation, *Native American Artifact Identification, Registration And Analysis with Resultant Identification and Classification of Cultures, and Domestic Enclave Locations Supported*

Through Relevant Technologies. That was it.

Trabue sat back and closed his eyes. Reggie was negotiating the first wave of Nashville's afternoon rush hour. The traffic was not severe by big city standards, but it had been steadily growing. Like all cities experiencing growth, Nashville was slavishly devoted to the automobile. Even if one wished, alternatives were few and poorly supported. Public transportation had all but died. The freeway system was steadily expanding regardless of cries from residents, old and new alike, that Nashville not become "another Atlanta." However, like it or not, Nashville was becoming what it longed to avoid. It was just another post-modern city eating its charm, history, and distinctiveness like the Chinese dragon eating its own tail.

The historical preservationists were still attempting to save what remained of the city's past, but the wind had been taken from their sails some time ago when the governor's mansion was demolished to make way for a fast-food franchise. A city once known as the "Athens of the South" was becoming less Athenian and southern each day. Even its stint as the home of country music was ending.

In Music City, U.S.A., the industry executives on famed Music Row played golf, drank bottled mineral water, and reported to corporate higher-ups in Tokyo, New York, and Berlin. Real country music was still played and appreciated around town, but now on a specialty basis. The youth of the city were listening to hip hop, new wave, and heavy metal.

Nothing lasts forever.

In its time, Nashville had been many things: a shared hunting ground for southeastern tribes, French Lick, Nashboro, Nashville,

Athens of the South, and Music City. Today, Japanese cars and computers were being manufactured only miles from "Old Hickory's" Hermitage.

What's next for Nashville? wondered Trabue. *A spaceport?*

Chapter 15

Lawrence Hart was not happy. The call from his daughter identified yet another detail threatening his plans. The detail had a name: Trabue.

That same detail was quickly earning a reputation of nosing around and Hart was certain that no good would come from it.

Hart had developed the opinion long ago that you could do just about anything you wanted if you didn't let anyone know what you were doing. In fact, keeping a low profile was engineered into the Hart lineage. That, and taking advantage of every piece of information he could collect, had made him the powerful man he was today.

It also didn't hurt to have influential friends. And he wasn't afraid to call in favors. And he knew how to seed the right pockets with cash. Also, when called for, he was never hesitant to apply force.

Hart's great-great-great grandfather was the first of the clan to cross the mountains and to enter Tennessee. Some said right after Daniel Boone himself; long before it was even a state. Others said immediately prior to Andrew Jackson, Old Hickory.

Exactly when Zeb Hart arrived was uncertain. But what he did once he arrived was well-known. His actions set the mold for the following generations. Having an aversion to any form of purposeful or consistent labor, Zeb gravitated to providing the wherewithal for the vices of others.

When Zeb got to Nashville, it was still called Nashboro. It had originally been called French Lick after the nearby salt lick that was the terminus for the game trail commonly known as the Natchez

Trace. The actual beginning, or end, of the Trace was several miles west of the river-front village where Zeb set up shop.

Hart's Tavern was a favorite spot for the wilder crowd. Legend has it that Old Hickory, in his race horse days, auctioned all his clothes at the tavern and bet the proceeds on his own stallion to beat a local favorite.

Zeb overheard the strategy and bet with Jackson. Zeb also lent the future president additional funds and the favorable outcome of the race fared both men well. Zeb was rewarded in many ways by befriending "My General" as he liked to call Jackson.

Zeb's best personal reward came some years later in the form of his Cherokee bride. As a casualty of Jackson's less than enlightened policy toward Native Americans, Zeb's wife almost died on the protracted forced march of her people.

The Trail of Tears saw most of the Cherokees pushed west on a torturous trek to what was known as Indian Territory, or Oklahoma, as it was later named. Thousands died of hunger and exposure.

Zeb's wife was plucked from her people by a traveling defrocked Methodist preacher, with a taste for corn liquor and an aversion for staying put. He soon tired of her after she successfully fended off his advances, and dropped her off at the tavern. No one fully understood how or why this "undesirable" could have altered the otherwise cold-natured Zeb. But she did, and she stayed. Rumor had it that she was as cold-hearted as Zeb. In any event, Hart's blood mixed well with the Cherokees'. Zeb always referred to her as "the Princess."

Old Hickory did not forget Zeb's backing and rewarded Hart with a role in the development of Memphis. Jackson made a killing speculating in real estate, and Zeb Hart got his share.

Over the years, Zeb's clan grew as his fortune grew. Yet, Hart never became a public figure. Always, the Harts were in the shadows—in and around events.

During the Civil War, Zeb's son sold guns, liquor and women to both sides. His grandson then parlayed the war-time gains to even greater advantage during Reconstruction and the Jim Crow years that followed.

One detail was constant: Strings were always attached to Hart deals and relationships. No politician, of any party affiliation, was without obligation to a Hart. More importantly, the public was almost completely unaware of the name. No Hart ran for office, and few even bothered to register or vote.

Civic lessons in the Hart home were brief. Find some information to use as leverage and use it. A concluding point would sound like, "Don't ever be afraid to hurt someone, and be quick and silent about it."

Few opponents ever recovered from a "Hart attack."

By the 1920s and Prohibition, the Harts were doing well on both sides of the legal system. Every aspiring governor or senator had paid their respects at the Hart dining room table. Of course, they were well versed in what was expected and most importantly, what was owed. No exceptions! Such was the high-end of the Hart regimen. Tennessee's leadership may not have liked it, but they played cards with a Hart dealing.

On the lower end were the unsavory individuals to contend with. The Harts had other people to deal with these types, but the

family always kept a hand in direct actions. "You can't control thugs if you can't beat them down yourself," was old Zeb's teaching. Each new Hart generation learned from the bottom up.

When the Italian crime bosses wished to move their sphere of operations southward to include the Hart home territory, they learned first-hand how ruthless a Hart could be. When emissaries from the mob left an introductory meeting with the Harts, they had, wrongfully, assumed that their take-over message was successful. The Italian boys never got home to tell their version of events.

Every additional emissary sent south failed to return. Whether sent to restate the original message or to search for the growing number of lost predecessors, they were never heard from again.

After a time, no more were sent. The Mafia viewed the Hart's turf as a black hole from which no one returned.

Lawrence's father had told him of these events, so he was certain they were accurately recounted from personal knowledge.

His father had been the last of the "old Harts."

Zeb's tavern techniques were kept and improved upon by Lawrence's father. It was he who established Peggy's Club, an after-hours bottle club located near the state fairgrounds.

Such clubs were common during the years of blue laws when liquor licenses were hotly debated topics in the South. The respectable folks limited the number and the hours of taverns. After midnight, drinking had to be done at home, or, as in this case, at Peggy's.

Ostensibly the club was private with each patron paying a cover charge, or membership, to enter. Patrons were expected to bring their own bottle. The club overcharged for mixers in order to operate. Food was basic, and if a patron had no bottle of his or her own, one would appear by magic. Patrons that were observed going in empty-handed and coming out loaded would testify that other club members shared their liquor.

Most of the club's patrons were the town's elite. When Lawrence was growing up, he often peeked in. He saw a lot. Later he helped out and learned the ropes of the Hart family business. It was at Peggy's that he met mayors, governors, and judges. Many similar clubs were established, but the Harts perfected the use of the watering hole as a listening post.

Comings and goings of all patrons were noted. Eavesdropping on conversations was an art form. Later, technology took the Hart approach to new levels. All information, however gathered, was measured against one standard—how it might advance a Hart objective. No unsavory activities were conducted on the premises. But a tight-knit, tight-lipped, and extremely loyal staff guided each requestor to the appropriate Hart-affiliated enterprise. All proclivities were noted. Information from the club was fuel for the Hart machine.

Such was the environment that spawned Lawrence Hart.

★ ★ ★ ★ ★

Lawrence Hart sat at the power table in the Capital City Club. It overlooked the Cumberland River and peered into the new NFL stadium. To sit at the table meant that you were one of the chosen, one of the city's real leaders.

The club was a private eating and drinking establishment. Lawrence's father had helped found it, partly as a replacement for the old Hart establishments, and partly as recognition that late-night activities, no matter how popular, were viewed as unseemly. This gave the Harts a venue to gather information during daylight hours downtown.

All the unsavory vice-related activities remained distributed among associates, friends, and an odd assortment of relatives and past employees. Long ago the Harts had learned that control was more important than actual ownership. They also knew that distance from vice equaled respectability. It also reduced scrutiny.

On the other hand, virtually every illegal activity within seventy-five miles of town provided some form of compensation to the invisible Hart empire. A kickback here, a payoff there, a silent share over there. Always, the relationship was vague and untraceable. The Harts could always claim sheepishly that they were unaware of the true nature of any small investment that was negatively perceived. But of course, over time, the number of such activities and the links to them were details left to others. Lawrence Hart only dealt directly with the most important of projects, and this one, the one that prompted the call from his daughter, had been his main concern for over three years.

I will not let some outsider, some nosy busybody, look into my affairs. Especially now, with this project, was his thought. *The outside talent that Jan brought in for the job was incompetent. This intruder is a loose end. I'll have to take care of all the details.*

He called for James, the ever-discreet maitre d', who greeted all the club members and their guests. James knew who had clout and always kept one eye open for a summons from Mr. Hart. A raised finger brought him to the corner table.

"Yes, Mr. Hart?"

"James, I'll need a private dinner party arranged for this evening. Three or four max."

"Of course, sir. Will you be ordering off the menu or shall I alert the kitchen?"

"No, the menu will be fine. Just keep any other diners at a distance. I'd like some privacy, but prefer not to move into one of the private rooms."

"I understand, Mr. Hart. I have only two groups coming in tonight. I'll move them to private rooms. You'll have the entire dining room to yourself. I will handle all the details personally."

"Thank you, James." Hart appreciated James' smooth style of kissing up without being too obvious. "Oh, and James..."

"Yes sir?"

"Could you bring me some of the club's stationery? I'd like to write a brief note for a special guest."

James nodded and moved toward his podium workstation near the entryway. In a few moments he was back at the table's side, placing stationery and a fountain pen before Hart.

"Thank you, James. I'll need you to call my office and tell them to send over a messenger. I'd like this hand delivered as soon as possible." Hart did not look up. Instead he focused on the task at hand.

In a bold print-style of writing he began: "My Dear Mr. Trabue."

Chapter 16

The angle of the late afternoon sun tinted the water in Stone Harbor with an orange glaze. Trabue was always gladdened by the sight of the *Awfria* resting in such colored water.

"Just the right look for the old girl," he said.

Trabue was thankful for Albert's guidance, closer to constant nagging, which had mercifully ended with the boat's purchase and subsequent restoration.

In his old school manner, Albert had preached "a man should have meaningful work, a good woman as his companion, and a hobby." He was born to lecture, as his packed classrooms testified to his skill.

"And Trabue, you have never worked in a conventional manner. But that's fine, because anything you ever did was meaningful for you. Now, as to companionship, you'll work that out again someday. So, that leaves a hobby, and I suggest you buy a boat! You've always been around them. A boat will get you to use your hands and it will bring adventures into your life. Not that you need them. It also will provide a change of venue. I must say, as much as I love the old hotel, it is sometimes more a zoo than a home."

Trabue experienced a mental chuckle when he thought of Albert's description of the small hotel that he called home.

Home. He had not thought of it in days. Not since he had found Karen.

Amazing how events can push the thought of something as fundamental as home to the back of your mind, he mused. Albert was right. The boat brought adventures. However, the current adventure was not what Trabue had imagined.

The good do die young and the innocent fall first. Who said that? he thought. *Some old forgotten sage, or maybe just a good observer of life.* His thoughts were interrupted by Reggie.

"If you don't mind, I'll wait around here for a while. I have a feeling our day isn't over."

Trabue gave him a quick nod of agreement.

Trabue scanned the dock area hoping to locate Eddie. *I'm surprised that during our many chess matches he never let on that a development was planned for next door. Maybe he is in the dark,* thought Trabue.

As he approached the *Awfria,* Trabue heard the sounds of domestic activity. Win and Amelia had relocated to the galley. An apron-clad Amelia greeted him as he stepped aboard.

"We've taken over your boat."

She was smiling widely. There was no indication of a person in crisis. Like Win and Trabue, the death of Karen had tremendously altered Amelia's life, yet she appeared so normal.

Amazing that we can adapt so quickly in the midst of this insanity, was his thought.

"You're just in time to sample our work." She urged him to join them in the galley. As he slid into the dining booth across from the stainless steel combination sink, stove, and fridge, she spooned a fragrant bowl of steaming gumbo and placed it before him.

"You've got all the makings here on the boat for some great food, so we decided to experiment. I believe cooking is nothing more than applied chemistry. What's so interesting about it is that

each creation can be subtly different, kind of like a lab experiment gone awry, but in a good way. So, how is it?"

Again, there was no indication that this vibrant person had just escaped death, left home, and joined a band of strangers in a quest that would lead to who-knew-where.

One woman died and caused another to assume a radically new life in an instant. This is too deep to think about right now, Trabue told himself.

He tasted. But, before he could comment, Win slid into the opposite seat.

"We've been told I can get Karen's body tomorrow." He looked somber. "I'd like to take her home." Win choked the words out.

"I'm going with him in the morning," added Amelia. "I know the process all too well. I'd like to help Win get through it as easily as possible." Her words helped Win.

"I'll be able to get into Karen's apartment then," he said.

He asked Trabue, "Have you made any progress?"

Social time is over, thought Trabue, *back to work!*

"I'm not certain what I've stirred up. Karen found or knew something that cost her everything. My afternoon visits convinced me that it's a Fellows project, at least on the surface. Amelia's close call and other acts are sure signs that we are closer than someone likes."

Amelia looked worried. The safe new world she had created in less than a day was being assaulted.

"As I explained to Win, by asking, probing, and just by being somewhere at the right, or maybe the wrong, time makes those responsible anxious, and they always react. Look at what just nearly happened to you!"

Her smile was gone. She knew that for her there was no safe crack in the rock, no hiding hole. The incident in the park was proof.

Trabue went on, "I went to see Karen's boss, Kenneth Forsythe, but he's gone."

"Gone? What do you mean gone?" asked Win.

"Missing. He's disappeared. He's been gone since Friday and his office manager has no idea where he might be or why he's gone. She assured me that it was totally out of character for him to just disappear, and thus, highly suspicious. Tie that to what happened to Karen, and what might have happened today, and we've got something. But I don't know exactly what yet."

In a tone of meek defiance laced with hope, Amelia asked, "How can you be certain that my close call was not an accident? There's always that possibility, and there's no obvious link to Karen." She was hoping aloud.

Trabue looked at her. The scientist was asking for facts. But, in reality she longed for something else. She wanted a world where belief could overcome facts.

Facts were often ugly. Without the ugly facts she could remain safe in the world she wanted.

"Amelia, you can't hide from the facts, and you can't wish a hiding place into existence. The problem is that ugly facts don't believe in anything. They find you. That is what they do."

Trabue felt terrible. *I've just informed a grown child that Santa is not real. Yes, the ugly fact found her, because that is indeed what happens.* Trabue felt soiled.

Win stepped in to lift the atmosphere. "Good can come from this! We can't let them do it again to someone else. Right?" It was half statement, half plea.

"The question is: Who is 'them?' Also, what are they hiding?" Trabue responded. "And will we be strong enough to..." He abruptly halted in mid sentence. Before Amelia and Win could react, he was out of the galley booth and moving up through the salon's entrance.

Trabue had sensed the *Awfria's* slight tilt that meant a visitor had stepped on board. Neither of the others had noticed.

A surprised Eddie was met on deck by Trabue.

"Jeez," Eddie exclaimed, "you startled me." He put forth an envelope. "Two guys brought this by the office; not the usual types to be delivering mail. They demanded, no pretty much threatened, that I get it to you ASAP."

The envelope was standard-sized with a gold-embossed seal that was meant to impress. It was hand addressed to: Mr. R.C. Trabue, *Awfria*, Stone Harbor Marina.

Before Trabue could query him about the messengers, Eddie's phone beeped.

"Got to take this, and oh! Just as I was leaving the office a guy called for you. Sounded like Darth Vader. He said, 'Tell Trabue that the wide body will land at or about 8 p.m.' It was weird. He wouldn't tell me his name or give me a number. He just made me repeat what he said. He told me you'd know. Got to run! The reception stinks down here on the docks."

Trabue examined the envelope. It's rich and heavy texture was like card stock, substantial ivory linen. The gold emblem was a stylized weave of three letter Cs. Embossed below were the words "Capitol City Club, Nashville." The note was a handwritten invitation to appear this evening at 8 p.m. at the club. The signature was bold, crisp, and in the same writing style as the invitation text: Lawrence Hart.

It didn't feel like an invitation as much as it felt like a summons—a challenge from the adversary. The postscript made that challenge a certainty. One of those ugly facts, noted Trabue.

It read: "PS: Extend my regards to Mrs. Jackson."

★ ★ ★ ★ ★

Below deck Trabue addressed his companions. "We have poked the beast. I'm off to meet the power behind the Fellows Corporation. I briefly saw the front man and found out for myself that he is fluff, just as you said, Amelia. His father-in-law must be the puppet master. I've been summoned."

He held the envelope in his hand, but was not about to share the postscript.

"Eddie said that Albert is arriving tonight at 8 p.m.; you'll have to meet him. I don't know the flight or airline, but Amelia, you know the good professor, so just stay together, get Albert and return here. Please be careful."

Trabue left the dock and returned to the parking area. Reggie was lounging in his seat chatting on the phone with Elvira. "Sure, baby, I know. I understand." He was merely accenting her non-stop approach to communication.

When he saw Trabue, he said, "'Bye baby! Got to go now; I'll be home late."

Reggie turned the phone off and placed it in the glove box with the battery dislodged. "Double safety," he told Trabue. "Elvira's been known to raise a caller through solid concrete." By the glint in his eye Trabue knew that it was not a dis, but a statement of awe, wonder, and love.

"We headed out?" asked Reggie.

"Yeah, did you get a good look at the two guys who delivered the message?"

"Message? Guys? When did all this happen?"

"About ten or fifteen minutes ago."

"Must have been when I took my plumbing break. A man my age can't hold it like the young ones." He gestured toward the marina's restroom and shower facility. "I didn't see anyone on the dock or at Eddie's office-shack. But I did notice another plain brown, cop-type sedan up near the entrance. Maybe our friends are doing double duty. Dropping off a message and being the tail."

"Makes poor sense, the message says where I'm going because it's an invitation, or more like a royal summons. Why tail me if they know the destination?"

"Beats me, but if that's not a tail, I'm a bus driver."

"Well, let's roll. Nothing slick this time. Just get me to the Capital City Club," Trabue instructed as they began to move.

"Nice, real nice. Can't say I've been there, but Elvira says it's tops. She knows just about everybody who works there, but then again Elvira knows just about everybody who does anything anywhere. I just wish she knew who was driving that car tailing us."

Chapter 17

Neither man spoke on the way to the club.

Trabue reconstructed the facts and prepared for the confrontation that was coming. He also knew that the nicer the venue, the meaner the outcome.

He prepared by reciting names. The list included all the admirable leaders of lost causes and out-numbered battles which inspired Trabue. He started the list, *Leonidas, Spartacus, Sitting Bull, Ghandi...* It strengthened him to imagine that each individual was with him, providing support.

Reggie was consumed with driving and scoping out the tail. "Who are those guys?" he asked. "They stay back, disappear, and then reappear. Quality work, real pros."

Across from the high-rise structure where the exclusively privileged sat, Reggie pulled into a parking facility.

"I'll wait here," he told Trabue. "I know the owners; they'll let me park nose out. If you need a fast break, I'll be set."

There wasn't a place in town that didn't know Reggie or owe him a favor. Forty years in town had taught him how to build a network of good friends. Guys to watch your back. Guys to trust. Elvira's network and his friends proved helpful. As Trabue walked across the street, Reggie waved to his pal on duty, slipped into a parking spot, and pulled out his phone. He'd get Elvira to send some backup.

Maybe they'd need it. He hoped not.

★ ★ ★ ★ ★

Trabue's ride on the elevator was routine if being escorted by three suited gorillas with steroid-laced muscles was considered a normal routine.

He was in an armed camp. Security was tight. Trabue suspected that he was on camera. There was no going back, maybe no way out.

In the club's lobby Trabue was gruffly asked by the first guard to stay put while the second guard sought Mr. Hart. The third guard eased into an alcove down the hall and peered out from the shadows. The plush décor and design of the club was a sharp contrast to the escorts. Trabue stood in silence and waited.

"Well, well. Good evening, Mr. Trabue." The voice came from an ordinary-looking small man in his sixties. The speaker did not extend his hand, nor introduce himself. He seemed confident that Trabue knew who he was. By not saying the obvious, he appeared ominous, despite his small stature.

He circled Trabue in a predatory manner.

It's always the little guys, thought Trabue. *It never fails. The bad ones are always squirts.*

"You came tonight hoping to find something," said the man. "Well, you've found me and I'd like to show you something. But first let me say, you have nothing to fear *for now.*"

Trabue could not help but notice how Hart slowed his pace and emphasized the "for now" portion of his statement. Was this the first threat? No, it was a second threat. The P.S. on the invitation had been the first.

Hart motioned for Trabue to accompany him into the main dining area of the club. It was vacant. The view was superb.

It was dusk, and Nashville's lights were coming on. From its perch atop the building, the club looked down on the sparkles and out to the ring of hills encircling the city.

Trabue knew immediately which table was Hart's. The best view, the corner, the power spot. They're always the same. Standing near the power spot were three people: John Fellows, Otis Jackson, and a tall, well-proportioned woman in her late thirties.

The woman had the blackest long hair Trabue had ever seen. It was definitely not in style but it was clearly her style. She was beautiful, very beautiful.

But something was not right about her.

At first Trabue thought it came from the extremes of her jet black hair and white skin. As he approached, his opinion changed. She was strikingly different alright. It wasn't beauty, it was attraction. Raw gravity.

Trabue and Hart approached the trio. John Fellows and Otis Jackson stayed near the woman, in orbit around her. She was their center. They were her satellites. They both knew it. John Fellows did not seem pleased about something. In contrast, Otis beamed.

Both men eyed Trabue. There was no recognition, just observation. They waited for a cue from Jan.

"Mr. Trabue, I'm Jan Hart-Fellows. I'm sorry we missed each other this afternoon at my husband's office." She extended her hand. The men still did not move.

"Good evening." Trabue reached for her hand.

She removed her hand before they touched.

Trabue thought, *Bait and switch?*

Lawrence Hart intervened. "Thank you, Jan, for saying hello to Mr. Trabue. I'm certain that he will remember tonight."

She nodded and walked past Trabue, dismissing him entirely.

"See you around?" quipped Trabue.

She turned. "I doubt you'll want to."

She left and the two men followed. Neither Otis Jackson nor John Fellows had spoken. The trio camped at the bar across the room and set up an observation post.

Definitely not a good sign, thought Trabue.

★ ★ ★ ★ ★

Hart spoke. "As I said, you will remember tonight. So let us proceed." Hart motioned for Trabue to follow him to the glass-walled corner of the room.

With a sweeping motion of his arm toward the window view, this small, undistinguished man assumed a magisterial countenance.

"You see out there? This is my city as far as you can see. Even farther. Nothing, I mean absolutely nothing, of any real importance occurs that I don't know about. That is the way I make it. Mr. Trabue, you are not a part of this place. You are an intruder, a small business owner on a boating vacation, a nosy vacationer."

Trabue listened and let him go on. *The show is part of his act,* he told himself.

Hart continued. "My business is fulfilling other people's desires. I get what they want and sell it to them. I do it legally or not, whatever is required. In the end it's all the same to me, as long as their money comes into my pocket. My virtue is in feeding their vices."

Trabue showed no reaction.

"I understand you have important friends. They can protect you only so much. You cannot stonewall me, Mr. Trabue, so listen. You will stop your inquiry and you will leave." For emphasis Hart spoke in single words. "You... will... obey."

Boy, thought Trabue, *he is a whack job. What's next, another threat?*

But Trabue was jolted. He had never expected a demonstration.

Hart pointed. "Look below. See the plaza? Do you see that man—the tall one?" Trabue's eyes took a second to focus on the scene many floors below. In the growing twilight he could make out the image of a tall, thin man carrying a briefcase as he walked across the plaza.

"Do you see him?"

"Yes." Trabue felt, in a very sick way, that this single word would initiate something vile, something very wrong.

"Good!" Another single word.

Hart snapped his finger. The guard in the alcove made a call. The demonstration began.

"Watch!" Another command.

Trabue strained his eyes and focused on the man. He noticed movement at the man's sides.

First the left, then the right, two forms came out of the twilight shadows. One was large and dark—muscular and ominous. The second was smaller, lighter, and fast. Big-and-Strong working with

Small-and-Quick. A lethal pair.

The thin man was absorbed in his walk, not expecting an attack. It was not supposed to happen in places so public. Wasn't it known to all that some places are just safe? But not this place, not now. The ugly facts will find you.

By the time the man recognized the threat, it was late, much too late for him to do anything.

The small quick one moved first.

From the left, the small man openly approached the target. He struck with what appeared to be a flick of the wrist. Then, with almost equal speed, and with massive intensity, the bulky man struck. It was over quickly.

The attackers disappeared before the thin man touched the ground. It happened that fast. Erect one moment, then a crumpled mass in a pool of blood the next.

Trabue's stomach ached. He felt it all the way from twenty-five floors above. Pain, and probably death. He caused it. He was the captive audience.

Trabue turned to Hart, looking directly at the small man, the accountant, the mid-level bureaucrat, this regular little man.

"Why, why him? Is he..."

"I don't know," was the reply. Its tone and inflection also said, "I don't care." Hart added, "It was Jan's idea. She thought you'd need an incentive to leave. She's brilliant! Ah, here she is now!"

She had crept up.

"Well, Mr. Trabue, I'm certain from your expression that you know how important it is to us that you go away. My, you look queasy." She made a low purring sound. "I'd just love to see you puke." She poked his hand with her finger. Her touch was cold. Her voice was colder. "Your interest in our matters is disturbing. You really should leave town quickly. Please realize we are serious. Next time, it won't be a stranger. Next time, I'll work on you myself."

She stepped past him and motioned.

In an instant, the ever-lurking James appeared genie-like at her side, ready to do her bidding.

"James, please tell Congressman Lowry and the Governor that John and Otis are about to leave, and that Daddy and I are here at the table ready for our dinner with them."

"Yes, Mrs. Fellows."

"And James, please escort Mr. Trabue to the exit."

Game over, thought Trabue. *No dinner. Just a show, and I hope there's no second act.*

Trabue was soaked with sweat. He wanted to retch.

These people are beyond my limit—way beyond. Karen Blaine is dead. These people did it. They'd do anything to have a vacant playing field. I'll be lucky to get out of here alive. Trabue prayed.

Retreat is not a dirty word. Thank God Albert's on his way. I'm in too deep. He fought to hold back his vomit.

James pushed him toward the exit. He could see Lawrence and Jan's images in the elevator doors' reflection. Sitting with their minions, they looked the perfect pair. They appeared so normal.

★ ★ ★ ★ ★

At street level there were sirens and lights. Reggie wheeled the cab out of its space. Trabue was inside its safety in a moment.

"Big doin's down the street," Reggie began. "It's..."

"You don't have to tell me. I saw it all! Just drive. Get me out of here. I need to think."

Reggie quickly put the commotion behind them.

Several blocks into a quieter zone, Trabue asked him to pull over. Trabue opened the door, leaned out, and retched until he approached blacking out. When he leaned back into the vehicle, Reggie's extended hand held a tissue. Trabue grabbed it and wiped his mouth. He motioned with a wave for Reggie to drive on. In a few more moments he called again for a halt.

"Go home Reggie," he said as he left the cab. Leaning back through the open door, he repeated, "Go home Reggie, take care of your family, your business. Go home!" He slammed the door for emphasis.

Reggie nodded and complied. Trabue turned on his heel and began to walk without looking back.

A dark muscular figure deftly trailed him. And two others, in a nondescript sedan, followed them both.

Chapter 18

There were two possible flights from Tampa that Professor Albert Bryan have could taken. Since Win had strict orders not to let Amelia out of his sight, they found a spot central to the baggage claim areas of both flights and together kept a keen eye out for Albert. Amelia had met Albert previously at a forensic medical conference and was confident she would easily recognize him. As Amelia scanned the passengers in the baggage pick-up area, she spotted Albert grabbing a single large flight bag.

Albert, although quite large, moved with the grace of a ballerina. He sensed her gaze and connected with her eyes immediately. His smile was warm and filled the air with the recognition of kindred spirits.

I knew it. Trabue does that to people. He brings the similar ones, the good ones, together, was Albert's thought.

He began to glide through the crowd, a beardless Santa with wings. He arrived, dropped his bag, and with the graceful ease and charm of a courtier, simultaneously brushed a kiss on Amelia's cheek and extended his hand to Win.

"Amelia, you look tremendous considering recent events, and you are obviously Mr. Blaine; my condolences on your loss."

"Thank you, sir." was Win's military reply. Amelia's reply was a silent blush.

Sweeping his massive arms around them, with his flight bag dangling, he nudged them forward by saying, "Let's move on quickly. From what Trabue has told me, we are Albert, Amelia and Win, three

crusaders on a search for truth, also three easy targets. Now tell me all you can as quickly as you can. I need an update since this morning's call from our leader. I'm a very fast learner and we have no time to spare. I assume that his not being here means something in itself."

Amelia understood why Trabue swept her up in the park and said, "We are calling Albert, now!" Albert's presence was reassuring to such an extent that she was absorbed in the moment. Amelia dropped all worry that life as she knew it was over. She also forgot that her husband was in all probability a dupe, a liar, a criminal, and a hypocrite, and might in some way be involved in murder, and attempted murder.

Win was comfortably in the sphere of a superior. He could trust Albert because Trabue trusted him. Also, Albert was bigger than life in more ways than one.

The next thirty minutes, the time required to retrieve Win's pickup and drive to the marina, were a blur of questions and comments, followed by more questions. Amelia had been around many intelligent minds throughout her life, but no one had impressed her with the ability to absorb with such speed as Albert Bryan.

At the marina the three compatriots each fit into a place on the *Awfria*.

Win prepared his bunk forward in the crew's quarters. Amelia, as the lone female, had the quiet berth at mid-ship and Albert invaded the salon. In silent recognition of their leader and his stature, no one ventured near the captain's quarters. With the nesting process complete, Amelia made coffee for them all and they convened in the salon amongst Albert's pile of belongings.

Win marveled at how one bag of moderate size could hold so many items. It was magical, similar to the fun car that produced the endless stream of clowns at the circus. Albert's bag was filled with a number of toys.

"Just to make me feel at home," Albert explained. "I'm really an introvert and I hate to be out of my element. My bluster and bravado is merely my way of dealing with the intellectual side of my nature. It allows it to act freely. However, at my core I'm a shy quiet man." He sighed. "Hard to believe, I know. But Trabue made it all too true and real for me once."

Amelia used the last remark as her long awaited opportunity to grill the professor about Trabue. All their lives were circling about Trabue. She wanted to know more about him; maybe it would help her to understand why, in such a short time, everything in her life was so topsy-turvy.

She interjected, "It seems odd that you and he are such close friends. You have to be twice his age."

Albert willingly took the bait.

"Would you like to hear the story?" They all laughed, knowing the question needed no answer.

"Trabue is older than he looks, in so many ways," he began. "I met him years ago in New Orleans. In the process of busting a car theft ring, I took a nick by a pissant .22 caliber weenie gun. I was given mandatory light duty and had to make a choice: sit all day filing papers and answering phone calls, or take a temporary assignment in a soft spot like the school truant system. I took the school job. Most days were filled with dropping by the usual kid hangouts and

scaring them back to class, but one day was different."

"How so?" asked Win.

"Well, I was late so I dropped into the assignment office to see what was up. Being the last one in, I drew the toughest assignment. It was Trabue. Then he was called Two-thirds Trabue, that's why I've nicknamed him T.T. It also serves as his emergency access name to reach me through any secretaries and gate keepers. If T.T. calls I know it's mega-important."

"What does T.T. really stand for?" Amelia asked. "Two-thirds of what?"

"In the school system there are 180 days of scheduled classes. If, for any reason, a student misses one third or more of the class days he or she cannot be advanced, regardless of grades or class standing. It's a mandate for state and federal money. You need the head count. Well, Trabue was famous for skipping out on as many days as possible in a school year and just making it under the limit. His closest year, the one in which I met him, he missed fifty-nine and three-fourths days. He always made his two-thirds, but always just barely."

"So did you cure him or something?" Win leaned forward to catch the response.

"Cure him? Well, I caught him, but only after he let me. Trabue's very good at studying the system and then beating it. After not catching him for a couple of days, I was mad. Intrigued, but mad. He was a kid and I was a detective. At the time I was really beginning to make a name for myself. How do you think I felt being duped by a truant? My street rep was at stake; especially after word went out that I wanted to stay on the school gig until I nailed him."

"That sounds serious!" Amelia leaned in too.

"It was! I couldn't figure him out, but I was determined. Later, Trabue explained it to me. I finally found him because I thought like him. He lived without any preconceived notions of life. I was in the fish bowl trying to figure life out by looking outside rather than where I was, in the bowl. Trabue is good at explaining all that. Well, to go on, one day I realized no one caught him because they started too late and at the same place. By the time any assigned officer was on the case, Trabue was long gone, to where he spent his days. He was always alone and never where you'd expect."

"So how did it happen, how did you find him?" they were both hanging on the story.

"I caught the early bird by getting up earlier. Trabue sometimes left his home as early as 4 a.m. Sometimes he didn't start there because he had not gone home. But in the end, I was camped on a stakeout worthy of a major investigation. I tailed him to the Audubon Zoo that day."

"The zoo! What was he doing there?"

"At first I thought he'd try to blend in with the tourists, but no, he made for one spot and stayed there."

"Where?"

"The wolf exhibit. I sat back and observed him as he watched and took notes. You would have thought he was attending class. That is until he popped up, walked over and invited me to join him."

"What did you do?"

"I joined him. Why not? My cover was obviously blown. Like I said, he let me catch him. We had a great time. He was no kid. At

fourteen he was easily my equal, and probably my better. He showed me how the wolves related to one another. He had names for each one and a detailed log of their behaviors. He told me, 'watch Fred, he can't cross over in front of Tony unless Big Jake, the top dog, allows him. Sometimes Jake denies him the right until Fred pees in his own space. It's tough not being top dog.' I remember us laughing at that. We spent the better part of the day talking, laughing, just carrying on. Late in the afternoon he got up and headed toward the gate. When he was about ten feet away I asked him if he thought I was going to bring him in. He turned the question back by asking me the same one."

"What was the answer?" They tripped over each other asking the same question.

"I told him 'no', and he said, 'You're right!'" Albert gave the last statement special emphasis by accenting it with both hands tossed palms up.

"He wasn't agreeing with me! He was merely approving my conclusion!" Again Albert sighed. "Boy did I find something that day. What a friend. And at such a young chronological age, what an old soul he was. From then on I was doing all I could to not turn him in. But, the heat was on. I was under the gun and Trabue learned of it. So, instead of us watching people at the mall, at Jackson Square or sitting in a tree..."

"A tree?" Amelia blurted.

"Yes, a tree. That was one of Trabue's favorite places. He, later we, would find a good strong tree with enough visual space between branches to sit in. He'd read and then talk to me about his observations.

A lot of the time he'd just watch the world go by. He was a very unusual person. He was brilliant beyond his years."

Win asked, "How did it end? What happened? You said Trabue found out about the heat you were experiencing."

"He ended it. One day he showed up at the office just as I pulled in the parking lot. He said, 'Big Al.' I was startled because no one called me 'Big.' No one dared mention my girth. He said, 'it's time to get you back to solving some real crimes. Your vacation is over!' Trabue went in with me, sat down at my desk and forced me to get back to work. I had no excuse for not going back to my old assignment. Of course, he went back to his old ways too!" At that Albert had a good laugh. "You know, he actually slowed down after that, only missed thirty to forty days a year until he graduated from high school."

"How did you keep up the friendship? Did you know his family?" Amelia's interest was genuine.

"His family was a bit peculiar to say the least. His parents didn't seem well-suited for each other, but I guess it worked for them. Trabue's father was a jack-of-all-trades: barge man, off-shore driller, and boat mechanic. He was a blue-collar type, but only on the outside. He was very well-read and a damn good fiddle player. Everyone liked him, but he disappeared in a boating accident. That's the cause people mistakenly attribute to Trabue's quirky nature. But, it happened long after T.T. was a reality."

The mention of family took a brief toll on Win, his recent loss coming back to him full force. In an effort to mask the hurt, he urged Albert to go on. "What about the rest of his family—his mother, any

brothers or sisters?"

"He has an older brother. Trabue idolized him as a kid. Barton Trabue was a jock, local football hero, and all around nice guy. The boy's mother, Carolyn, was very close to Bart, or Bub, as he's called."

"He's still around?" asked Amelia.

"In a way. It's part of why and how Trabue is so special to me." He leaned back, laced his fingers behind his head, and squinted his eyes. "This is hard to tell, so bear with me. I kept a watchful eye on Trabue for a good four years. He buckled down as I said, but in his own way. The new T.T. way was skipping one or two days a week instead of three or more. We saw each other, but not like before. I had my job, which was getting to be something big, and a family of course. His mother was focused on getting Bub through college. Football didn't pan out the way Bub expected—a bad knee—and in no time the cash was gone. Carolyn converted their old home, The Colonnade, into a bed-and-breakfast. It's what Trabue calls home now. It's been expanded into a small cloister-type hotel that is posh to a point, uses word-of-mouth advertising, and is staffed by a quirky menagerie. Trabue had no interest in college. What does college offer a kid like him? Jeez, he read encyclopedias for fun. Plus, he has street knowledge that a career criminal would envy. He just *knows* people. Anyway, he traveled, worked everywhere, and tried just about everything. I got a card from him from forty-six of the fifty states. At twenty-one he joined the Army and the cards stopped coming."

Win perked up at the mention of his new friend being a fellow soldier. "I knew it, I just knew it. Something about him made me think he'd been in the service!"

"Well," continued Albert, "he served, but I'll bet it was in a unit that no one really knows about. It wasn't regular Army."

Albert caught himself. "I am not overly fond of secrets, and regardless of the cause, I feel strongly that truth needs to be in the daylight. It may seem like an odd stance for a ex-undercover officer. But, we all have our blind spots, especially about ourselves."

Albert continued, "Remember the first Gulf War?"

"Oh, yeah!" answered Win. "Been there, done that!"

"Well, Trabue was there too, real early. Someone had to be on the ground prior to all the action on CNN. He saw and did some 'close work' as they say. He was seriously wounded and spent a stretch in an army hospital in Germany. Long and short of it is that it ended his military career and started what he thought would be the best part of his life."

"How so?" asked Amelia.

"He met a nurse, a rehab specialist. The boy was in love. He got struck big time. He courted her while being treated. She was a hard case, but he never let up. In the end, he had his way, or as they say, he chased her until it was time to be caught. In any event, they married and all seemed set. He called me the day of the wedding. He was about to be released for a stateside facility. Jody, his wife, headed for New Orleans to start a job and stay with Bub and Carolyn at The Colonnade. Trabue was on top of the world. No, the universe."

"What went wrong?" asked Win.

"Everything and nothing," was Albert's riddle-like answer. "Things were good with Jody, Bub, and Carolyn. The wrong came from outside: Trabue's father had a business agreement with a shrimp

boat clan. The deal had been set up before his death. People say his partners were behind his boating accident.

"The shrimpers came from the coast and were seldom seen in the city. The clan's patriarch showed up in New Orleans just about the time The Colonnade started to make a little money. He claimed that Mrs. Trabue owed him fifty percent of the hotel, based on some dubious records. If Carolyn had been alone, she might have fallen for his demands, but Bub would have none of it. He threw the claimant out the hotel's front door all the way over the porch and halfway to the street. Bub knew how to make a statement. Bub roughed the man up pretty good and seriously damaged his pride, and more importantly, his reputation as a player in the shadow world of semi-pro crime."

Albert rose and walked about the salon restlessly as he continued. Both Amelia and Win knew that telling this story was not easy for him, but they both sensed that he wanted to share the information with them. After all, they were now in a no-going-back situation with Trabue leading the way. They said nothing. Their body language urged the storyteller on.

"There's no proof; there never is in cases like this. Trabue was expecting a good life. He'd paid his dues. Instead he got two funerals and a lot of waiting outside a critical care unit which eventually produced a paraplegic Bub."

"Oh no!" gasped Amelia. Win just looked down.

"Like I said, no proof, especially no witnesses; Carolyn, Bub, and Jody were headed for a Sunday picnic in the country. Hit and run, but who hits a car so bad that it kills two and maims one and can still run? All of it was a set-up. The investigation was a sham. But, out in the bayou parishes, local heat is controlled by local semi-pros as often as not. I tried to help, but I had some serious issues of my own. Those issues later were what brought T.T. back to my life full time. In the end, Trabue was himself. He observed. He logged what he saw. When he was certain who was responsible, he acted."

"How?" both of them said together.

"I can't say." Albert looked down. "Let me correct myself. I won't say. I promised Trabue I would guard his secret. He burdened his soul for what he did. All I can tell you is that when angered, a person as good as Rutledge Campbell Trabue can become as violent and dangerous as anything ever seen in nature. He will never harm the innocent, but trust me; he will not spare the guilty. The clan and its minions paid dearly. No one who participated or covered up the act was overlooked by Trabue. Men just disappeared. They paid the price, but he paid it, too."

At this point Albert slowly sat down. His great frame seemed to absorb the chair.

He resumed. "Like I said, I really was of no help. I failed my friend. Just before it all happened, my ideal career ended. I came home one day and had to use my cell phone to call into my own house. My wife had changed all the locks. It was her subtle way of telling me it was over. There had been warning signs, but I was blind to them, or chose to ignore them. In a nutshell, I fell apart. My reaction? In three months I drank and self-medicated to oblivion and back. If it were not for my previous record I would have been tossed out of the police force, and I might add, rightly so. But, some friends

used their clout to have me medically put out. And by put out I mean out, for good! I woke up one day in the sunroom at the local rehabilitation facility. Years ago, we called them funny farms; now insurance pays for them so we have more polite names, but it's all the same. I was institutionalized."

"How sad." Amelia touched his arm to convey her concern.

"That's when we linked up again, me and Trabue. Unbelievably, he was there, too."

"Trabue, in the funny..." Win caught himself.

"No, it's alright to say it; it was a funny farm, not a rehab. We were really out of it. At first, I thought my old friend was there to visit. But he was there everyday and at all hours. So as I came to, I realized he was sitting with me, staring out the window because he had a similar big pain to deal with. I had forgotten completely about the circumstances of his tragic losses, had lost touch. One day he spoke and I listened. The next day we reversed roles. We just talked. Still do, in our own weird language. In the end, we cured each other enough to get released. You could say we were the best thing that happened to each other, and we knew it. After we got out, Trabue took me to The Colonnade. I was still a bit of a mess. There at his own home, Trabue recovered faster than me. I was not too good for quite some time. I had lost my pension along with my family and everything else. Trabue not only cured me, he fronted the expense of my Masters Degree, my Doctorate, and basically my career and current life. We reversed our previous roles. I needed a protector and he was it. At the hotel, I was the combination yard boy, fix-it man, and bellhop. I lived in one of the smallest rooms in the western world. Trabue rode me like a bronco. He never let up. In the end my doctoral dissertation also became my first book: *The Mind of the Street Criminal*. It did quite well."

"Well? It's a standard!" piped in Amelia to let Win know how modest Albert was. "It's used as the basic text in more courses than anything else in law enforcement!"

"To be honest, everything came from those early days with him. I just mimicked his style of watching people and applied it to the streets. *Voila!* An instant classic. I owe him everything! And when the University of South Florida offered me a post, he tossed me out, bag and baggage, and forced me to go. I wailed, I cried, I was scared, but he forced me back, all the way back to being a live human being. And the kicker is this: Whenever I've tried to say thanks, he shuts me up. He gets smart-ass with me, tosses around some names, and avoids being serious. That's why I came here so fast. He called and left a message as 'T.T.' I knew it was time for me to help him. I'm here to pay back, and right now I'm getting anxious about his whereabouts. God, I love that boy. He's a man now, but he's T.T. to me. Imagine my big butt in a tree with him all those years ago! He taught me not to avoid doing something for the fun of it! He taught me that you may learn something while having fun, and God knows, the people who love life don't hurt others unless they've got it coming."

Albert's emotions welled, "Where is he? Where is he? I'm worried. Trouble clings to him because he's so good!"

Chapter 19

Trabue walked. In normal circumstances he would know exactly where he was. He liked maps, always did, studied them for fun, just like he read encyclopedias, but now he was unaware of his exact location or immediate surroundings. His mind and heart were racing—the world around him was a blur.

Every few steps his stomach erupted. A reflux of gastric juices rose volcanic-fashion up his throat. His body was in revolt. It was not fear. It was worse. His body knew what his mind was fighting to forget. His body was releasing his soul's pain.

Trabue had known and fought evil. First, for his country. Later, for his family. He held no pride for his role in either encounter. He did not seek to be an instrument of justice. He simply longed for peace. He mourned for Bub and his mother. He ached constantly for his lost love, Jody. He also mourned those who met his vengeance.

Trabue's thoughts moved between vengeance and justice in an audible debate. "Jeez, got to stop talking to myself, or they'll put me back on the sun porch, this time without Big Albert to chat with."

"I hope Albert and the others are safe. I need his help, but if anything happens to him or the others because of me..." he stopped. "Damn Fool! Because of me some tall thin man, an innocent man, is now a crumpled mass in a pool of crimson. He may have lost his life because I poked the beast. What did I think I was doing?"

He stopped abruptly. His thoughts forced a bubble to burst. It was time to plot a course back to the marina. He was focused again, headed for the *Awfria* and his friends. However, Trabue remained

unaware that behind him lurked a dark, well-muscled observer.

★ ★ ★ ★ ★

Now that his quarry seemed more alert, the observer dropped back and increased his distance from Trabue. Yet he continued to stalk.

★ ★ ★ ★ ★

Still further back, a plain sedan sat beneath a canopy of trees. The occupants watched. They too would follow, but with night-vision glasses they could keep back and still easily watch. "Yes," one said, "that same guy is tailing him. We'll stick close to both. Over!"

★ ★ ★ ★ ★

At Trabue's pace he believed it would take approximately one-half hour to traverse the Nashville neighborhoods to the marina. For any other hiker it would take at least twice as long. Trabue's stride was efficient and he was on the move.

★ ★ ★ ★ ★

Damn! thought his tracker. *This guy is fast. How can I keep up with him without running?*

★ ★ ★ ★ ★

"Looks like they're both headed for the marina and that means so are we. Over!"

They all headed to Stone Harbor.

Chapter 20

This time Trabue only saw her lights. But, the elation he felt was immense.

Serenely beautiful by day, the *Awfria* was seductive at night. He felt no less a thrill than a man dying of thirst would feel glimpsing an oasis. This boat was his sanctuary and his source of relief.

Trabue's pace quickened as he approached the dock. He could see movement in the salon. The massive shadows could only be due to his large friend. *Thank God, he made it*, thought a tired yet very happy Trabue.

On board, Albert was behaving like a father on prom night, waiting without appearing to be waiting. However, when he saw Trabue he was anything but reserved.

"My boy! God it is great to see you!" They embraced like father and son. The feelings they had for each other were simple and direct. Each held back nothing.

"God yourself! Have you put on weight?" chided Trabue.

From anyone else, the remark was an insult. But from Trabue, it was laced with love and respect.

Their communication went beyond words. It was a language characterized by a certain accent of tone, inflection, and positive energy. Oh, how Trabue missed conversing in it.

For a few moments they basked in a swirl of mutual energy. No meter could detect that energy. However, it was as evident as their smiles.

"Our companions crashed about an hour ago," stated the large

man. "Win is all done in. I think Amelia slipped him something to help him sleep. She's zonked herself."

Albert got serious. "So, you've kicked over a can of snakes. Let's not get bit. You talk."

"Snakes, I'd take," was Trabue's rebuttal. "The opposition is beyond snakes. Let me tell you about my evening."

Trabue assumed Albert had gleaned all the available, useful information from Win and Amelia, and he was right.

To an outsider, their conversation for the next ten minutes was bizarre and perhaps even alien. They continued in their private language with bursts of descriptions, asides, and fragmented sentences. Trabue spewed forth a babbling flow, accented by gestures, shrugs, nods, winks, blinks, and even scratches.

Albert's hand signals nursed the speed and direction of the discussion. He accented everything and kept the pace moving with "uh-huhs," "yeahs," and "go ons." This marvel of communication was born of their mutual confinement and long talks on a sun poorch. It was theirs alone. With finality Trabue asked, "Got it?" and Albert half-burped a "Yup!"

Mystics and closely-bonded marriages produced similar modes of communication.

"Well, we certainty are playing hardball, but it's no game," stated Albert. "I am so sorry that you had to witness the demonstration. It must be painfully disturbing."

Trabue said nothing, just nodded, ever so slightly. *Albert understood. Understood, oh so well*, he thought.

"They are not the slightest bit afraid of you, or now us," muttered

Albert. "Such an act shows not only their disregard for life, but also their arrogance. It's a demented statement but in it is where we shall find their weakness. I can assume that the only reason they have not gone directly after you is me. Jackson carried the information to them about you and the connection to me. Whatever it is that Karen found, it is certain that they had no restraint in killing her. However, if you disappeared, or came to an untimely or improbable end, they know I'd be around to investigate. Now that I'm here, the threat of my involvement is gone. Remember a threat is only so good. Once it's a reality, it loses so much. We must be careful."

"Careful? Careful is my middle name, also scared, tired, and sick. I'm only in this because, well, Win doesn't deserve this. Karen didn't deserve this. You should have seen her."

"In the water? No thanks."

"I believe she summoned me."

"Some things are meant to be. We are all here because of forces we cannot explain, and because you called."

"Thanks. I'd just like it to end." Trabue meant it. His soul cried out for it to end.

"Don't we all," was Albert's punctuation. Nodding to the rest of the boat he said, "What do we tell them? About tonight? How much can they handle? You said Amelia was on the edge this afternoon. Could she take knowing that her dear hubby was in the enemy camp tonight? In the camp when a totally innocent bystander was brutally attacked just to make a point? No, not a silly point! An overkill statement, if I may use grossly dark humor."

"Ugh! That was at the limit! I'd say you should be locked away

again for that remark, but we both know that it didn't work the first time. I would have preferred a modern version of 'get out of Dodge.' Alive or dead, that victim was just a show." Trabue paused and said, not for Albert, but for him, "We are dealing with real evil here."

Albert added, "Like I said, we've got to be very careful."

Changing focus, Trabue asked, "Speaking of which, how's your supply of gadgets? I know you get a kick out of doing the demos and yakking your butt off about the wonders of technology."

"Here." He tossed Trabue an item. "It's the latest."

"Wow! An electric razor! Let me see. It looks like you've got a real winner in your famous crap collection!" He razzed him. Albert loved the attention.

"Right, it is a razor, fully functional, cuts a bit close actually. But it also has the latest chocolate chip." He was referring to brown technology. "Not quite the black ops level stuff you used in the Gulf, but almost as good and almost as rare."

"The microprocessor chip in this is fantastic. It allows me to zap out everything lingual within fifty meters."

"Lingual? How so?"

"Don't know for certain. I have at least one intern on staff each semester that's a wire-and-chip geek. The current one could maybe explain it, but it would take until next semester." He chuckled. "Trust me, it recognizes language patterns, you know, and scrambles the signals, the audibles, something like that. I'll set it up later to protect any conversations we have on board. It's NSA-type stuff, hush-hush and hard to get."

"How did you get it?" asked Trabue.

"Stole it."

"Really?"

"Yeah, at a conference and, as a demonstration of the criminal mind in action, I went through the exhibit area with all its high security and just filched all I could—right under their noses! Then at my lecture I emptied my pockets. It was a simple but effective teaching method. I believe you taught me the technique."

"Not me," Trabue protested in a show of mock alarm. "Never did an illegal, immoral, or stupid act in my entire life! Well, nix the stupid, I did befriend a crazy cop once."

"Watch it! Watch it! You'll hurt my feelings." They smiled. It was so good to be bad to each other, regardless of the circumstances.

"Ledge, you've got to invite me for a visit sometime without all the drama. How about we just hang out like when we first met? Maybe take a cruise."

"Sure, I think we can do that. Kind of go full circle. You know, friendship, nut house, murders, and then back to friendship. What do you think?"

Trabue added, "Honestly, Albert, I hope we get to the other side of this soon. But right now I need to hit the sack. I'm played out."

"Yes, you've had quite the day," agreed Albert. "But first, let's discuss tomorrow. I'll be up and out early. I plan to hit the bricks again seeing my ex-comrades on the street level. Win and Amelia will try the apartment again. And of course they will make the arrangements for Karen. You, my boy; what will you do?"

"I'm at the library"

"For?"

"I need to check out the dissertation lead. I also plan to bone up on some land use and development issues. Stone Harbor Marina of all places," he motioned around himself, "may fit as a piece in this puzzle."

"Sounds like a plan to me."

"See you in the morning."

"Oh, by the way, I added three motion sensors to your existing electronic array. We are super safe here tonight. Matter of fact they are so good I had them calibrated to detect that gimpy leg of yours. I could tell it was you approaching."

"That's not possible. How could it tell it was me?"

"Your steel implant makes a click. I recorded it with a micro mike last time I saw you in New Orleans and, like I said, the sensor was set for you. It worked!" he beamed.

"Another thing. Let's be careful not to talk off the boat; I'm not certain how far down the dock my gadgets will work. I tried not to fuss with your existing items so the range of protection might be shortened. Also, GPS technology is getting too good. If the bad guys have enough dough, we could be under satellite view any time and that means we'll need to weigh anchor and offer them only a moving target. When we talk it should be while moving and below deck."

"No problem. After all, it's a boat, and I like moving it. I move it every few days no matter what. So let's plan on meeting back in the afternoon and go on a safety cruise. I'm off to bed, no more!" he said holding up his hands.

"Good night, John Boy!"

"Good night, Mother!"

★ ★ ★ ★ ★

"They've still got us blocked," said the voice in the sedan. "We'll maintain post, second subject is also on the property."

★ ★ ★ ★ ★

"Damn bugs! Eating me alive! I can handle the watching, but sleeping outside has never been my thing," the muscular observer said to himself. "Lights out. Guess they're down for the night!"

Chapter 21

She was cold, and motionless. Just what you'd expect from a corpse. She was also exceedingly beautiful.

Her glazed skin shimmered under the florescent lights. Tears dripped down Win Blaine's face as he surveyed his sleeping child.

Hey Daddy! See me, see me? I can fly! Ouch! Don't tickle! I'm scared! All of her came to him in an instant. She was still alive in his mind.

Always will be, he thought.

He told Amelia, "In the hills where I come from, we have feuds and grievances that go on for generations. Somebody slighting someone else makes some people hold a grudge for a long time." She held his hand. "But this, this is something else. There's no sense here, no reason. She was perfect. So special. Why?" He broke into uncontrollable sobs.

"Let me help," she said. "I'll get my friend, we'll fast-track this."

Amelia led him to a place to sit where he could not see the final preparations for moving Karen. She knew he could not handle strangers attending to his beloved only child. The process was all too familiar for her. This had been her life.

"Win, let me take care of this."

Amelia may have lost her husband, her home, and her old life, but not her clout—at least not yet in this building.

Her personal close call the day before had given Amelia a new perspective on what she had been doing. All her life was focused on death. Now she knew she would never do it again.

To help Win she personally attended to as many of the details as possible. She prepared Karen for her journey home. For the first time ever, she cried while she worked.

As the mortuary's van pulled away she felt drained—then relieved and reborn. She wanted to be a healer.

She found Win and took him to Karen's apartment.

★ ★ ★ ★ ★

Amelia had never been to Karen's apartment, yet upon entering she knew instinctively that things had been altered. Subtly, yet undeniably altered. She sensed violation of Karen's space as if it had been her own.

To a casual observer the violators had tried to make everything appear normal. But Amelia could sense their invisible tracks. Their intent was to leave no clues, no residue of their presence. But, by merely being there, they had soiled Karen's space.

Win sensed it also. "Something's not right," He exclaimed. "It's the same, yet different."

In searching Karen's place, the intruders left their invisible marks, their evil scent. In attempting to sanitize their actions, they voided Karen's influence.

"Let's see what they left us," Amelia offered, trying to ease his obvious discomfort.

"No, no. Whatever was here is gone. I know it. They got what they wanted." Win turned and walked out. No sifting through personal items could produce his daughter again. He had no interest in what was left behind. His loss was spiritual and permanent. No item,

no material object, could fill the void. He would have none of it.

"Let's go," he said.

Amelia felt the certainty in his voice.

They left in silence.

Amelia paused at the door. She thought she heard a child's voice, *Don't tickle me! See me? See me? I can fly! 'Bye Daddy! I love you!*

Chapter 22

Albert felt young again, young and thin. He loved the streets. His cerebral life in Florida had been acceptable but the pavement was what spoke to him. The streets were real.

It did not matter to Albert that he was on a vague search. Whatever was important, he'd find it.

Talk and sift, talk and sift. Then sift some more, talk again. It was a constant process of obtaining information and sifting it. Just talk and sift, talk and sift.

Sounds simple?

Yet, if you cannot fit the scene, you weren't allowed to talk. Can't sift a thing. So, you've got to know how to identify, approach, and engage the sources.

Albert knew how to do just that. He drew up a mental list of those sources he would approach. *Let's see,* he thought, *I'll need a representative sample. No, no, that's the professor talking. Do a Trabue! Think man, think like a street citizen again.*

He began again. *The streets have cliques; each clique has members, leaders, hangers-on, and snitches.*

If you've got the right amount of cash, any group can be pierced. The traitors, they sell out. But cash is dangerous, it draws attention and trouble and the information obtained with cash is less reliable than information which is given freely. A snitch only wants the cash, not to share information. Hangers-on are the ones to hit quick and hard. They will give it up for the status—the appearance of having been accepted by the group they are spilling their guts about.

The members are the hardest to crack. They value what little they've got and want to protect it. If you have the time, can spend it to build up trust, the leaders are the best source. They will deal information for power.

Albert did not have the time.

He thought, *The opposition is so bold it attacks just for demonstrations. That is evil at its most brash. Everyone in our group, especially Amelia and Trabue, is vulnerable. We don't have time to waste. I've got to work fast.*

Albert's antennae were tweaked. The detective in Big Albert came fully alive. He'd start with the cab drivers, since it was too early to talk to the bartenders and the other night owls. Reggie was his first move.

Reggie was a real find. Trabue's life was full of Reggies. They gravitated to Trabue. Last night Albert made a mental note concerning Reggie. He bet himself that Reggie would show up at the marina in the morning. Sure enough, while the others slept, Albert had crept off the boat and introduced himself to a waiting Reggie.

A cup of coffee with Reggie Shavers at the cabbies' meeting place was gold for Albert's credibility. As requested, Reggie introduced Albert to several of the blabber mouths and then drifted out of the picture. By the second cup of coffee, the professor had enough information to fill three lecture schedules. Talk and sift, talk and sift.

Next came the hotel valets.

Albert snatched a ride with a new pal to the central business district's commercial hotels. His ride refused a gratuity so that all watchers would know that this new guy was 'a good dude' and his money was no good. In plain view Albert chatted up the crew at one hotel and then made the rounds.

Talk and sift, talk and sift.

After the valets came the hotel maids, desk clerks, and the city bus drivers. He saved bartenders and waitresses for the end. Talk and sift, then verify with the local police. In one day of constant motion he was able to obtain an impressive amount of information. Taking it to his fellow police officers was the fastest way to place a relative-truth value on what he'd amassed.

Talk and sift, talk and sift.

If time were more plentiful he would add some of the less savory groups—the hookers, druggies, etc. They could add the spice and fill in the smallest of gaps. But, time was precious. Innocent blood had been spilled, more than once.

While Albert sniffed the city, he wondered about Trabue and the formal research, but would not have traded places for anything. Albert was in his element. Like a lumbering bear, Albert's omnivorous tastes were being satiated as he meandered through his new territory. Albert felt good on the hunt.

Chapter 23

"What's a seven letter word that ends with 'D' meaning aquatic siren?"

The question came from Aunty. She was standing in the doorway blocking the entrance to the adjacent den that she more or less occupied on a continual basis.

"Huh? What?"

Elvira was uncharacteristically caught off balance. She had never seen Aunty away from the TV when "O" was on. She rebounded quickly at the sight of a vertical Aunty so far from her recliner.

"This is a first!"

"Don't change the subject!"

"What subject? What subject?"

"You not being on the phone. That's why I am missing 'you know who' for the first time ever! When have you known me to miss *Oprah?*"

"I thought you asked about a crossword puzzle."

"Yes, but it was only a sign."

"A sign?"

"Yeah, I was lookin' at today's puzzle." Aunty always looked at the puzzle, but she never completed one. Seldom did she put a word down or across. For her, it was in the looking that the signs appeared.

"Tell me; I'm all ears."

"Mermaid, that's what! That dead girl, she's a mermaid! Which is, and I quote, 'an enchanted being that lures men to their destinies.' I saw it in the crossword. Now, that is a sign if I ever saw one!"

"You know Aunty, you can find anything you want if you look long enough and believe what you find. If it's what you want."

"Huh?"

"I liked you better when you read tea leaves. Cut out seeing the signs in the crosswords."

"And I like you better chattering away on the phone! You haven't called anyone in fifteen minutes. Now that's a first! What's wrong?"

"I don't know. I'm just feeling so uneasy, like there's something about to happen and it's not good. I'm afraid. That's it! I'm afraid."

"Of what?"

"I don't know. That's why I'm not calling anyone. I'm not certain who, or why I should call anyone in particular."

"Well, it can't be the mermaid causing it."

"Why not?"

"Her stuff works only on men."

"Now, you're getting scary. I bet if you look at the same puzzle you'll find another sign. There have to be a lot of them in there— probably even one sign for each word."

"Don't make fun of me! I see what I see."

"And I feel what I feel." Elvira reached for her phone. She was going to call Reggie, Sam, and the remainder of her family. She felt that something bad was out there and she wanted her family to come home. She'd explain things to them when they arrived.

From inside the den Aunty called to Elvira, "I got another one."

"Fine, tell me!"

"Seven letters, and 'E' is the last one."

"I'm still all ears."

"T-R-O-U-B-L-E," Aunty spelled out.

"Are you happy now?" asked Elvira.

"Ain't a question of happy. It's a question of what's eating at you!" She was back at the doorway. "Should I be preparing for one of your rants?"

"No, this is different. One of my storms can't match what I feel."

Flicking the remote and leaving the TV black, Aunty fully entered the office. "Elvira, we've been together, friends, for as long as either of us has memory. I've never seen you like this. Now, I'm afraid. What is the matter?"

"I don't know! I just have a feeling."

"Trouble is the word. I told you not to make fun of my crossword signs. There's trouble around all the time. Now it's around closer. That's what you feel. Maybe it's because of that other word too! That mermaid girl is trying to talk."

"Whatever it is, I'm getting my folks home. As fast as I can! Now, go watch TV. I've got some calls to make."

Chapter 24

Trabue envied Albert.

The exciting and fun part of an investigation was out in the streets. Not inside. But, Trabue had his work to do.

Truth be told, he could not match the big man's uncanny street act. When they had first met, Trabue was amazed at Albert's natural ability. Trabue could watch and observe, but Albert became part of the street.

I'll bet he's having fun.

Trabue's pleasant thought suddenly ended. He remembered Karen floating and the thin man crumpled in blood. *Attend to the work,* he reminded himself.

He must become, if not an expert, at least a competent amateur authority on Native American artifacts and anything else remotely associated with Karen Blaine's work. He attacked the library and began to consume information.

Trabue set up camp at a corner table in the graduate research assistant's section of the library. He was granted access by the librarian. He knew how to act.

By donning a pair of glasses and holding a satchel of papers, Trabue presented the perfect image of the older grad student sent on a research mission for his dissertation advisor.

"Excuse me," he began as he addressed the librarian. "Professor Bryan is letting me house-sit if I draft an outline and do some prelim research. Is it alright if I camp out in the corner for the day?"

She had seen a countless parade like him and hardly gave him a

second glance.

"Sure, slow day, nobody is clamoring for space, it's your table." He assumed a thankful pose, causing her to add, "If you need anything, just ask."

He's cute, she thought. *You never know...*

She returned to her work and tried to put the attractive stranger out of her mind.

Trabue claimed his space by placing items on his perimeter. A note pad here, an open book there, a wad of paper over there, he clearly marked his territory. Several latecomers approached his borders, but backed off at his obvious signs of inhabitance. One younger male lingered a bit longer than the others, but quickly retreated after Trabue's watchful gaze met up with his. More curious than aggressive, the intruder mumbled an apology and scampered for safer ground. No further sorties were encountered. Trabue could delve into the information he sought to comprehend and master.

He set about his work in an orderly and meticulous fashion. He took notes to remind himself of interesting trail heads to be explored if a current path proved fruitless. He scanned documents and absorbed data at a pace which would awe any student. He did not waste energy on any act, no matter how small or trivial. He moved only to turn a page, click the mouse, or make a key stroke. Expending energy took time. He was very aware that he and his companions had little time. Once the opposition realized that the gruesome demonstration had failed to end the investigation, they would act with escalated force.

Trabue needed to know what it was that they were so focused on

protecting. He had to find what they valued so that he could understand their weakness. "What was so dammed important to them?" he
asked.

One thing was certain to Trabue: They did not value life. He
shuddered at the thought of how easily they could end life. The thin
stranger. Karen. The attempt on Amelia. Who was next? When? And
why? *Why?*

From across the open bay of the research wing and through a
stack of books, the gaze of the muscular observer was focused on
Trabue. *He doesn't move much,* was the thought. *Something has his attention.*

Chapter 25

Jan drummed her fingers. Each digit moved in a mechanical fashion with keen precision. Trance-like, she was thinking. It was her signature method of contemplation.

Jan was in her private world. Her complete world. She had begun its construction on a bright November day as a second grade truant.

★ ★ ★ ★ ★

Miss Michaels was focused on the chalkboard. If she had noticed Jan's vacant seat, the teacher would have paid it little attention. For, often following the morning recess, Jan would not return to the room with her classmates. Once or twice a week, Jan would exit the schoolyard and cross the lane into her own backyard.

The Ellsworth School sat in the midst of an affluent West Nashville neighborhood. Many of the students were within a stone's throw of their homes. However, only Jan Hart routinely left the school's well-manicured campus for a midday visit home. Her breach of the rules was never mentioned and was openly tolerated. Lawrence Hart made more than an ample contribution to the school's annual fund drive.

On this day Jan was gone again. Such was her privilege. Such were the beginnings of the private world of Jan Hart Fellows.

So, with her crayon masterpiece in hand, Jan walked through her yard and continued until she reached the busy street that led toward the city's center and "Daddy's Office."

The eight-year-old was on a mission. Her depiction of the Pilgrims' first feast was special and she wanted Daddy to see it immediately. She was precocious, had money, and knew how buses worked. Getting to the building owned by Hart enterprises was not difficult, even to a second grader. In fact, it was easier than she had imagined. Getting to the office on her own was special and she wanted it to be a surprise.

Upon arrival Jan was disappointed to find the outer office vacant. Mrs. Thorpe, the receptionist who always answered Daddy's phone, was not at her desk. Jan peeked into her father's office and, likewise, it was empty.

Undeterred, Jan was prepared to wait. Jan had heard Lawrence Hart refer to Old Zeb's Cherokee wife as the "Old Princess." Jan was her Daddy's "Little Princess." Jan's artwork was her portrayal of herself and her ancestor as contemporaries directing the Pilgrim Fathers at the first Thanksgiving. Jan's dark hair was drawn as being very long like an Indian princess', just as she would wear it in the future.

Jan's plan to surprise her father appeared to be a failure. She did not wish to retrace her path and return to school and, without an audience, staying seemed to have no purpose. She had so looked forward to surprising Daddy.

It was November and she remembered that on this day Daddy had left the house wearing an overcoat. She checked his closet. No overcoat; he must be out.

She decided to surprise him on his return by waiting in the closet. She giggled when she imagined his surprise on opening the closet and finding her there. She wanted him to see her picture and

know that she remembered his stories about the Indian princess that was her ancestor. She fell asleep in the closet.

Jan never knew or cared to know how long she napped. It was what she saw and experienced upon awakening in the dark that mattered most. It was the most influential day of her life.

She heard voices. Loud, angry voices.

She peeked through the keyhole and watched. No, she *absorbed* the events taking place before her.

Her hiding place had been undetected. Her father's coat was draped behind him over his chair. He had entered the office with the angry men and immediately sat down. She could see him directly before her.

Two men, with their backs to her and the closet, were now seated facing her father. Their angry voices, the ones that awoke her, continued. She heard:

"Larry, you don't get it," from the one on her left.

"Yeah, yeah! Don't get it!" mimed the other. "We are the ones!" He pointed back and forth to his companion. "We, not you!"

"Sorry, Larry," the other said with obvious mocking in his voice. He was attempting to make her father seem weak and insignificant. Jan disliked the way the men spoke to her father. They seemed to enjoy being mean. She could hear it in their voices. She was shocked that her father was so quiet. It was not like him to appear so meek.

Then she noticed he was drumming the fingers of his left hand. The movement was deliberate and exact. Its precision soothed her. She was relaxed and excited at the same time. She absorbed more.

"Larry, Larry, Larry," the left one jabbed. "You don't seem to get it." More of the mocking tone.

"Yeah," chimed in the other.

"You did give us some help at first. But we run things now!"

"Yeah, now!"

"We recognize that you are still a friend, and we don't think anything in the future will cause us to think or feel otherwise. But we need to part company—go our own way."

"Yeah, our way."

"Larry," again the tone. "Larry, it's our time, get it? It's time for a change!"

When the two men became quiet, they noticed the methodical rippling sound of Lawrence Hart's fingers. It had been going on all during their talking. Only now did they notice. One-Two-Three-Four came the thumps.

One, Two, Three, Four.

One, Two, Three, Four.

One, Two, Three, Four.

One, Two, Three, Four.

They watched and listened.

Jan watched and listened.

Lawrence Hart kept thinking and drumming his fingers.

Jan sensed he was about to do something special.

"Yes, you are correct. It is time for a change." Lawrence Hart stopped drumming and reached for the switch to his office intercom. "Mrs. Thorpe, would you ask Mr. Collins and Mr. Drake to join us, please?"

"Yes, Mr. Hart," was the reply. "I believe they have been waiting

for you." Jan heard the respect in Mrs. Thorpe's tone of voice when she said, "Yes, Mr. Hart."

Two very large men appeared from the corner doorway at the rear of the office. Their instant materialization caught the angry men off guard. The pair of angry men had assumed the summoned two would enter through the same doorway they had used. Instead, Collins and Drake were behind the seated visitors in positions of strength. The angry men became alarmed.

"Larry, we don't need..." The angry man on the left started to talk, but did not finish. He stopped mid-sentence when the swoosh-sound came from behind.

Jan could clearly see what happened. One of the large men took something from his coat pocket. With a flick of his wrist he snapped the cold hard steel to its full extension. The arching motion of the police baton produced the swooshing sound that cracked the upper arm of the man seated on the left. He screamed.

A second swoosh was heard as the large man's arm arched again, this time meeting the left man's other arm. There was no second scream. Instead there was a low, long moan. It excited Jan.

It happened so fast that the other angry man's reaction began only as the second swoosh hit its mark. He attempted to move forward and up, but was unable to do so. The second large man behind him had also moved. The seated man's shirt collar and tie provided the perfect means to pin him against the chair. He could not help his companion.

"You son of a..." started from his mouth, but he stopped when he heard the crunch begin. Pivoting his head toward his friend, he continued to hear the crunching and saw the gruesome reason for the sound.

Lawrence Hart had signaled with a casual motion of his hand traversing his neck in the age-old sign of death. The first large man had obeyed and the crunching of cartilage was the audible affirmation of death. In an instant it was over. A rag doll now replaced the angry man on the left.

Lawrence Hart rose behind his desk. He was not very tall, but his physical stature belied his power.

He said, "Well, let's continue our talk about change!"

He quickly continued. "First, never call me Larry, unless you have no respect for yourself either!" He motioned with his hands, coaxing a response from his terrified audience. Nothing happened. Only a pitiful gagging sound could be heard.

The gagging sound continued and increased in volume with the man's contorted effort to rise up. He was attempting to respond and escape at the same time.

"Sit!" ordered Hart.

The man withered, fell back into his chair and whimpered.

"Listen!" commanded Hart. "I have two things to say." He leaned forward across his desk and intently eyed his prey.

"First, I am Mr. Hart! Got it?" He waited before repeating more loudly, "Got it?"

"Yes, Mr. Hart," came faintly. It was less than a whisper and near a sigh.

"AGAIN!"

"Yes, Mr. Hart," came the voice at a faintly higher level.

Del Staecker

"Good! Good! Now second, you are not going to die. Not today." Hart smiled again. "So let's proceed, shall we?"

"Yes, Mr. Hart," came a weak response.

Hart then motioned to the two large men. He brushed his hand absently through the air at the rag doll.

"Gentleman, please remove our silent friend. Since he is no longer required at this meeting, make him disappear."

Quickly and silently the two large associates removed the lifeless body from the office. Hart was alone with the terrified man. Or, he presumed so.

Jan had peered in silence, learning from a master of fear. She had watched her father's timid acceptance of behavior bordering upon abuse. Then, minutes later, she was awe-filled.

She saw him become decisive, strong, and respected.

She watched him make trouble go away.

Jan continued to absorb.

★ ★ ★ ★ ★

"Now, let's continue our discussion." Again Hart motioned.

Again came, "Yes, Mr. Hart."

"Good, very good! You know I removed your friend because he was a bad influence on you." Again the coaxing motion.

"Yes, Mr. Hart."

"Excellent!"

Jan could see that her father was enjoying the proceedings. She ignored the room's other occupant and focused solely upon her father. He was magnificent!

She watched as Lawrence Hart opened the middle drawer of his desk and withdrew a sheet of paper.

He briefly glanced at it, then peered over the top edge and said, "I was prepared for today's meeting. Did you know that?" He went on, not waiting for a response. "There are ten names here. No, wait." He grabbed a pen from the holder on his desk and, with a motion across the paper, continued, "No, there are only nine names." He turned the page toward his frightened guest. "See?"

The terrified man squinted at the page. His focus was slow, but even from the rear of the room Jan could tell when he recognized the names. His fear filled the room.

"Surprise!" said Hart. "Nine names, all known to you. All family and friends. People you worry over. Your wife, your kids, your parents. Understand?"

"Yes, Mr. Hart." It was clear.

The meaning was obvious, yet Hart continued. "I'll make this crystal clear. If I ever need to meet with you again—ever—three names from this list will disappear. Just like your late partner! Do you understand?"

"Yes, Mr. Hart!" The answer was followed by another moan.

"And should you feel that a brave act could change things..." Again he motioned, coaxing the desired response.

"Yes, Mr. Hart."

"If any harm should befall me, should I be threatened, or should I so much as suspect disloyalty from you..." again he motioned.

"Yes, Mr. Hart."

"...then everyone on the list will disappear."

"Yes, Mr. Hart," came without coaxing from a hollowed-out man who only minutes before had been full of defiance.

"Good, good!"

Jan could see her father's pleasure and wished to share it. She wanted to open the closet door and rush to him. But also, she wanted to enjoy it alone.

She waited in the dark.

"Now, there's only one remaining item. Payment. Yours."

"Yes, Mr. Hart." Again, motion was not required.

"You will double the percentage of our previous agreement."

"Yes, yes, yes, Mr. Hart." The man had nothing left.

"And, you will pay twice a month. It makes sense now that you have no partner!"

"Yes, Mr. Hart." The voice was faint, so weak it may have come from a ghost. Hart had not only won, he owned the man's spirit.

"You can go!" was Hart's final command.

The man slowly rose. There was no life to his movements. A mere wisp of the former angry man backed to the office door.

With head bowed he uttered, "Yes, Mr. Hart," and disappeared.

Chapter 26

Jan wanted to remain in the closet longer. For her the experience was so good she wanted it to last forever. Jan's adventure had led to independence, excitement, pride, and now pleasure. She lingered, not wanting it to end.

While reaching for his overcoat, Lawrence Hart thought he heard something. He abandoned the coat and moved toward the sound. He hesitated at the closet door. He flinched as it sprung open. His defensive motion was halted immediately when he recognized his daughter lunging toward him. Quickly she was upon him, waving her drawing.

"Daddy! Daddy! Surprise!"

His world froze.

For a man who had so recently been in charge of such an intense situation, Lawrence Hart, even momentarily, was at a loss for a response. For a brief moment he was as hollow as the man he had just discharged.

What did she see? was his horrified thought. *What have I done?* drilled a hole in his brain.

Up to that time no Hart female except Zeb's squaw, the Old Princess, had any involvement in the "doings," as they were called. Wives and daughters were excluded from all details of the Hart empire. Jan, at eight, was unexpectedly in the middle of it. He did not know what to think.

As later life would witness, Jan provided the solution. She eagerly jumped in.

"Daddy, they were bad! Those men were bad! I'm so glad you made them go away!"

Pushing him to the office sofa she again waved her drawing before him.

"I wanted to bring you this, Daddy. I hid. I hid in the closet. Do you like it? Do you?"

Regaining his composure, Lawrence Hart sought to engage his daughter in a line of conversation far from recent events.

"Yes! Yes, dear! It's beautiful! Is it? No!" he feigned surprise. "It's the Old Princess, and who? Is this you? Is this my Little Princess?"

He clutched the drawing like a drowning man gripping a life preserver in mid-ocean.

"Let's celebrate your drawing and your surprise!"

In ten minutes, Lawrence and Jan Hart were seated before the counter of their favorite ice cream parlor discussing flavors and toppings. Lawrence Hart was relieved.

The relief was premature.

Between spoonfuls of scoop number three Jan calmly asked, "Daddy, have the bad men gone away for good? Really gone away?"

Lawrence Hart hesitated.

Jan jumped in before he could fabricate another distraction. "If someone is bad, you say and do things, and then they are gone. That's good! Really good! Can I have more ice cream, Daddy? An Indian princess should get more." She smiled and he motioned to order again.

The waitress, upon catching Hart's summons responded, "Yes, Mr. Hart."

Jan squealed with delight and laughter.

Again his world froze.

Lawrence Hart looked at Jan. She was smiling and playfully tapping a spoon of ice cream. In a giggly voice she said, "Yes, Mr. Hart! Yes, Mr. Hart! Yes! Mr. Hart!" Abruptly she stopped and Jan looked up at her father. Their eyes met.

Up to then Lawrence Hart thought he had seen it all. He had become callous and immune to surprise. But, Jan surprised him. It was with her eyes.

At that moment he saw something new. It was dark, inviting, and irrepressible. His daughter, yes, his Little Indian Princess, had the darkest coldest eyes imaginable.

Were they always like this? he wondered.

No, he could never have overlooked them. They were new. Today's events had caused her evolution.

When she had finished her second serving of ice cream, Lawrence Hart said to Jan, "Come on, Princess, I'd better get you back to school."

She giggled and said, "Yes, Mr. Hart."

★ ★ ★ ★ ★

On one side, Lawrence Hart was saddened by Jan's abrupt loss of innocence. Yet, he was also excited by her stark coldness and matter-of-fact acceptance of events.

Could she become his heir?

He seriously thought about Jan as head of his family's business.

Hart saw his Little Indian Princess from a new perspective and vowed to pay closer attention to Jan's activities and behavior.

That evening, prior to the family's dinner gathering, he made a point to ask Jan about the remainder of her day. Hart was extremely curious about what effect the events of the day would have upon her. He was amazed at Jan's casual recounting of what transpired on her way home from school.

"I walked around the block; the long way, Daddy."

"Yes, tell me why."

"That lets me come through the side yard, away from the Castners."

"The Castners? Does anyone there bother you?" Hart was surprised by the protective surge in his voice. He had previously possessed fatherly feelings; now he was acutely aware of Jan as his heir. "If anyone ever hurts you, tell me! Tell Daddy!"

"No Daddy, no one hurt me. And he can't; not anymore."

"Who? Who tried to harm you? Who? Jan, who?"

"No Daddy. It was only Bennie!"

"Bennie?" His mind had stopped. His memory fumbled. Blankly he repeated, "Bennie? Who is Bennie?" His expression was as blank as his mind.

"Bennie," she whispered. "You know, Bennie. Mrs. Castner's little Bennie. The little dog Bennie."

"Bennie," he muttered. "Bennie."

Hart visualized the four-pound miniature Doberman Pinscher and sighed with relief. Bennie was the hyperactive and totally irritating inhabitant of Mrs. Castner's property. Until now, Lawrence Hart would have been hard pressed to recall the animal's name.

"So tell me, has he been bothering you?"

"He's gone."

Hart had heard this message before. It was clean, brief, and final. He never expected it to come from Jan.

He had to know the details.

"Tell Daddy," he whispered.

Jan leaned forward and whispered back, "He always chases me, bites at my feet, but not anymore." She giggled softly, adding, "He's gone."

"What happened?"

"I took the long way so he would follow me to the side yard."

He motioned for her to continue.

"I smashed him with my book bag."

"Go on."

"He fell down and looked like he was asleep."

"And then what?" Hart asked.

"I twisted his neck—like the man in your office."

She was calm, speaking softly. Hart looked into his daughter's eyes. Black, cold, and perfectly at peace with her actions. Hart felt pride in her purity.

"Where did Bennie disappear to?"

"I put him in a bag, Daddy. A paper bag. Then I put the bag with Bennie in our trash can."

"That's good, Jan." And he hugged her. "Now, go and get ready for dinner. I want to make certain that Bennie is gone forever."

Jan returned the hug with enthusiasm and skipped off for the

dining area. Hart exited the house through his study's doorway, stopping only briefly to grab a small flashlight and a trash bag.

In the alley, Hart peered into the smaller of two trash cans. He had guessed correctly. A child would opt for the shorter receptacle. On top of several bags of kitchen trash sat a brown lunch bag from which two hind legs and a small clipped tail protruded.

Hart placed the bag and its contents into the opaque plastic trash bag and quickly stepped into his garage. With a toss, Bennie was in the trunk of Hart's car and would never be seen again.

As Lawrence Hart returned through his backyard, he could hear the faint and clearly distraught summons of his neighbor, Edith Castner.

"Benniieee! Bennnnnieee!"

Hart smiled and joined his wife and daughter for dinner.

★ ★ ★ ★ ★

Each day brought Lawrence and Jan closer.

Over time, Jan learned how to disguise her cruel nature perfectly under the watchful eye of her father. The swimming accident and her mother's fall were two slip-ups and reasons to cause Hart alarm. Jan required supervision and tutoring. When left to act on her own, he feared she went too far, too quickly.

The competitor in the pool, and even her mother felt Jan's cruelty. On these occasions Jan crossed the line set by her father for her own protection.

The marriage to John Fellows was part of Hart's protective plan.

Fellows was an excellent foil for Jan. "Even a slow turtle wins some races," Hart liked to say. "And John is really a sleeper."

Lawrence Hart worked hard to prepare Jan to assume leadership of his empire. He was proud of how hard Jan worked in the community. She smiled and appeared everywhere. She volunteered and led every charitable cause that would ask. She became the beautiful face, the clean cover, the smooth veneer of the dark enterprise she would inherit.

And she loved it all.

★ ★ ★ ★ ★

Jan continued to think. Her fingers moved. Just like Daddy's. However, her motion was sharper, cleaner, and more pronounced than Lawrence Hart's.

Click, click, click, click.

Jan's well-manicured nails made each impact more machine-like. She had learned from a master and had improved, in many ways.

She reached for her phone and hit the speed dial.

"Yes?"

"I've been thinking," she said.

"Yes."

"It's time for Mr. Trabue to disappear."

"I agree. Will you arrange it?"

"Yes, Mr. Hart!" Jan and Lawrence Hart both laughed at their long-standing private joke.

"Good-bye, Princess."

"'Bye, Daddy."

★ ★ ★ ★ ★

Jan gazed out the window and whispered. "Yes, yes, it is time you disappear, Mr. Trabue."

She resumed her thoughts.

Click, click, click, click.

Click, click, click, click.

CLICK!

CLICK!

CLICK!

CLICK!

Chapter 27

Amelia draped the thin blanket over Win as he slept. His hand, rough but tender, absently touched her thigh. She did not blush, and she did not attempt to move it. Rather, she delicately bent to reach it with her lips and gently kissed it. He sleepily murmured her name and drifted away.

The universe had split. She was in a new clear half and she was happy. *Very odd!* she thought.

She assessed her companion. His face was handsome in a manly, outdoorsy way. His eyes were surrounded by crow's feet. Years of hunting and fishing gave him a faded look, like old blue jeans. She liked it.

She liked him and she had eagerly shown it. Upon their return to the *Awfria* she had guided him to her bunk. He knew. She knew.

It had been soft, very soft, and tender.

No words were spoken. All messages were demonstrated. It was beautiful and she had no reason to regret its quick development.

"Events can change your world in the blink of an eye," her father had told her.

This is a good change and I am happy, she thought.

She rose and made her way forward through the salon.

The blink of an eye, she thought. Her attention was drawn to the flashing lights from Albert's gadgets. *What's this?* her thought began.

She was interrupted by a greeting coming from the salon doorway. She saw a small man move quickly toward her.

"My, my, what doooo we have here!"

At the same time she heard Win call her name as he entered the salon.

"Amelia!"

He was dropped from behind by a larger, darker presence.

A cloth was placed over her face.

Amelia's last thought before passing out was, *Oh Lord, please! This can't be good!*

Chapter 28

All the information pointed in the same direction: Stone Harbor. So, Trabue returned to the marina.

A Shavers Express cab pulled away and again its driver had refused payment. *Poppa Reggie is looking out for me,* thought Trabue.

Rather than walking down to the dock, Trabue headed around the entry along the perimeter fence toward the marina's boundary. During his previous stay and the recent comings and goings, he had noticed a gated entrance to the adjacent wooded area. The gate was recessed from the road, and the driveway appeared unused.

Deceptive, mused Trabue. *It's a construction site, but from the look of things it's a project someone wants to play down. It's made to look less active than what it really is.*

Although the site was now vacant, there were distinct signs of recent efforts. Footings were dug, foundations were poured, and a myriad of supplies were positioned for each phase of what appeared to be a commercial structure of some sort—several structures, in fact.

The information that had been shared with him and all subsequent references that he had found at the library had identified a small residential condominium project, but this was no ordinary residential site.

Yes, he observed, *this is an ongoing, major project.*

His senses heightened when he heard someone approach. There came two, no, three people, and they were circling him cat-like. They were hunting.

"Guess the prey and win a prize," he said softly to himself.

He had an uneasy feeling in the pit of his stomach when he saw the briefest of images dart between piles of bricks and rebar. Small-and-Quick was moving.

Where is Big-and-Strong? Trabue thought as he took stock of his situation. *Not good. I have been in worse spots, but not by much.*

He was in a precarious location. The predators had played the terrain well. He was on a berm of gravel that sloped sharply down. He could traverse it, but he would expose his back while he negotiated the sloped, loose ground.

I'm an easy target, he said to himself. *So, best take a stand. Make a fight on my terms.*

He looked for a weapon.

Just as he spied a likely piece of rebar and reached for it, they made the opening move.

Splitting up, he said to himself.

Small-and-Quick was on the left. Big-and-Strong stayed right. He could only hear Number Three.

★ ★ ★ ★ ★

The small one came into view. His face was damned ugly, pock-marked greasy topped by fair thin hair. He held a nasty-looking knife.

He wanted Trabue to see the knife.

Blades instill dread. A bullet is too fast to fear, too quick to think about. But a blade is something to dwell upon.

That's why the ugly little man used it, to get his prey thinking.

Think about it while Big-and-Strong eased in for the kill.

Sometimes the big one used a knife. Sometimes, because he liked to, he used his hands. This time he had a gun.

Trabue grabbed for the rebar as soon as the little guy moved.

Even well-practiced teams make the occasional error. This time the Number Three team member caused the error.

A foot slid on gravel and a blurted, "Wait!" interfered with their timing.

Small-and-Quick lunged, but was distracted by the shout. It was enough for Trabue to whirl the rebar across the little man's arm above the wrist.

Crack!

That should hurt! thought Trabue. He felt and heard the rebar crush bone.

The blurting voice also put Big-and-Strong's aim off target. His gun spoke loudly, but slurred the message.

Trabue felt the zip of something pass through his shirt, just below his armpit.

Trabue whirled in a full circle, bringing the rebar around with as much speed and force as he could, hitting Big-and-Strong and propelling the big man forward to the gravel berm.

Big-and-Strong dropped his weapon as he collided with Quick-and-Small, who was howling in pain. Both fell over the berm and cascaded down the loose gravel. At the berm's base the pair found level ground and an escape route.

As the duo fled, Trabue dove for the gun. He was unsure of Number Three's location.

Everything told him to act quickly as he came up ready to defend himself. He aimed as Number Three's head came into view.

With arms up and a terrified look, Number Three pleaded, "No! No, Mr. Trabue, don't do it! I'm Sam. Sam Shavers. Reggie is my daddy!"

Trabue exhaled the longest breath of his life. Had he not heard the name "Reggie," Trabue would have acted. He was relieved beyond measure that he hesitated. So was Sam.

"It's good that I don't think you look dangerous," said Trabue.

"I bet I look more scared than anything," Sam replied.

Trabue was looking at a young Reggie Shavers. No denying the relationship. Reggie had a younger double in his son.

"Man, was I scared lookin' at you lookin' at me! All I could think about was my wife and how I'd miss her."

"Well, Glory Be!"

Trabue smiled and they both broke out in laughter.

Trabue shook Sam's hand and then added a "guy hug." The near crisis brought their lives together. Trabue knew he'd met a solid friend, the kind you keep for life.

"Poppa Reggie told me to take care of you. I've been following you since early yesterday. Did you know?" asked Sam.

"Not a clue," Trabue replied. "I believe in guardian angels. Never met one 'til now. Thank you Sam! You saved my life. Those two are killers; I was pretty certain I'd have been their next kill if you hadn't thrown them off. Really, thanks!" Trabue gave him a second hug.

"Now doesn't that look sweet?" was the remark. It came from one of two police officers. Both had their weapons drawn and aimed.

"Drop the gun, back away and grab some dirt! Now!" was the command.

Chapter 29

Trabue never liked handcuffs, especially the way they were applied this time. He and Sam had complied with the officer's directions and hugged the dirt. The cop and his partner enjoyed the arrest drill. They relished pushing the limits, cuffs too tight, knees-in-the-back, stepped-on fingers. Trabue and Sam were roughed up on the ground and on the way to the patrol car. It was intentional.

Trabue thought someone must have heard the errant pistol shot and called the police. When Otis Jackson rolled up in a city car he hoped for the best, but feared the worst.

"These cops aren't back-up for the two thugs," assured Trabue. "We're alive. If they were in on the attack, we'd be gone by now. Jackson must have been lurking in the area. He can't do anything unless these two go along."

Sam was nervous. His experience with police had taught him many lessons, mostly to be nervous. His former activities brought him in frequent contact with guys like these and he wanted no part of them. Trabue understood.

"Don't worry Sam," was Trabue's advice. "We've done nothing wrong and this is too public a place for us to be disposed of."

"Disposed? That's a great word. Just the one I needed to hear. Last night the bugs ate my ass. Today, I almost get shot, not that you really would have. Would you?"

"No, Sam. I'm too old and slow," kidded Trabue. "Besides, it's not Saturday and I only shoot people on Saturdays. Now, relax and take it easy. I'm trying to lip read and I need to concentrate."

Trabue had been staring intently at the three cops. Only now were their mouths visible, but it was too dark in the shadows for him to make anything out. Instead, he observed body language and gestures. Jackson was not pleased. He looked confused. Maybe he had not even considered an option that included Trabue being alive. Sam was the wild card and had saved Trabue's life.

The meeting broke up and the cops returned to open the doors of the patrol car. They roughly pulled the occupants out.

This is not good, thought Sam.

His alarm was unfounded.

Abruptly, the cuffs were removed. By the time Trabue could massage his wrists to start the blood flow, the two wayward public servants were spraying gravel as they sped off.

Otis Jackson remained.

"You were lucky today," Jackson said.

"Don't try to play me! I know you are dirty! It's just a matter of how dirty. When I figure out your role, I'll get a piece of your behind!"

"Mr. Trabue, don't threaten me! You've been warned! There will not be a fourth strike in this game for you!"

"Fourth? I count two so far, not three. Last night's sick show and now," countered Trabue.

"I'm counting Amelia," Jackson said with no emotion.

It was then that Trabue knew it was real bone-depth evil he must face. *Imagine,* thought Trabue, *he's counting an attack on his wife as a warning to me. He's beyond dirty!*

Trabue stopped and took one step back. He wanted Jackson to

see his gesture. Trabue held up both hands, palms out.

"You've made your deal with the devil, Jackson. I'll cut you no slack and I will see you in hell!"

"You've been told. Leave town or die."

Jackson started his car and left.

As Jackson turned on the main road leading from the marina he passed a non-descript gray sedan parked facing the spot he where had left Trabue and Sam.

★ ★ ★ ★ ★

"They missed. We will continue our surveillance," was spoken into the car's scrambled radio.

Chapter 30

Otis was not happy about the exchange. His thoughts were glued on Trabue. *He has no idea of what he's dealing with.*

Jackson reached for his police cell phone and punched in the number of his local informant. When the line picked up he attacked. "I don't care what your excuse is!"

"But..."

"No buts, no excuses!" he brutally overrode his listener, adding, "If anything moves, I want to know about it!"

"Yes, Yes. I'll stick to it."

"No excuses!"

★ ★ ★ ★ ★

"He's getting careless. That call was in the open and on the work line," said the driver of the gray sedan.

"Yeah, he's fried. Things are getting messy," was the reply.

"We'd better stay close."

"Yeah, but not too close."

★ ★ ★ ★ ★

"No excuses! Shit!" Eddie repeatedly slammed the phone into the cradle.

"Shit! Shit! Shit! Shit! Shit!" he yelled each time he banged the phone. Anger, coupled with frustration, oozed from him.

A simple grass bust, he thought. *A little weed, and it grew into this!*

Eddie collapsed into his chair and surveyed the marina. *I like Trabue. But I could lose all this!* He felt soiled by his actions. Watching and reporting had escalated once before when the two guys worked on the girl. He feared a repeat.

I'm afraid I could lose it all! Eddie knew he was in deep. *But, how deep?* he asked himself. *Will I ever get out?*

He now understood that his drug bust had been a setup. The guy that set up the transaction conveniently disappeared. *He probably was not even a real person.*

One of the transient boaters brought up the idea. "Do a deal. Move a few bags of weed through the marina. Who would suspect an inland, fresh-water marina?"

"Right," muttered Eddie to an invisible audience. "The deal fell apart in a bust and I'm Jackson's bitch!"

His memories were poison. Eddie had tried to make a little extra money, not for himself, but for the marina. It was the place he loved. The only place he ever felt at home. It was home.

The cops had been on him in an instant.

The boat, with the weed, pulled in, and wham! Jackson and company were in his face with lights, evidence, and then a deal. Play along and the dope charges go away.

"Right," muttered Eddie.

But they never went away.

The only thing that went away was Eddie's freedom. And now it was his home that might go away.

Eddie exited the marina office and walked to the end of the main dock. He could see a push boat moving its load downriver past the marina entrance channel.

"Boy, I'd love to be on that rig." He caught himself, realizing that now his dreams and desires were based upon escape from his beloved marina.

The reluctant snitch looked up toward the northeast rim of the old quarry. In that direction above the marina was the boundary to the construction site.

I was supposed to save the marina, he thought.

After the drug bust, it was Jackson who had broached the idea of how Eddie could escape jail time.

"When the lawyers come, you sign. The marina development will save your ass from jail time and showers that could get ugly."

Eddie had no choice, or so he believed. So, sign he did. And nothing improved. The drug charge was "still pending." The marina was slipping away. He was a slave of his own making.

Before the girl was found in the river, Trabue and his boat had been off limits. Trabue was just passing through. Now things seemed to be focusing on Trabue and his growing army of friends.

Eddie didn't like spying on Trabue. He was afraid that things would escalate, like before. He didn't want anything to do with harming anyone again. Karen Blaine's face was in his nightmares, and he found it almost unbearable to have her father around.

Eddie wanted to explain it all, but was afraid. He saw no way out. Eddie knew his fate was in the hands of people who used an Assistant Chief of Police as their messenger. The worst part was that Eddie had no real idea who was pulling his strings. He sensed that when the end

came, he would never see it coming.

He watched the push boat clear the channel and take his dreams of escape downriver.

Chapter 31

Sam used the phone in Eddie's shack to arrange for a pick-up. He beamed at the sight of Glory Be and, with her chattering, they sped for home.

Trabue relaxed only after they were out of sight, which occurred simultaneously with the appearance of Reggie driving Albert into the marina's parking lot.

Reggie waved with the phone in his hand. Trabue guessed that Sam was already filling Reggie in on the events.

The cab came to a rolling stop and Albert quickly bailed out. Reggie waved again and gave Trabue a thumbs-up and sped out the way he came.

"Elvira put out an 'all points bulletin' for the Shavers clan to convene," stated Albert. "Reggie told me to thank you for not shooting his favorite son. So please, tell me what's going on. I feel left out." He pouted and stuck out his lip.

After Trabue finished his story, Albert said, "To the boat! We can talk there. It's safer and we need to devise our game plan."

They proceeded to the *Awfria*, finding it empty. On board they located a note printed in what appeared to be a woman's hand.

"Ledge and Albert, we are going out for dinner. We'll be late. See you. Amelia."

"I'll have to assume they know what they are doing," remarked Trabue with a bit of irritation.

He was naturally worried, but Win was an ex-military cop and Amelia in his care should be safe.

"Perhaps they are helping each other. We need to focus on a plan; let's talk."

Trabue sat in the salon while Albert tinkered with one of his gadgets.

"This one seems to be on the fritz. I'll fire up the spare and we'll be secure."

Trabue was never a patient person. Although he was able to sit motionless for countless hours as an observer of all things, he could never totally overcome his patience flaw, especially in stressful situations. His gut ached.

"Tell me what you've found by sniffing the pavement," he asked. He knew it would get Albert going.

"Yes, yes!" an animated Albert began. "I did my thing like in the old days. You know, talk, sift, talk, sift, talk. I was in the zone!" He was getting excited. "I'll cut to the chase; I know you, you'll push me there, so I'll get there fast on my own."

Trabue chuckled. Albert knew how to unwind his impatient friend. He felt better already. He always felt better with Albert.

"Long and short of it is that the Hart empire is in big turmoil. It's pulling back and squeezing at the same time. Boy, they are into everything and I mean everything! Amazing! You have got to admire and wonder at it. I thought I was overreacting at first. You know, being off the streets for so long, like I was overestimating them because I was a born-again novice. But no! This operation is something else. It's big and subtle. It's everywhere and nowhere. There's no evidence it even exists, but it's real. When you told me about the demonstration, I held back some of my thoughts. 'No,' I said, 'it's a fluke, a spasm, an over-played reaction.'" He stopped, looked directly at Trabue and slowly said, "I was wrong, very, very wrong."

Trabue looked directly back at him and said, "So, what are you saying?"

"We are in deep shit. We are neck high in shit."

Trabue had sensed it. His stomach had ached for days; it was retching at this moment. To hear Albert admit how he felt made it worse.

"At least I'm not nuts," he said. "We are facing something that we are right to fear."

Yet in a way he was relieved. Their mutual fear and embarrassment to show it was out in the open now.

"What the hell, Al, you want to live forever? The worst fate in the world would be for you to get old, loose your teeth, and have to suck oatmeal through a straw."

Albert laughed. He patted his ample waistline and countered. "I've spent years making myself into a large target; I'm okay with being one as long as we do this thing together. Now, tell me about your side of the search."

Trabue recounted his library efforts. "The issue is somehow tied to Native artifacts. Karen was becoming an authority on the identification and analysis of all the items found in North America. She was 'the source.'"

"Please explain," asked Albert.

"Well, let me paraphrase a quote from one of her professional articles. She said that although the computer could speed along the analysis process, a flaw was ingrained in the computer itself. We toy

with falling too far into the data web." Trabue paused.

"Go on."

"Numbers. She said computer data is just numbers, binary numbers, zeroes and ones, just zeroes and ones. The numbers could represent people and their actions, but the numbers were not actual people. They are only symbols. And she did not want to lose sight of the actual people. In the end she became a philosopher—an ethicist. She was very concerned about what it all meant. Data, numbers, information meant nothing to her without the people connection. She was honest and wanted the data to honestly represent real people, and that probably got her killed."

"How so?"

"I'm not certain. But the answer is on the property next door. At least it might be. That's why they sent the two guys to stop me. I think the construction process unearthed some artifacts and Forsythe was hired to gloss them over, discount them, or in some manner alter their meaning and influence. Karen wouldn't go for it. She was poised to contact officials in Washington, probably to be the whistle blower. That's my read."

"Did you find anything on the site?"

"No. Before I was attacked, I searched the area accessible from the land side. But there's one spot left to examine. There's a shelf of land above the river formed into a point above a ledge. It's got a double layer of fencing with razor wire on the land-side approach. We can try reaching it from the water."

"Well, there's no moment like the present. And I feel we have no time to waste. Our opposition is adept at eliminating all threats. We can't sit around, right?"

"What about Win and Amelia?"

"If we are successful, we'll be back before them. If not, it doesn't matter."

"Good, I'll let Eddie know we're moving the boat. I'll tell him where we plan to anchor. In a pinch he can find us. You can act as deckhand." Trabue gave the last statement a bit of a twisted emphasis just to move Albert into a response. He was notoriously lazy about the boat.

"What, me? I'm not certain I'm skilled enough to..." he was cut off sharply by Trabue.

"Can it Albert! That act won't float. Float, get it? It's a nautical term. You know, like as in the two years you were a deckhand after high school."

Albert tossed up his hands and searched the ceiling with his eyes. "Oh, God! Please, can I have one secret from you?"

"Get your butt moving Albert, there's no time to waste. I want to be out there to check the site and be back before dark."

"Aye, aye," Albert responded with a quick salute which he flicked into an extended middle finger.

Laughing, Trabue said, "No mutinies! I'm a tyrant with the crew."

In mock outrage Albert marched out of the salon. Then deftly, with the utmost grace and agility, he changed direction in mid-stride and with cat-like speed scaled the portside hand holds up the emergency route to the flybridge. In seconds he had the twin diesels started and proceeded to prepare for departure.

Trabue jumped to the dock and headed for Eddie's office. He

looked back and shouted, "You're fat, you're fast and you're fired!"

Trabue found Eddie and quickly filled him in on their plan to move the boat.

When Trabue returned, the *Awfria* was purring and rigged to run. Albert stood on the dock and prepared for the push off.

"Take the helm Captain Trabue; your loyal crew awaits your commands."

Trabue climbed the ladder to the flybridge.

Albert nudged the *Awfria* ever so slightly and they were off.

Chapter 32

Triple O, Obvious Outcome Osbourne, was more than nervous. "Two unsavory jobs for the M.E.'s office in such a brief time. This is too much exposure!" He fumbled his keys and ground the car's starter. He knew he was being watched.

★ ★ ★ ★ ★

"You think we can trust 'em?"

"Sure, sure, don't worry Leon, and quit looking out the window."

"Just makin' sure he don't run out to a cop car or nuthin'."

The big man turned toward his bandaged friend, letting the curtain of the motel room's front window fall back in place.

"I just don't like this. We never needed a doctor before." He motioned toward the small man's arm. "You gonna be good?"

"You have no idea how good I'll be," smiled the little man with the greasy pock-marked face. "This might be a blessing in disguise."

"Huh?"

"Never mind, never mind." He leaned back and closed his eyes. The little man waved his good arm, signaling that he needed to be left alone. The big man shrugged his massive shoulders and backed his huge frame into a chair. He was accustomed to being shushed.

Bertie Powell had been telling him what to do for nearly a decade. Up to now all had gone as Bertie said.

Ten years ago they were just two punks. Two loser punks going nowhere at break-neck speed. Leon Jenkins was big, strong, black,

and not very smart. Bertie was white and weak, but fast with his wits and a blade.

Landing in juvenile custody ten years ago was good for both of them. At least that is how they saw it. If everything had happened a month later, it all might have turned out differently, because passing their eighteenth birthdays would have made them adults and their nowhere paths would never have crossed. But, luck prevailed and a week before their birthdays, they both screwed up and landed in the county's care.

Bertie had tossed a knife through a crowd in his high school cafeteria and Leon had stolen a lawnmower. Separate actions resulted in the same trip to the detention center.

In the detention center, Leon had heard two guys talking about "the smart ass, little white dude" and how they were going to "fix his ass." With no TV to watch, Leon thought he'd tag along for the show.

Bertie Powell had been even greasier and skinnier back then, but he was already quick. Leon arrived just as the two guys overpowered their smaller prey. Powell saw the big tag-along and sized Leon up perfectly.

"If you ain't in on this, I'll give you twenty dollars to get 'em off me!" Before his assailants could act, Bertie upped the offer by adding, "Each!"

Leon was never good at math, but he reasoned that two times any offer is good. So, he moved in on the two attackers.

What happened next was the foundation of all future actions taken by the Bertie-Leon team. The two attackers assumed that Bertie was an insignificant threat, so they pushed him aside. That was mistake number one. They reasoned that together they could handle Leon. That was mistake number two.

With a comb for a blade, Bertie zipped a quick raking action across the cheek of one of the thugs. It was enough to make him wince and also cause the other to look his way.

Then Leon hammered them. They were hit together and dropped together. Leon's arms were the size of most men's thighs and denser than granite.

Physics dictates that two heads and two torsos cannot occupy identical space. Several bones had cracked on each side of the collision. Powell stepped over the moaning mass and said, "Sweet! We'd better get out of here, fast!" He attempted to leave, but Leon held his arm, stopping his departure.

"Where's my money?"

"Can't pay it now, But I'll double it if you stick with me!"

Leon went for it again. Dropping his new friend's arm he asked, "Double?"

"Yeah, double! And there can be plenty more if you trust me!"

So Leon trusted Bertie. There was more, but Leon never knew how much.

They were released together on their co-birthdays.

In "juvie" they had lived well. Bertie made the deals and Leon enforced them. If anything went wrong, Bertie provided a quick distraction and Leon provided the muscle. Their trademark was Bertie's quick moves followed by Leon's overwhelming might. It was a simple and very effective strategy. For nearly a decade it was a formula that worked. Today was their first failure. Neither of them liked the

way it felt.

In their early days they provided reliable collections for drug dealers in several cities. As their reputation grew they branched out into other areas of enforcement, moving up to the big league with their first contract for a hit six years ago.

It was Bertie's idea to come to Nashville. He had set up the move, as he always did, and up until today it had looked good. Except for that thing with the woman not going down as planned. It was somehow tied up with the guy today. Bertie knew all about it. Leon was just the muscle and Leon trusted Bertie. Bertie took care of the details, such as money.

Leon wasn't certain, but he thought they were close to their goal. Bertie had explained it to him many times:

"See, Leon, we are what is called labor."

"Yeah?"

"Yeah, we do things, things we are told to do, for a price."

"The deals, right?"

"Right! We perform the labor and get paid."

"You're good at settin' things up!"

"Yeah, right! So, one day we need to get out of the doin' part and into the 'tellin' others to do' part."

"Yeah, not labor."

"Right! So, real soon, we're gonna get something on our own, a business, maybe a bar or a strip joint."

"Strip joint!"

The thought of an unending supply of strippers always caused Leon to smile. He would kick back, close his eyes, and daydream about "his club and his girls." Without fail he would ask Bertie, "How much more money do we need to get a club?" The answer was always the same: "A little more, just one more good job and we've got it!"

"Partners, right Bertie?"

"Yeah, partners, Leon!"

"My half and your half make us partners!"

Of course there were no halves.

It was one whole. And it was all Bertie's. Bertie placed the money in several accounts in banks with exotic addresses. Only one name was on the accounts.

Leon would have been surprised, and certainly broken-hearted, if he had known the facts.

Fact one, Bertie had all the money.

Fact two, there never would be a club.

Fact three, Bertie was ready to end the partnership.

Bertie thought, *It's time to end this. Getting hurt is the signal. I've seen it coming. We've lost the edge. One mistake is one too many. We do these jobs for the long-haired freaky chick and her spooky father. Then we get the money and I'm off to the Caymans, without Leon.*

Bertie had never liked Leon. *He's big, strong and stupid. Saw that in juvie, still see it now,* he thought. *He'd get lost on the way to the toilet. I'm out of here by myself this time.*

Looking over at his long-time companion Bertie saw a meal ticket and security, nothing else.

He continued with his thoughts. *It just goes to show, we never should have tried anything outside our specialty. Needless daylight work is not for*

us. And Leon is getting slow and careless.

Blaming Leon made his pending act of betrayal seem alright.

"My arm hurts," he exclaimed.

"Huh," came from a startled Leon.

"Shut up! Just shut up! I'm hurtin' bad and I've got to think."

"You keep thinkin', Bertie."

The small greasy man closed his eyes. The pills given to him by the quack doctor started to take effect. He sat back on the bed and leaned against two soiled pillows. As he drifted off, he instructed Leon. "Be alert for a phone call. We might get another try at the guy who did this!"

In his dreams Bertie was tall, good-looking, and popular. He spent a lot of money, alone. Bertie's dreams had no Leon in them.

Chapter 33

As is often true, getting to a location by water can be tricky. The river's current was inconsistent due to some eddies and back flows near the spot where Trabue could best tie up the *Awfria*.

As they neared the shoreline, Albert prepared the boat for docking against the cliff's lower edge. His years as a deck hand were apparent. He inflated several large fenders, hung them properly, and pre-set all the required lines in quick economical motions. Trabue knew he could rely on Albert to assist on board, but the need had never presented itself. That is why he had allowed Albert to play stupid about boat duties.

As Trabue expertly worked the twin throttles, the *Awfria* came to the exact spot he desired. His estimate of the current was correct and the boat held stationary as Albert found two tree limbs, one forward, and one aft, for a secure docking. The fenders barely touched the cliff's rock edge.

"Perfect landing," commented Trabue. "A good sign. I hope this is the beginning of the end."

He cut the engines and put the anchor light on. *Just to be safe,* he thought. *Dad would be proud of that docking maneuver.* How he loved being on a boat. For a brief instant he was extremely happy. *Boats take you away from all the crap in the world,* he mused. *They bring good thoughts to mind; simple good thoughts.*

"My Captain, my Captain," taunted Albert. "Are you going to dream away the daylight?"

Happiness faded to reality and Trabue once again focused on the

task at hand.

"You stay on board. I'll climb up the cliff to that ledge about twenty feet above us. I'm certain I'll find something. What, I don't know. It shouldn't take too long, but if for any reason I'm gone over thirty minutes, clear out. Got it?" Trabue loved giving orders to Albert.

"Maybe." Albert was hesitant and clearly not in total agreement.

"So, what's your plan?" asked Trabue.

He answered firmly, "If you're not back in ten minutes I'm going to shinny my large butt up this rock and find out what's keeping you. Got it?"

Trabue was warmed by Albert's genuine concern. "I'll hurry," and he proceeded to depart the boat and start climbing. He joked, "Just don't break anything while I'm gone."

Chapter 34

Trabue traversed the rock wall easily. He did not look back or down when he reached the top. He moved ahead.

Immediately before him was a canopy of lush green leaves. He pushed them aside and found a small clearing. The area was man-made and of recent origin. Several mounds were surrounded by a hodge-podge of wooden boxes and airtight shipping crates.

Trabue warily approached the nearest pair of crates. On their sides were labels showing Forsythe's office as their final destination.

Trabue popped the seal and opened the nearest crate. It contained what appeared to be native artifacts. Bowls, bead work, tools, and the like were packed inside. He closed it and opened the second one.

The smell was over-powering. Holding back a gag he replaced the lid quickly. *Well,* he thought, *now we know where the missing Professor Forsythe is.*

Trabue had seen enough. He retraced his steps and headed back to the *Awfria*.

As he pushed the leaf canopy aside he heard the unmistakable sound of unfamiliar boat engines. He continued to the cliff's ledge. He looked down and did not like what he saw.

Rafted to his boat was a larger, sleeker, and much newer Euro-styled yacht. It pinched the *Awfria* to the ledge.

"There's no escape, Mr. Trabue," was the remark from below.

Trabue recognized the voice. It was the little man, the nondescript fiend of the night before, Lawrence Hart.

"Come down and join us. We'll wait for you on my boat."

Although the sun had just set and twilight abounded, Trabue's eyes were seared by a search beam. There was no escape.

When Trabue touched down on the *Awfria's* deck, he had two options for his route to the other yacht. He could go up and over the flybridge, or through the salon.

Up and over would place him in sight of the other yacht all the way. Through the *Awfria* meant he might have an opportunity to do something to improve his odds. Grab a weapon, trip one of Albert's gadgets, something, anything!

He opted for the salon route.

It was an outright bust.

They had thought of the same thing. As soon as he entered the salon, he was greeted by an extremely powerful and well-aimed blow to his much-abused stomach.

"Hello, bitch!" was Big-and-Strong's opening. Trabue dropped to his knees, breathless.

"Easy, Leon!" the words came from Bertie Powell. He was sporting a cast on his arm. "Mr. Hart said no rough stuff, yet."

Trabue liked the "no rough stuff" comment. It was the "yet" he didn't like.

"Sure. Sure. I'll wait, but I'm not happy 'bout it. He dissed us good. Nobody gets past Leon Jenkins, nobody!"

Leon spat on Trabue.

From his deck-level vantage point, Trabue could make out the remnants of a struggle. Albert must have gone to the other yacht reluctantly.

Good for Albert! I was only joking about breaking things, was Trabue's thought. *I hope he is okay.* He feared it was not so, but wished for the contrary.

"Drag his ass next door; we got work to do," ordered a familiar voice. It was Eddie telling the duo their next move.

Eddie? I didn't see that coming, thought Trabue. *I believed he was a good kid.*

Jerked to his feet by Leon, Trabue found his arms pinned, then tied behind his back. He was hustled aboard Hart's boat and deposited before the waiting boss.

Leon did not miss the opportunity to elbow Trabue's face, bang his head on a rail, and stretch the limit of "no rough stuff." Trabue was disoriented when he was tossed on the yacht's sofa.

The landing was cushioned by Albert's great bulk. *At least I know where he is,* came into Trabue's fogged mind.

Trabue slid partially off Albert and was jerked upward and then tossed down again by Leon.

"I said no rough play, and I meant it." This time the voice was female. Trabue recognized it as Jan's.

Standing before him were Jan, her father, Otis, and Eddie. Big Leon and Bertie stood guard at the door.

"We gave clear warnings," Jan said. "You and your friends went beyond the limit."

Trabue could barely see or hear. The blows and knocks from Leon took away his edge. The edge came back when he saw the needle in her hand.

"Your oversized friend, the Professor, has already had one of my cocktails." She tapped the syringe, letting him know that it was full

and ready to go. "Before we say good-bye, I want you to know that it has not been a pleasure to deal with you. You flustered my husband so much that I decided to take control of things."

Her black hair shimmered all the way to her waist and swirled when she turned to address her father.

"Right, Daddy?"

Hart nodded to her and smiled a thin lizard-like grin.

"I'm afraid you are just another detail to be removed. I am going to make you go away." There was a finality in her tone that made Trabue certain she had done this before and enjoyed it.

"All this over real estate?" asked Trabue. *Just keep her talking! Think! Think!* he screamed inside his mind.

"Ha! Real estate! You must be joking," she replied. "You really think it's about that? What a shame, what a real shame. You're taking a big plunge in the river and you don't even know why!" She enjoyed discovering that he was not in the know.

Good, thought Trabue. *Good! You go girl, get excited. Keep talking while I think. Think! Think!* his mind kept screaming.

"Tell me, Otis," she asked. "Is he stupid or playing a game? I'm sorry John isn't here to play dumb and dumber."

Otis shrugged. "It's your call, Jan. I told him what was what and he kept pressing. He's persistent and that's not good. You should end this and fast. I think you should..."

She cut him off with a quick and sharp wave of her hand holding the syringe.

"Oh! Really!" She was excited.

Next she mimicked him. "I think...you should... I told..." her voice became a shriek. Something he said or how he said it touched her off. "I'm tired of you and your opinions. Just like John's. None of them are good! None work out. Remember? It was you who thought that doing the girl was a good move. She wouldn't go along with Forsythe, so you had her drugged and dumped. What good did that do? It just freaked out Forsythe! We needed him at least for a while longer. Now he's UPS freight up on the hill and just another disposal problem!"

She was working herself up and Trabue needed to keep her going. Trabue engaged her again.

"So what's so important about whatever is up there?"

She wheeled around, her hair swirling like a black lace shawl.

"Important? Everything! That's what! We've got over three hundred million dollars tied up in what's up there. I'd say that's important enough!"

"Artifacts? They can be worth that kind of money?" He was groping.

"What!" She looked incredulous. "Trabue! I thought you were smart! It's not about either, not artifacts or real estate. It's about gambling! Money! It's always about money!"

Otis tried to cut in. "Look, we should..."

He never finished.

Jan swung her arm quickly and decisively. Her jab hit him between the ear and jaw line. She plunged the entire contents of the syringe into him.

Otis Jackson gasped. There was an amazed look across his face. His eyes rolled back and as he fell, Jan moved aside and let him drop.

"Sorry, Otis," she said. "I'm not up for an argument."

No one said a word or moved. Even Lawrence Hart was shocked by her cold and brutal action.

She pulled up a chair and sat in front of Trabue. Her eyes were vacant and black. She had gone somewhere else where something unworldly was guiding her. Whatever she had become was totally and completely evil.

Trabue stopped ordering himself to think. It was useless. He could only stare and listen. They all listened. Was it fear, or were they hypnotized?

"Look, it's simple. We didn't find artifacts, we planted them. The land above overlooks our property across the river, right Daddy?" He too was in her grip and could only nod.

"The land next to the harbor and the harbor itself will be the base. From there we'll ferry people across the river to our two thousand-plus acre resort and casino on the other side. Right, Daddy?" This time she didn't look to see the nod.

Her father was hypnotized by her evil.

She continued. "Years ago I went to my first Nashville Steeplechase. It's a charity event. I saw all those sweet, dear community people having so much fun. They were dressed up, cavorting, and, for one day, they were able to legally gamble in Tennessee. I saw how much they loved to gamble. So, I got creative."

Trabue winced. The last time she had been described as creative was following the demonstration at the club. When she got creative innocent people paid for it.

"I asked myself, 'why should people not be able to gamble all year long?' I started planning, and it turned out to be simple. The annual portion of gambling money in this country that goes through reservations is huge, over twenty billion dollars. Daddy has so much money and so many important friends; it was easy to get started. I'm almost done now, right, daddy?"

Again no look, but also no nod; her father was really out of it. She was both a narcotic and a charmer for him.

What a pair, thought Trabue, *no wonder the mother drank herself to death.*

"Do you like to gamble, Mr. Trabue?" she asked. She needed no reply. Her voice continued.

"People are going to like gambling at my place. It's mine, all mine, and it will be special. You see, that's how the Indian artifacts help out. There's no reservation in Tennessee or Kentucky. Did you know that? We pushed the Native Americans out, or they never lived here. Whatever! I'm going to create my own casino resort. The gambling will be all mine to control. So, I had to bring some proof in and I had to create a reservation too! It's such a good idea! I'll get to run it all!" She was amazing, even to herself. Especially to herself.

"That girl, the one who worked for Forsythe, didn't think it was right. What did she know? She wanted the artifacts to tell the truth. I just want what I want. I am going to have a tribe of my own, and a reservation. It will be easy—just pay the right people, hire lawyers, and bribe the judges. Right, Daddy?" Trabue saw that whatever had her, had her good.

"I'll be the new Native Princess, right, Daddy?" He did not react. "Oh Daddy! Come on! Stay with me!" she waved at Hart and he

began to emerge from his trance.

Trabue and the others continued to watch in a daze.

Trabue had no idea if her disorder could be diagnosed, but it existed because the power and money were there to fund a sick mind. Money and an indulgent father were a lethal combination when added to whatever Jan was.

Trabue prayed for a miracle. It came as a slight movement from beneath him.

Is Albert playing 'possum? he asked himself.

Jan resumed, "So anyway, I'll get some politicians to readdress the whole Trail of Tears thing, or whatever." She went on, but Trabue was not listening. He was focused on Albert's show of life and wondering how it might save them.

As he wondered and hoped for a miracle, Jan refilled the syringe and seemed to notice the fallen Otis for the first time.

"Daddy, I could use a small amount of help over here. Please get the boys to move Otis."

She leaned toward Trabue and said, "Need to lighten the work force a bit. You know, too many people knowing what we are up to. I just make them go away! Right, Daddy?"

Hart came to life and motioned for Eddie, Bertie, and Leon to come further into the salon. Eddie was the first to come closer. That was his mistake.

Jan looked at Eddie. He was her next victim.

She motioned to Leon by pulling a finger across her neck. Leon knew what the signal meant. So did Eddie. He saw it coming, but did not react quickly enough.

Leon was faster than Eddie. There was a crunch. Leon liked to use his hands. Eddie fell to the floor without further sound.

"Over the side with him," Jan instructed.

Leon and Bertie removed Eddie and Otis from the salon. Trabue heard a single splash. He assumed Eddie was now a bobber. Otis would not be found in the river. *Faked heart attack?* thought Trabue. It made no difference. Both he and Eddie had paid the price for being around when Jan lost it.

"You seem to have an excess of bodies," Trabue chided Jan.

Again he thought, *Maybe, if I can just keep her going I'll find a way out of this.*

Albert moved again, ever so slightly.

"Don't you imagine for one second that I'm pleased with myself for doing that to Otis," she explained. "I spent a lot of time and money getting him ready to be our first African-American mayor. I just got tired of his constant advice and second guessing. He's been screwing up lately, so I had a plan for getting rid of him. Yes, I've got a few extras around, but he's no problem any longer. The boys have taken him home. They'll set up a sex and drug thing at the condo. His wife and your pal are already there. Voila! Problem solved. Three more annoyances out of the way! And, a juicy bit of gossip to circulate at the next Chamber of Commerce meeting." She giggled.

Trabue felt his stomach revolt.

Her illness, whatever it was, had consumed her soul. She was raw evil. Her eyes, those vacant, black-hole pinpoints zeroed in on his.

"Now, on with your part of the show! Do you want it in the arm, the leg? Where?"

"How about in December?" he quipped.

"Funny, real funny." She motioned for Daddy to assist.

"Get him off the big guy; I need a clean shot at a vein. He's going to go fast, I promise."

Hart came around his daughter and bent over toward Trabue and Albert. It was then that the sleeping giant emerged with a roar to match a rutting bull elephant. With sudden energy akin to a volcano, Albert elevated the entire gathering and propelled all of them toward the yacht's salon door.

For Trabue, the sequence of actions appeared in slow motion. He saw looks of startled surprise on Hart and Jan. He saw glass shards from the salon door glimmer as they flew slowly through the air.

He saw Lawrence Hart's face contort as his back hit and broke the yacht's railing. It was Albert's great bulk that pinned the smaller man against the railing, just prior to its giving way. Trabue heard a sickening crunch. Even the sounds he heard were in slow motion.

The slow motion enabled Trabue to read the warning label on a life jacket hanging near the door. As he flew past, Trabue thought, *Is this for real? Is this how your mind acts just before the end?*

Everything had been altered by Albert's expenditure of energy. The big man's surging, renewed life-force had bent the space-time continuum. It was, *Hello, Mr. Einstein, good-bye boat!*

They all hit the water.

Chapter 35

In the water Trabue had a new problem: sinking with bound arms. He felt air bubbles pass his face so he kicked his feet to follow them. Just then he felt Jan grab his waist.

Yeah, the ex-swimmer, he remembered. She was strong. She wasn't going to give up easily and let him go. She was taking him down.

Trabue was determined not to go gently. He startled her by wrapping his legs tightly around her and making like a sinker. Trabue became a lead weight trying to burden her.

If you want to go down, we go together! I'll die, but so will you Jan!

She was startled, but her response bewildered Trabue as she nestled close and tongued his ear. She released a small diabolical laugh with a few escaping bubbles and then she drove them deeper.

She's the swimmer, she's stronger, he realized. *She's going to win. She's just toying with me.* In his last moments of life he became more alert than ever.

His brain knew it, but it was his skin that experienced it—the chemical formula for water. Good old $H2O$. He could feel each molecule as his skin separated the river's pollution from each atom of oxygen and hydrogen. He also felt something else. He felt the hand of God. No, it wasn't a hand that touched him! It was a branch—no, several of them!

Together and all at once, a multi-fingered alien hand with a hundred fingers touched him. It touched her too! She giggled at the first touch—a tickle. Then she flinched. Not a tickle! It was a grasp, a grope.

Months before, somewhere upriver a tree had fallen. *Did anyone hear it fall?* was his thought. Sound or no sound then, the fallen tree was now silently introducing itself. More exactly, its limbs and branches—the tree's fingers—reached out and grasped Jan's long shimmering beautiful black hair.

She released Trabue to free her hair. Her motion increased the tree's embrace. She was frightened.

Trabue's breath could take him no further; he was spent. From above he sensed, then saw, a light.

Is this the tunnel they talk about? he wondered. *But, it moves. Oh, it's a spot light. Maybe they'll find me as a bobber.*

He looked at his arm and saw the syringe. It wiggled free, half empty, to find its buoyancy point, remaining suspended below the surface—just like the sunken tree.

As Trabue's life faded, the light from above enabled him to have a final vision. The syringe hanging in the water was very still, in contrast to Jan's frantic motions to free her hair from the tree's fingers. She released a huge column of air bubbles, stopped moving, and drifted out of sight. The scene was haughtingly beautiful.

Chapter 36

You know, thought Trabue, *being dead isn't so bad. It's dark, but it's not bad.* His brain had rebooted. *It's dark, and it smells strange, like the nurse's office at my old elementary school. What's that?*

He sensed movement about him. *Angels? Must be angels. And they are big, much bigger than me.* He drifted again.

Sometime much later, he thought he was actually awake. He looked over and, *Yes! The big angel is still there.*

The big angel moved. The rustling of his newspaper and shifting of position produced comforting sounds. The angel looked up and said, "About time you joined us."

Trabue playfully gave the angel the finger. He drifted asleep, feeling safe to do so. He knew he was being watched over.

Albert summoned help. He could relax now.

After reinforcements arrived, Albert left to stretch his legs. He'd been sitting guard for five days. Other than maintaining basic hygiene, consuming minimal food, and changing his clothes, he had not left his post.

Fortunately, the press had not been very persistent. Albert had taken care of them. The mostly young and inexperienced reporters took the police statements at face value. His own utterances were treated as gospel. The news pieces read like they had never seen an editor. In effect, there was no real examination of events.

The police were almost as easy to handle: not quite as devotional in their demeanor as the reporters, but still respectful to Professor Bryan. The police assigned for follow-up did not dig for answers.

They jotted down Albert's story and that was it.

They should at least go beyond the basics and ask a few skeptical questions, thought Albert. *Am I really that formidable? Is my reputation truly that good?*

In the end, Albert's battle between Trabue's personal privacy and the public wanting to know the truth leaned toward privacy. Until Trabue's condition improved, Albert really did not care about the public's need to know. He fended off the press and had sat guard at the hospital.

Now that Trabue was finally showing signs of recovery it was too late to change the record even if he wanted to. The news cycle had moved on.

★ ★ ★ ★ ★

"What's next, Professor?"

It came from Reggie, who had been standing guard almost as loyally as Albert.

"We let Amelia and her medical colleagues do their thing. Trabue needs to heal."

"No, I mean is it over? Is it finished?"

Albert rubbed his eyes and stretched. "Don't know exactly. I have some mental loose ends to tie. I believe I've got a handle on them, but five days is a long time. Another end may unravel, but I think I've identified them all."

"Sure hope so," replied Reggie. "I'd hate for anything to come back and bite us, or anyone else."

"Trouble is, it's always the unseen snake that bites the worst. It's the pebble sitting in the open that you trip on. When he's up to it, I'll speak with Trabue. He filled me in on everything as we went along, and I saw a lot first hand. Right now, I can't see a fault in my thinking, but..."

"But that's where you could make a mistake," Reggie finished for him and added, "Professor!" to emphasize his point.

Albert laughed, "I stand corrected. The perfect plan allows for a mistake. I should assume that we don't know everything. I'd just feel better if Jan's body was found and the loose ends were tied up."

"It's still whirling in my mind, too. I was there for a lot of it, and trust me, after Sam told me his part, and after five constant days of Elvira on the phone sniffing details, I'm ready for a break. That's why I've decided to pull the plug and retire."

"What! Retire? You and Elvira together all day long? Can you handle it? Could anyone?"

"It's time to let things be handled by someone else, that's all."

"Someone else?"

"Yeah, Sam's ready."

"Really?"

"Yeah, he's been tossing ideas at me for as long as I can recall. I've more or less gone along with them all because he's been right more than wrong. I have faith and confidence in Sam's ideas. I'd be a fool to stand in his way. It's time for me to step aside and go fishin' like I've always talked about. Also, I believe that Elvira needs a change. If I go, she'll follow, telephone in hand!" Laughter invaded them both.

"You'd never be able to retire without a cell phone," Albert said

with a smile.

"Yes, I know. Elvira, living without a phone, is not possible. I've learned that she sleeps with her phone!" Both men laughed again at the well-known joke about Elvira's sleep habit.

Sam arrived and wondered why his father and Albert were laughing so freely. Their high spirits looked good to him. Sam's smile was interrupted when Albert leapt as if hit by a lightning bolt.

"Cell phone!" Albert shouted. *"Cell phone!"*

"What phone?" Sam questioned.

"No, its phones, not phone! I've got to talk to Amelia, where'd she go?" Albert sped off to where he had seen her speaking with Trabue's other doctors.

Reggie pointed after him and instructed Sam, "Go, go on! He's on to something important. I'll stay to watch Trabue. You go and back him up, drive, do whatever—*go!"*

Sam sprinted down the corridor and caught up to Albert who was still repeating, "It's phones, phones! He had two phones!"

When Albert sighted Amelia, he slowed down and completed a mid-stride transformation from excited investigator to calm professor. At first, Sam thought he'd seen a time warp or some other anomaly. Such was Albert's speed in gaining composure.

Professor Bryan caught Dr. Jackson's attention with a raised eyebrow and a tiny hand gesture. It was a marvel to behold, a perfect display of miniature semaphore and eye contact.

Sam liked watching the Professor in action.

Amelia removed herself from the gathering with calm grace and dignity, but her eyes belied the extreme interest she had in the appearance of first Albert and then Sam. She wanted to know what they wanted to know, fast.

"So, what's up?" Amelia asked quizzically.

"Amelia!" blurted Albert. "I'm sorry, but I've got to know something. It's very important—extremely important." he hesitated, "Something about Otis!"

For Amelia, Albert's words took a second or two to sink in. "Otis?" her mind was momentarily blank. "Oh, yes Otis. What about Otis?" She was slightly embarrassed at her slow response.

"Do you recall the list?" began Albert. "The list of all the items found on him when he was killed?" he paused. "You know, the standard list the M.E.'s office gave you?"

He was certain she would remember. She had prepared hundreds of similar lists in her career. She had it with her when she treated Trabue. Amelia had shown it to Albert, commenting that one of her colleagues had pirated an advance copy. Professional courtesy, she called it. A heads-up to side-step any embarrassment at being surprised by a strange or quirky object being found amongst a relative's final possessions.

Amelia had remarked to Albert that the gesture from her professional friend was thoughtful, but not needed. Otis had nothing of interest on him. Albert had scanned the list, and his police mind must have placed the number of cell phones in a mental compartment for later analysis. It had popped out, or up, or into view when he had joked with Reggie about Elvira and her phone, her one phone. Even a world-class phone talker like Elvira required only one phone. With all the options, two phones were not necessary. Not necessary unless

you wanted to hide something, be totally safe from caller ID, or you and somebody had another reason for using an extra phone.

"Amelia, what about the phones? There were two cell phones on the list. Why did Otis have two phones?"

"Two? I'm not sure. He had both with him all the time. I thought he needed two because of the police work. Don't police need dedicated phones?" She paused. The multiple options made available from current technology slapped her in mid-sentence. "No, no! He had no need for two! But, he used both! I saw him, but I never actually heard him use the second phone! The second phone was always the one he jumped for!" She was remembering back to the days of her old life before Trabue, Win, Albert, and all the rest.

"Yes, go on Amelia, go on," Albert coaxed her with a gentle, smooth voice.

"He kept it with him all the time. At the bedside, even in the shower—always near. Whenever it rang, no, it never rang, it vibrated. Whenever it moved, so did he. He'd excuse himself, find a private place, take the call and then afterwards he would be different."

"So what does it mean?" Sam asked. "What can having two phones mean?"

"I'm not certain, but it's a big loose end. I was too close and I missed it!" remarked Albert.

"So did I," piped in Amelia.

"So?" came from Sam.

Albert asked Amelia, "So where's the second cell phone? Can we get it?"

"I'm not sure, but I think so. No! I'm positive. I haven't signed a release, the phone should still be at the M.E.'s office." she paused.

"Unless someone, the people who called him, got to it already!" finished Albert.

"We'd better get moving," added Sam.

The three of them headed for the nearest elevator.

Sam said, "We'll need to get there fast. Glory Be is outside. I'll have her drive us."

Chapter 37

The trip to the M.E.'s office was classic Glory Be—a total blur.

Sam took it in stride. Amelia and Albert were in wide-eyed shock as the cab rolled up to the M.E.'s office. It took them a couple of moments to reenter the non-Glory Be world.

"Lord, have mercy!" exclaimed Amelia.

"No, it's Glory Be!" exclaimed Albert. "I'd never have believed it. Trabue told me, but I did not believe it could really be that wild! Sam, where does she get all that energy?"

Sam just smiled and shrugged, "I can't explain it. She's a wonder, isn't she?"

"A wonder? No! She's outright amazing! It's a miracle that I never had her on the table at my old job." blurted Amelia. "Sam, don't you worry?"

"Amelia, I've tried to tone her down. No such luck. I've come to accept the fact that her energy is like a force field. It protects her in some bizarre way. So, I've come to live with the fact that I'm married to a human hurricane."

Sam pointed to the parking lot and exclaimed, "Look, she's already parked! Any other driver would be only halfway there!"

Glory Be waved back to let Sam know all was well.

"Let's move!" broke in Albert. "We've got to find that phone!"

Inside it took only a few minutes for Amelia to chat up her old co-workers and get them to retrieve the items. Both phones were with Otis' effects. Amelia removed the phones from the container and quickly replaced the lid. She avoided looking at any of the remaining items.

"They look identical to me," observed Sam.

Albert reached for the closest phone.

"Here, I'll do a call-up for the number." As the display lit up he read the number to Amelia and asked, "Sound familiar?"

"Yes, that's his work number. I had it on my speed dial at my office and at home, but I remember it, that's definitely his regular police number."

"So it's this other one. I'll need to take it and the container with me. Is that okay?"

"Sure, fine, that's why we're here, right?"

"Right as rain. Now, the fun starts."

Outside the building, Sam flagged Glory Be's attention. In an instant the quartet rolled back to the hospital, retracing the route in even less time. At the hospital's driveway the passengers bailed out.

Amelia told Sam, "You are correct in thinking there is a force field of some type! On at least three occasions I thought we were goners, but there seemed to be an impenetrable bubble around the cab. I'm amazed!" She looked to Albert for confirmation.

"Don't look at me." His hands were over his eyes. "I was too afraid to even look!"

As the three of them crossed the hospital's lobby, Albert informed Amelia, "Your job's finished. It's now up to Sam and me to chase this loose end."

She did not protest. Albert knew that she was focused on Win and her new future. She was more than ready to break clean from Otis and the past. Albert had seen her obvious discomfort with the

container of items that had belonged to Otis. He had said nothing when Amelia refused to look into it. His taking the container was a gesture for closure. He had no plan of giving it back to her. Albert knew she would never ask for it. It was full of the past.

Sam broke the awkwardness. "I'm headed up to check on Dad and Trabue. Amelia, maybe you need to wake him up or check to see if I could visit?"

Albert motioned as if he were guiding chicks to safety as he said, "I'll need some time to have this phone checked out. You go on to the room. I'll meet you there in about an hour." He headed immediately for the bank of pay phones. He wanted a hard-wire line for his call to Tampa.

Chapter 38

"No problem, Professor Bryan. I can do it all from here."

"How do we set it up?"

They were discussing the "mystery phone" found in the container of belongings.

Leonard Wheeler was Albert's best techie grad student. Whenever Albert had an equipment need it was Lennie who had the answers. Albert had been slow to accept technology. Slow until Lennie appeared on campus. Lennie loved gadgets and computers. He was also a natural at taking things apart and getting information from inanimate objects.

"So all I do is call you? I just use the phone in question and you'll strip it like that? It's that simple?"

"Well, yes and no. It takes a lot of backup, which we have here, or I can arrange. It's really very complicated but, with all this gear, it's also very easy."

"I think that when I get back to the campus I'm going to check all those papers I signed—all those grant requests. I think you've created an empire right beneath my nose." He could hear Lennie suppress a laugh.

"Don't worry Professor; it's all legal, I think."

"Who cares if it's legal? I'm pulling your leg about the grants. I just want it to work!"

"Oh, it'll work all right. Just push in the numbers I gave you. The phone will hook up to me by satellite and I'll do all the rest from here. At least I'll guide the process through all the gear here in

Tampa." He paused. "Seriously, Professor, you don't think I've got too much stuff here do you?"

"Lennie, if you find out anything that I can use here I'll sign all the requests you can generate."

"Give me a little time. I'll call as soon as I'm finished."

"I'll be waiting."

★ ★ ★ ★ ★

Albert Bryan hated waiting. He had learned how to be patient. Stakeouts, the talking and sifting, it all taught him that it was good to wait. But he still did not like it.

In this instance his discomfort was doubled. He had to wait and he was afraid that he had failed. He thought, *If I've missed something and someone gets hurt... Stop it, Albert! Deal with it when you know what it is!*

So, he sat and waited, overcoming the fear of failure with patience. The illuminated cell phone in his lap shot data up to a satellite and the satellite dropped it on Lennie.

Albert whispered, "Take what time you need Lennie! Do your magic, but do it right!"

Chapter 39

The vibrating phone brought the sleeping bear out of his nap. Albert glanced at his watch and calculated the time it had taken Lennie to do his thing.

"Twenty-nine minutes. Not bad, not bad at all."

He got up, walked over to the pay phone and dialed his grad student. Lennie did not answer his phone with the customary greeting. Rather, he started right in with, "You were twelve feet from the pay phone, by my estimate. Pretty good, huh, Professor?"

"What?"

"Twelve feet. Nine if you were seated. You'd have to get up and it would take an additional second or two."

Albert looked back at the lounge area where he had been sitting and counted nine standard floor tiles between his current position and the chair.

"Lennie, how did you do that?"

"Impressed?"

"Maybe. You could have called the lobby and had someone peek over here and then set me up. So, tell me your version. If it's good, I'll be impressed."

"Sure, but first, please, say hello to Vicki."

"Who? Vicki? Say hello to whom?"

A voice cut in and said, "Hi Professor Bryan! Remember me? Vicki Sanders? I interned a couple of years ago at USF with Lennie."

"Oh yes! Vicki! Vicki, how are you?"

"Fine." She was interrupted by Lennie.

"We can chit chat and fill you in later Professor, but I got a lot of info, very fast, mainly because of Vicki."

"Why thank you, Vicki!"

"No problem Professor. I was really excited when Lennie asked me to help." Again, Lennie brought them back to the issue at hand.

"Sorry, Vicki! We can catch up later. Professor, first let me explain how I knew the distance thing. It ties everything together!"

"Fine, Lennie. You've got my full attention."

"I knew your exact location and I mean EXACT by the GPS chip in the phone."

"Lennie." The tone was disappointment.

"No, no! I know you are going to say that it's no big deal. All new cell phones have GPS. But not like this GPS!"

"Go on," prompted the Professor.

"The phone is special. Very special. It's government-issue and has a security GPS chip that is readable only from government security, or military GPS satellites. I knew the location to within one one-hundredth of a meter; that's about one third of an inch!"

"Whoa! Hold on, Lennie!"

"Nice, huh?"

"Lennie, back up! If it's government, and I trust it is if you say so, how did you activate the GPS?"

"Got your drift Professor. You don't have to worry!"

"Worry? Worry? You've gone through the military's system or the government's security system with a bootlegged phone carrying a GPS chip that can tell position within a dime's surface area and tell me not to worry? Lennie, have you gone mad?"

"Professor," the interruption came from Vicki this time, "it's cool, not to worry! Really! There's more of these out there than you'd imagine. The encryption codes were easy to knock and if you don't move the phone, well, I guess you have already, so hang on."

"Vicki?" Albert feared she had dropped off the call when she realized the situation, but she responded.

"Yes, Professor, I just had to lean over to my other console and do some cover-up work on what Lennie and I did to get the info about this phone." She was gone again. The line was silent for what seemed an eternity. Lennie could be heard breathing. Albert had used up all his reserve patience and was about to scream when Vicki returned.

"Okay, it's covered! I put a silencer on all the signals from the phone. It's black now. No one can see it or hear it. Boy! That was cool!"

"Good! Good!" exclaimed Albert. "Now, don't scare me like that again!"

"Sure, Professor. Sorry!"

"So, both of you, tell me! What does all this mean?"

Lennie started. "Looks top drawer to me. Not the latest, but close. I'd say from the phone records we pulled..."

"Phone records?"

"Oh yeah, forgot to mention the good stuff! We got sidetracked by showing off the GPS thing."

"Lennie! You are killing me!"

Lennie sputtered, "But, but..." Then he heard Albert's laughter, followed by, "Lennie let's start over. Give me an outline, then the

Del Staecker

narrative description of facts, and finish with your conclusion."

Lennie finished for the Professor, adding, "See, I did learn something in your classes!"

Chapter 40

Vicki allowed the more senior Lennie to perform the verbal report. Both Albert and she were impressed with Lennie's professional thoroughness. In response, Albert did a verbal recap for clarification. The professor was always teaching.

"We've got a government-issued phone with exact GPS capability that was live 24/7, meaning whoever gave it to the carrier always knew the location of the phone, and thereby was always able to trail its user. Correct?"

"Correct!"

"The phone was obtained from the manufacturer through the government purchasing system and, based on our best information, was a domestic security rig. We know this because the other phones that called it were both domestic, and the satellite tracking this particular type of chip is predominantly used by FBI and DEA, while they are in-country, and it's not NSA, correct?"

"You got it, correct."

"There is no link that we can find to terrorists and to Homeland Security, correct?"

"Correct."

"The phones it was called from were not calling each other, therefore we can assume one or both of the numbers calling in may not have known about the other, but we cannot be certain, correct?"

"Yes, correct."

"And, you can find one of the callers' phones based on its chip, which you believe is similar and may be from the same organization,

and this is the calling phone that is still very active, correct?"

"Correct!"

"Finally, we need to move fast if we want to use any of this info, correct?"

"Yes, that's correct. We have to assume that the blackout measures we've used, or possibly our multiple queries, will trip a security program. We are outside the usage parameters to a number of the programs. Someone will soon know that we hacked in."

"Oops!" cut in Vicki. "We didn't hack anything! We did an exercise for training. The result was the info, but we were just fishing, just training!"

"Will that cut it?" asked Albert. "Legally?"

"No, but it sounds good!" was Vicki's reply.

"Swell, let's go on. The conclusion is that we have stumbled upon a government operation, maybe a rogue one, but we cannot be certain. We can either proceed with the investigation or bail out now with the hope that we cover our escape route completely. Correct?"

"That's it, correct! I would add that whoever it is that is responsible for the extra cell phone, they have considerable resources. They are government, government-connected, or very rich."

"Excellent work! I am very proud of both of you! If something comes of this I'll fill you in as best I can, but for now, I'll just need to know the location of that phone, the one that is still active."

It was Lennie that replied. "Again, it's no problem, Professor. I'd suggest we ping the location just once. Then we close down everything and make tracks as best we can into cyber nowhere. I've been honored to help you!"

"Me too!" came from Vicki. "I said 'yes' in my head long before Lennie offered his apartment and use of his boat for my mid-winter escape." She giggled, showing a small amount of embarrassment.

"Lennie!" began Albert. "What enticements did you offer?"

"Don't be upset Professor," stepped in Vicki. "I wasn't bribed. Besides, I know Lennie doesn't have a boat and his apartment is a mess—I'd never stay there, but I was flattered."

"Lennie, I sense you two had another agenda going here," said Albert.

"Sorry Professor! She's so cute and I was carried away!"

"Vicki, I'll help Lennie court you by saying thank you as follows: He's a wiz at wallpapering the campus with grant requests, so I'll endorse one that includes you in a winter seminar on tech support as a guest lecturer. How's that?"

"Really!" She was ecstatic. "Professor, thank you! Thank you! Such a spot on one of your programs will fill my presentation requirement for my degree."

"Now disappear. I've got to talk some more with Lennie and your exposure ends now! 'Bye Vicki and thanks again. I'll see you this winter!"

"Good-bye Professor; see you Lennie." And she was gone.

"Lennie, give me one hour to get up a foolproof means of putting a tail on whoever has that phone. I'll call back on a secure line as soon as I can set it up. In the meantime, cover your tracks!"

"I'm on it already!"

"Good. Be ready for my call."

Albert cradled the pay phone, slipped the cell phone into his

pocket, and set out to find Reggie, Sam, and Amelia. He needed to put together a quick plan to spot, tail, and identify whoever had been talking to Otis on a regular basis.

I'm not certain I know what I'm looking for or how it fits into all this, he thought, *but this loose end may unravel something.*

As he approached Sam and Reggie outside Trabue's room he told them, "I may have overreached, but this phone is no run-of-the-mill item. I need your help to make certain we have completed the entire investigation into Karen's death."

Reggie replied, "So, what do you need?"

Albert explained his plans and asked both Reggie and Sam to obtain some more help and some additional equipment.

"Reggie, would you feel alright with Elvira joining in on this?"

"Elvira? Well sure! Just say how and when."

"I need a communication network with local eyes and ears."

In less than an hour they were ready. The Shavers cab drivers were prepared to transport Sam, Reggie, and Albert to any spot within the city. Elvira was set to reach additional spotters. All they needed was the tip-off from Lennie.

Albert placed the call. "Lennie, are you set?" Albert asked.

"Right on! I've prepared an immediate cross reference with the Nashville street map. All I have to do is ping that phone once and I'll give you an exact location."

"I'll need the closest cross streets and any landmarks!"

"No problem! Ready?"

"Do it."

In an instant Lennie responded.

"Professor, I'll skip the coordinates. Here's where the phone is now—it's at Third Avenue between Commerce and Union, mid-block on the right side of the street. I'd guess in a vehicle based on the co-ordinates. I'd say in the passenger's pocket! Good enough?"

"Perfect! Stay with me just a minute." Albert nodded to Reggie who had Elvira on the other line. Reggie gave the information to his talkative spouse. In a moment Reggie was back to Albert with, "Got a friend in the luncheonette at the corner. She's stepping out to take a peek down the street." He paused, waiting for the word or a confirmed sighting. "Okay, Professor, she's got a gray sedan in sight; she'll stick with it."

"Lennie," said Albert, "you go dark now!"

"Done! See ya!" and Lennie was gone.

"Reggie, let me talk to our spotter." Albert reached for Reggie's cell phone adding, "We'll need to get there right away, so I suggest we use Glory Be as the driver. I'll keep my eyes shut."

Sam made the okay sign with his left hand and grabbed his cell to call for a pick-up by his wife. Albert spoke to the onsite scout.

"Tell me. How many people are in the car?"

"Two."

"Both in the front seat?"

"Yes."

"Excellent! Now, is the car pointed north or south and is there anyone parked behind the car?"

He looked at his copy of the city map.

"It's pointed up the street toward the courthouse, I'm not certain, is that north? And there is a vehicle behind them."

"That will do. Just keep watching, but don't give away your activity. We'll be there very soon." Albert looked to Sam.

"Let's go. We can set up the action on the way. And I'll give it a final thumbs up once I'm able to take a look for myself."

Again the ride was quick. But this time Glory Be was silent. She was listening to Albert's instructions. When he finished, she sighed. Everyone was waiting for a burst of her usual, and this time she just sighed. They all knew the job ahead was important.

She dropped Sam, Reggie, and Albert off a block west of the target vehicle on Fourth Avenue. As the trio exited her cab, Glory Be said, "Sam, take care! You hear me! Take care! Look out for Poppa Reggie too! And Professor?"

"Yes, Glory?" Albert answered.

"Do you think I can do this?" her face was not wearing the usual energy-packed smile.

"I'm confident that you can do this, Glory. I've never seen a driver like you before! Have you ever thought of NASCAR?"

She cracked a huge smile. "Sure, I dream about it all the time. Imagine my fan base, got to be millions out there just dying for a black girl to mix it up with all those country white boys!"

Albert couldn't help but laugh.

"Glory Be, you are a wonder, a true Glory! Go on, show your stuff!" He waved her on.

As she sped away, she waved back. Even her simple hand motion had extra energy, and Albert felt the rush.

"Sam, you hook up with the other cab. Reggie, is our spotter still in place?"

"She's there, ahead at the corner, faking a long smoke break."

"Excellent. I'll do a final check and you coordinate the move as soon as I give you the go-ahead signal from my jumping-off spot."

"No problem. Sam and Glory Be should be in place by the time you're set."

Albert reached the corner as the spotter extinguished her smoke and ended her call. To even an expert observer nothing appeared out of the usual.

Albert rounded the corner. Upon seeing the target as described, he scratched his ear and kept walking across the intersection. Reggie took the sign and called for Sam and then Glory to move in with their two cabs.

Too late to stop it now, thought Albert. *I wonder what the penalty is for assaulting a federal agent. No, two federal agents.*

Chapter 41

Sam had a perfect view of Albert walking on the sidewalk, behind the target vehicle. The big man was making his way quickly to the car's door.

Good, he thought, *their view to the rear is blocked by the van behind them; Albert is not visible, or for a man his size, not too visible.*

Sam punched the accelerator and laid on his horn. The target car's occupants were surprised by the screeching of tires as Sam's cab noisily halted next them. The door handles on the cab were less than an inch from their vehicle, trapping them against the curb.

The second part of the surprise was in front of them. Glory Be's cab backed around the corner of the cross street in front of them and sped in reverse toward the parked car. No forward escape for them; they braced for impact. Instead, just as Sam's cab came to a stop, Glory Be's cab did the same. They were pinned in and they knew it.

Their reaction was to look right, toward curbside, for their escape. No luck! The exit route from the hemmed-in car was filled by Albert's large frame.

Boxed in, with escape blocked, they saw the big man reach into his pocket. The man nearest Albert moved for his shoulder-harnessed weapon. Before he could complete his move Albert shouted, "Hold it! I'm not armed!"

The shooter stood down, and slowly Albert extracted the cell phone from his pocket. He showed it to them both.

"Just thought you'd like your phone back!"

The men inside the car were relieved that an altercation was not eminent; however, their faces did not show any positive signs. They were focusing on the phone, viewing it, processing it, trying to put it in the right mental compartment.

"Need some help?" poked Albert. "It belonged to Otis Jackson. But, I believe it was originally yours."

Their faces showed recognition. Albert had their attention.

"No need to be hostile. I'll just slide into the seat behind you and we'll have a talk. They nodded together, signaling approval for Albert to join them in the car. He opened the curbside rear door and slid into the back seat. As he entered the car he moved to wave to Sam. The two men turned to face Albert.

"I'll not need my associates, correct?" asked Albert.

"They can go," was the reply from the driver's side of the car.

"Good, I'll let the street-side escort move on." he finished his signal to Sam. "But first, I'll need you to smile for the lady."

"What?" and "Huh?" came from the front seat at the same moment.

As Sam's cab moved away, Albert motioned for the men to look forward. Glory Be had exited her cab. With camera in hand she boldly walked up to the car, smiling at the occupants of the front seat. Through the driver's side window Glory Be leaned forward and aimed the camera. She snapped a shot of both men.

"I just want a visual record of our meeting. Hope you don't mind. My name's Albert Bryan, what's yours?" He leaned over to see that Glory Be had taken the shot they had discussed. She smiled. He knew she had it. Albert gave her a wave and she smiled again, turned, and returned to her cab.

"Guys, I'd like to make this brief."

Glory Be and her cab drove off. The occupants of the front seat turned around for a second time to face Albert. The scowls on their faces clearly displayed their ill feelings and extreme displeasure over their embarrassing capture.

"We know who you are!" the man on the passenger side exclaimed, "And, the phone is none, I repeat, none of your business!"

"Back up, friend!" was Albert's quick and forceful reply.

"Spare me the synthetic indignation. This is definitely my business! If I can find you, you screwed up; someone else can find you. Maybe Jan Fellows, if she's alive."

He tossed the phone over the front seat with enough speed and force to bounce it off the car's front windows. It landed on the dashboard, then slid to the floor.

"That's your phone! I'm returning it to you since you failed to take it off Otis Jackson's remains. I guess you were so busy taking credit for shooting those two retards that were stuffing him in a trunk that you failed to search his pockets!"

They were silent.

Albert went on. This was one interrogation he enjoyed.

"So," he began, "you were working Jackson, correct?"

They remained silent.

Albert was louder and very insistent. He repeated, "You were working Jackson, correct?"

"Maybe."

"No maybe about it. You gave him a phone. That one!"

"What phone? I don't know anything about a phone."

"Don't get me pissed! That phone is all you. It's been stripped and searched. It leads right here to you. You screwed up by not reclaiming it. I bet you were surprised to see that Otis was dead. You can't work a dead man, can you?"

"His death was not our fault," the driver said.

"So you admit he was yours?"

"I'm just saying we arrived and took out the two who were disposing of the body. That's all. No more, no less."

"I don't think that was all."

"That's all you need to know. Thanks for returning the phone, Professor. We'll be more thorough in the future."

"I thought they taught you better at Quantico."

There was no reply.

Albert assumed that the silence was affirmation that his unwilling hosts were FBI-trained. Albert broke the silence.

"Let's go on, shall we?"

"Nothing to talk about."

"Then let me tell you boys a story. Please stop me if I'm too far off the mark."

There was no reply, so Albert proceeded.

"Once upon a time there was a very slippery crime organization. It was shadowy, vague—almost not there, even if you looked right at it." He paused. There was no sign of recognition, approval, or disapproval, nothing. Albert took it as having started at the right spot. He went on.

"So the organization or whatever you wish to call it just went its merry way with nobody paying it much attention. After all, it was

local. It was not on anyone's radar. It was small time as far as the Feds were concerned."

Albert paused again. He could not perceive anything from his audience. *I must have it right,* he thought. *Or, I'm boring these guys to death.*

He went on. "Then for some reason—maybe the crime organization bribed the wrong congressman, maybe someone whined about lost tax revenue, or—well, it doesn't really matter. Just for some reason the Feds stepped in and checked out this group." He sighed.

"Guys, it's the same old story. You get involved when the street cops—the ones like me—like I was, can't handle the complexity, right?"

With the mention of the complex nature of the shadowy crime organization, Albert's audience responded.

"Okay, so what?"

It was small, but it was a response, and Albert knew he had something right.

"So what?" Albert tossed back the words, "*So what?* People get killed, that's so what!"

"What do you mean by that? Do you think we are responsible?" asked the passenger in the front seat.

"Yes, if you don't act. And you didn't. You had to know. You were working Jackson for a long time. You had him inside the Hart machine for a very long time! Right?"

"Maybe. What difference does it make?" the driver asked.

"All the difference in the world if you die or if a loved one dies. Ask Win Blaine about losing his daughter. Ask the kid who bobbed and bloated in the river!"

"There was a lot to learn. Jackson was in. But we were never certain that he was totally reliable. We waited. The risks seemed to be acceptable."

"To who? You? Not them! Not them!"

"Professor, you said it! You said it yourself—it's very complex. There is a lot at stake here—it's very complex."

"Try me!" demanded the Professor.

"There are several agencies involved. Everyone eventually gets the scent of a crime operation once it passes a certain point. If it's too big, if it launders too much cash, if it avoids too many taxes, or if it pushes on the wrong people."

"So?"

"So, there are fifty or more agents poking around—tax types, drug types, all the flavors of the federal law establishment, not to mention the state ones. It's complicated."

"You're telling me that the law machine is too complex to act?"

"No, we act. We act all the time when we get the go-ahead. It's complicated."

"You're incredible! You aren't cops! You aren't real to me!"

Albert knew that he was wasting his time looking for answers with these two. They were part of a machine that competed with the Harts. Lines between good and bad were blurred in their world.

"Professor, you're wrong. You're wrong because you don't know what you're really dealing with. End of statement, end of interview. It's over and good-bye!"

"You're right! But I'll decide when my part is over. It will be over

when I know everything I need to know. Maybe I won't learn it from you. Maybe it will take time. But I'll know!"

"Like, I said, Professor, you have no idea of who or what you're dealing with."

"I'll find out! That's what I do." Albert said it, but felt the hollowness of his words. *Can you ever know?* he asked himself.

Albert got out and headed to the cross street behind the interview's location. Reggie and Sam were waiting for him in the Shavers Express.

"You get what you wanted?" asked Reggie.

"Don't know. I'll probably never know for certain. As the man said, it's very complex."

Reggie put the cab in motion.

Albert instructed him. "Go past our pals on the way to *The Nashvillian.* I want them to know I'm a presence to contend with—somebody who will not just go away."

"I'll do the slow roll just to make a point."

As the cab passed the parked car, Reggie eased by at a snail's pace. Albert looked over. Two average faces looked back. "Xerox faces," remarked Albert.

"There goes a guy who thinks he knows what he knows," remarked the driver.

"The professor and his friend Trabue could be a problem. Think we should report this up the chain?" his companion asked.

"No! I've told you, stuff like this leads to more stuff like this. We're too close to retirement and the good life to do anything that will keep interest alive in what's happened."

"I just hope you're right. You know how the man at the top hates surprises."

"We've handled worse problems."

"If Trabue hadn't found her..."

"It would have still played out. Everything happens for a reason. Don't ever forget who you really work for."

Chapter 42

"How do you find anything?" asked Albert. He was looking at the pile known as Patterson's desk. "Does the Health Department know about this?"

"It's become a trademark. I'm not allowed to clean it up. The PR department brings tours through just to look at it," joked the reporter.

Patterson was bent over a cabinet behind the desk area searching for a couple of Styrofoam cups. He had offered Albert a drink upon the Professor's arrival and was trying to meet his obligation. The trouble was the mess. He could not locate his stash of cups.

"I know they're here—got 'em!"

He filled both cups with a mixture of coffee, cream, and a liquor that bore a Mexican label.

"Great stuff. The only positive thing to come from my misdirected excursion!"

"That's what worried me, your excursion," began Albert. "I gave your name to Trabue. He stopped in with a request, and *boom!* You disappear. What happened? How did you blow it? How did you miss being in on the biggest story in decades for Nashville?"

"Yeah, I missed it alright! The richest, most-under-the radar business man in the region is killed on his yacht. His daughter is missing and presumed dead. His son-in-law's remains are so disfigured that he needs a closed casket ceremony. An Assistant Chief of Police is killed. And out-of-town pro killers are blamed. It's big alright, the biggest—and I missed it!"

"How?"

"Ego, that's how!" Patterson took a big swallow and fixed himself another round. "Pure, simple, ego."

"Fill me in. It sounds interesting, maybe even tragic."

Albert tasted the concoction and decided he'd not go any further with it.

"Jan gave me the lead. I had cornered her at a community luncheon with a pointed set of questions concerning Karen Blaine and Jan's hubby. She played me. Boy, did she play me!" Patterson drained his cup again.

Before he could pour another round, Albert gave him the sign for no more.

"Why the concern? You and your pal, Trabue, solved the girl's murder."

"The story really begins or ends right here," said Albert. "Right here." He placed a small computer disc on Patterson's desk in the one spot clean enough for placing an important item.

"What's on it?"

"An interview. More like a conversation or exchange. It's a beginning, or, like I said, maybe it's the end. I can't say."

"Sorry, I'm a bit slow. Maybe it's this cup of Mexican juice. What exactly is on the disc?"

"A favor, that's what is there. A favor for you to perform. Call it payback for running to Texas or Mexico, or wherever it was Jan got you to visit."

"Fine! But please stop with making me feel like an idiot about Mexico. I thought I had the goods on John Fellows. You know, a real

scandal being squashed and me being able to uncover it. It would make a real headliner, and I need that. My column is slipping. Hell! The whole paper is slipping. No! The whole damn paper business is going down the tubes. Can't blame me for trying, can you?"

"No, no. I understand. You're a desperate man. Look at your desk. If this isn't desperation, then what is?" Albert chided.

They both laughed.

"Seriously, do you only chase stories now? How about doing some real work?"

"The favor?"

"Yep!"

"Explain."

"The disc has some conversation on it. You listen. Put two and two together. See what you think." Albert reached into his pocket and placed another disc next to the first one. "This has a photo on it. Just one photo. It's two regular-looking guys in a car. They may need some looking into."

"You know who they are?"

"Listen to the conversation. Take it from there, alright?"

"Yeah, sure, sure! Then what?" Patterson asked.

"Then you personally take the two discs to this address with this note. Do it quick! I'm asking you because I do not trust anyone, or any organization, to get it done. But, this calls for a hand delivery."

Albert handed the note to Patterson. Patterson looked at it, looked at Albert, and looked back at the note.

"Are you in some kind of danger? Is that why you want me to step in with this?" Patterson reached for a third drink.

"No, I do not feel threatened, as we speak."

"Then why this?" He pointed to the note.

"I'm just being cautious. And being a good citizen. If the higher-ups know what's going on, fine! I'm just a quirky pain in the ass. But, if these guys are off the reservation, then I've got some back-up. And if I do get hurt, there's someone who may show an interest. You get another chance, another tip. Call it my gift to you."

"I'll do it. I'll make certain this gets to the intended audience sooner, not later. Matter of fact, after missing all the action, I've been encouraged to take some additional time off. A trip to our nation's capital is just what I need."

"Thanks! I hope this is just my overreaction. I've been sitting up a lot, watching over Trabue, maybe I've over-analyzed things, wanting to tie everything together when there's no situation where everything fits. It's just that here and there, a loose end pops out of this simple investigation into the death of a young woman. The street cop in me wants the bad guys to fail and for the town folks to be safe. Our side won and I hope there's nobody looking for a rematch."

"So, what's your next step?"

"None. I'm not taking any more steps with this investigation. That's your call. I'm satisfied with the basic crime answers, we got the simple bad guys, and now I'm planning to enjoy my friend's company and help him heal. He's been through a lot. We're taking a boat trip on the Tenn-Tom waterway headed back to New Orleans."

Albert rose, shook Patterson's hand and departed. He left behind a shaken reporter, slightly drunk, sitting amidst a pile of trash masquerading as a work space.

Patterson muttered, "Maybe I'll sniff this lead. Maybe I won't. Hell, my last trip was just as ill-advised. Look what it got me."

He reached for the bottle, poured another large portion and quickly downed it. When he leaned back in his chair to doze he nudged the disc and it slid off the desk. Nestled in the pile, the disc found a home amongst the debris.

Chapter 43

Reggie was slumped in the back seat of the Shavers Express. He was asleep and looked worn out. Inside the cab, Albert asked of Sam, "Did Reggie fill you in on his plans?"

"He gave me the news and said he'd take a nap. Early retirement, he called it."

"He's serious, you know? He's letting you run the business and he's going to take Elvira fishing."

"He deserves it. But he's not taking Elvira near any body of water. She is strictly a land animal. She's also superstitious when it comes to things related to the water. She and Aunty think the girl they found in the water, the one whose death started all this..."

"Her name was Karen Blaine; let's not forget her," Albert reminded Sam.

"Well, Aunty thinks Karen was a mermaid or a water witch."

"How about an unlucky victim of some really bad people?"

"That'll do," agreed Sam. "Anyway, I think Aunty was stretching the mermaid thing a bit. Too much TV and crosswords jumbled in her mind. She can't see what this was all about."

Looking directly at Albert he asked, "What exactly is this all about, anyway? What did we get into? When Glory Be picked me up last week near the marina when those two killers came after Trabue and I was almost shot, I was shaken up, *really* shaken up!"

"It's perfectly reasonable to feel that way, Sam. Violence—or even the threat of it, is not pleasant. It shakes you up. It is violent!"

"Well I've seen and done my share of violence. But, that day I was

seeing it clearly, seeing it up close for the first time. I didn't like it. It shook me up because it was real and right in front of me. I could have been one of those guys, but I'm not. Elvira, Aunty, Dad, and Glory Be love me. I made a choice not to be like the guys who killed Karen and the others. That, I understand. But today, I don't understand. Why those guys? Why the phone? Why?"

"Nothing is as simple as it appears, even something as real, as right in your face, as those two killers were the day you stepped in and saved Trabue. It's complicated!" Albert grinned.

Sam looked puzzled and a little hurt.

"Sorry, Sam! It's just that I've heard it described that way already today. Let me explain as best as I can. We, or should I say Trabue, started out to solve the mystery of Karen's death. Along the way he enlisted friends like me, and he found a set of allies, like you, Amelia, and your family. All of us, in our own way, were trying to help Trabue make sense out of what was basically an evil thing. Your Aunt's explanation may be a bit out there, but for her it explains things. People are happy with the explanations they invent."

"So why today? What's your full explanation of Jackson and the phone?"

"It'll never be fully explained. I believe we were dealing with two forms of human activity—the Harts and something else. I think Jan and her father were as bad as bad gets. For a long time they stayed undercover, lied, pulled strings—called the shots on a lot of nasty activities."

"Like hiring the pair to go after Trabue?"

"Yes, they usually got someone else to be the muscle. Jan was a bona-fide sicko. Jan liked to get her hands dirty. It probably goes back deep in her. She had the need to hurt—she had the type of mind I could study for quite some time. But, I really don't want any more of her type."

"Do you expect things to change with them gone?"

"Yes and no, as they say. Crime, the kind they were behind, will be less organized around here, for a while. That's where the phone fits in, I think. The phone led me to the other organization."

"The other organization?"

"Yes, everything in life competes. I said there were two forms of activity. In this case both forms had their representatives. Jan and her father's enterprises were on one side and some form of the law, or government, was on the other. At least that is what I think."

"So, what's the difference? You seemed pretty ticked all of today. And you were, are, a cop. So, why the drama? Why the scene today with the guys in the car?"

"Maybe I was expressing my own opinion and trying to make it all fit my reality. I was mad. Still am mad. Trabue is in the hospital, Jackson is dead, and Eddie is dead too! Karen's death might have been avoided. Maybe all of this could have been avoided. Who can tell? Who can say how many people would still be alive if the so-called good guys, the government, had been more forceful and quicker in acting. Maybe I want too much out of people and the structures they establish."

Albert sighed. He was a weary warrior.

"Maybe I want the competing organizations to stay pure, keeping the fight focused and fast-paced. I just hate to think that some

committee, or bureaucracy, or agency was thinking of budgets, reports, and planning documents and not about real live people. It's good versus bad, no matter how we dress it up. There can never be a truce between virtue and vice. There's no clear-cut end that I know of. It can get personal, too! My life was at stake and I don't want to be just a statistic," Albert stated.

"It was real. Like I said about those two guys. For me, that day, it was real," offered Sam, "and for you it was real too! Not movie make-believe. Not some paperback thriller."

"Yeah, it was very real and simple. Easy to understand at the gut level, but remember I said it's still complicated?"

"There's more?"

"As much as you care to make of it. Nothing is as simple as it first appears. Look at the unique chain of events that got us all together. A lot of simple things all jumbled together—that's complexity!"

"So you're saying it's not over?" Sam looked puzzled again.

"No, I'm saying it goes as far and wide as you are willing to look. Eventually everything is interconnected. You can go on forever, or you can stop wherever and however you wish. Your Aunty stops with her mermaid tale. Win Blaine stops with knowing who killed his daughter and feeling the comfort that the killers are gone too."

"Where do you stop?"

"I stop when Trabue stops calling me!"

"What do you mean?"

"He's a good version of a black hole. He sucks in all that is good. Trabue attracts people worth knowing. Look at us! We are an odd lot. Who else could have pulled us all together, except Trabue! He's a touchstone for good. And I can't help but think that all of what happened took place for some purpose."

"Please!" came from the back seat. Reggie shifted his position and continued, "My head hurts with all your talk. This retiree needs a real bed for his first official retirement nap. Sam, take me home!"

Pointing at the passenger in the rear, Albert smiled at Sam. "See! Everyone has a comfort point within their own reality!"

Sam reached over to engage the meter. "Here's my reality." He looked into his mirror, caught his father's eye and asked, "You prepared to pay for this fare, Mr. Shavers?"

Before Reggie could respond, Albert pulled out his wallet and said, "This one is on me."

Chapter 44

Trabue remembered giving his guardian angel the finger.

Not such a good idea, he dreamed.

Later, totally awake but a little groggy, he recognized Albert as his watchful guardian.

"Don't apologize about the gesture," was Albert's comment. "I got over it. I'm just glad you're back. You have been gone for quite some time."

"How long?"

"Five days, and then some," was the answer.

"How are you doing?"

"I had one hell of a headache. But, I'm fine. You were the one we were worried about."

"We?"

"The five of us—Win, Amelia, Sam, Reggie, and me. And, of course, the entire Shavers Cab Company family!"

"Win, Amelia?" Trabue's worry rushed out.

"They're fine. They woke up in Amelia's bed with the same headache I had. Jan's plan was for them to take the fall for Otis' death. You've got to admit it, that she-devil had a sense of irony. Imagine the headlines—Outdoorsy Redneck Found in Bed with African-American Police Chief's Physician Wife, Corpse Nearby."

Trabue attempted to sit up.

"Whoa there, big boy!" Albert rushed to the bed. "You're not doing anything until the good doctor checks you out."

He scampered out the door to find some help. Trabue was deeply touched by Albert's concern. "Five days! That's a lot of worry time," he muttered.

Albert, Amelia, and Win entered the room. "Looks as if my patient is going to make it!" Amelia beamed. She was radiant.

Win leaned in to touch Trabue's arm. "Welcome back!" He was a different Win. Trabue did not see Karen's ghost haunting him.

"Hi! I'm sorry not to get up, but I'm glad to be here. What happened? Where are Toto and Aunty Em?"

They smiled. Amelia replied for the group.

"We'll let Albert explain, but not now. You need rest and a lot of it. Come on, Win, I've got to examine his charts and confer with the attending. Albert, please take care not to excite him." She grabbed Win's hand and led him out.

"Did I miss something?" asked Trabue. He watched their obvious closeness and affection.

"There's nothing to miss. They are a real item. I assume waking up in the buff was okay with them. It's a joy to see love in the flesh."

"I'm just glad to see anything. I've got to admit, they look fantastic. Tell me what I've missed in almost a week."

"Nothing much to tell. We knocked over the biggest crime ring in a dozen states, saved the new couple, solved a few murders. You know, the usual." He grinned.

"Really, what's the final score?"

"We started out to solve Karen's murder and that we did. Jan and Otis ordered it. Jenkins and Powell did the dirty work. It was all the news. Detective Evans got the credit for breaking the case."

"Evans? You mean..."

"Yeah, Doorstop. Even a blind pig finds the truffle. He did the only thing a rookie could do. He fingerprinted everything in Karen's life and by chance the odd couple, the big one and his greasy little friend, left some traces of their work."

"They in jail?"

"Nope, the morgue."

"What came down?"

"After they left the yacht with a dead Otis, the duo headed for the dock. They were going to set up Jan's sex party joke at the Jackson condo. They were stuffing the deceased Assistant Chief of police into the trunk of a car when a gray sedan with two FBI agents arrived. The duo became Dead-and-Deader when they drew down on the Feds."

"Gray Sedan? The one Reggie kept noticing?"

"Yeah, your tail."

"FBI?"

"FBI, as best I can figure. They'd been sniffing around the Hart-Fellows organization for quite some time. They probably had strict orders not to blow their investigation. I confronted the pair with a lot of help from Sam and Reggie. I reamed them over their role as peeping Toms. This whole thing is wrapped up as far as the man on the street wants to know, but you know me; I'll be chewing on this one for a long time. You and I need to re-hash it and re-live it. We were bait and I don't like being chum, no matter how noble the cause."

"We were expendable."

"Yes! Expendable. Truth be told, you and I were just part of the game. My esteemed federal colleagues, of whatever alphabet soup-named agency you prefer, were so hot to nab Hart and his crew that they endangered this distinguished author, professor, and criminologist extraordinaire."

"Wind bag and fat ass, you mean."

Albert laughed. "Only you are allowed such liberties." His face changed. "This was serious. You were the vortex of something that defies explanation. The events are only a projection of some hidden forces drawing or pushing us in, like Eddie."

"Eddie? What about Eddie? He seemed like such a regular guy around the docks. I was way off on him, right?"

"Maybe, maybe not. Like I was trying to say, he may have been drawn in. The guy was way out of his league. His body was found floating in the marina."

"Sad to know that you never can tell about the folks you see every day. He looked lost, always lost."

"Well, he wasn't lost for long. In a manner of speaking, he made it home. Like I said, Eddie drifted into the marina and was found at the end of his own dock. He made it home."

"Did they find Forsythe, too?"

"Forsythe? No! He's still missing. You got any ideas?"

"Look on the cliff, the second crate on the right as you approach from the water. He should be real ripe by now."

"I'll send the information on to Evans. The experience will, how do we say, season him."

"You like the kid?"

"Not as dumb as he appears. Kind of like you."

"Thank you, Albert. You can insult me any time."

"Don't worry, I will."

"I'm just glad we are alive. If I hadn't called you, I'm certain I would have screwed this thing up. My stomach was churning. I sensed the danger, but never thought it could be so bizarre."

"Well, we didn't wrap up all the stray lines. There are some that will never be tidy. But all in all, we were a B-plus effort."

"Thanks again, Professor. Did we make, or avoid, the papers?"

"We're pretty clean as far as public awareness is concerned, mostly due to the cloudy nature of that last night's sequence of events. With you out—and to be fair, I was not all there for most of it—the authorities could only hope to put the big pieces together. The real kicker is that Hart and company came out with a neutral legacy."

"Neutral! Come on! We saw and fought with real crap."

"Hold it, hold it. We won." He explained further. "Think about it, John Fellows was found the next day dead, at home."

"What?"

"Forgive me. I forgot that small detail."

"I guess when Jan said she left him at home, it was for good."

"Appears so. And I'm as sorry a reporter as Patterson. He tossed out the biggest lead of his career when he blew you off. Jan sent him on a wild goose chase when he queried her at some charity event. He's apologetic and owes us big time."

"Go on, finish with what happened with..."

"...our little adventure in recreational boating?"

Trabue rolled his eyes, saying, "Is any of this serious to you?"

"Dead serious. Just my way of dealing with almost losing my best audience. God, it is good to see you cranky!" He went on. "Remember, everyone was floating around in the river. Lawrence Hart was dead. He drew his last breath before he hit the water. My girth saw to that. Trust me, I will never forget the crunch from the collapse of his rib cage as we sailed through the railing of his yacht. He was the bug and I was the windshield."

"Sorry, Al, it must have been terrible!"

"Yeah, but I'll get over it."

"You sure?"

"No."

"Maybe we should finish later."

"I've shared worse with you before. Let's get this behind us." Albert continued, "Jan's idiot husband may be a homicide or a suicide. He was found with no face—shotgun blast. He was almost The Headless Horseman, a real mess! But who cares? If it's a murder, Jan was most likely behind it. She may have been tired of him. She may have been eyeing Otis as the next pony to ride. He may have ended it himself. We'll never know for certain. Like I said, we noodle it some more and later, we close the book when we are satisfied. We've done it many times before with our other experiences. Anyway, Jan is probably crab meat."

"Probably? Haven't they found her?"

"Not yet. I'll be a lot happier when she's found. But, let me finish! In any event, John Fellows died and left a ton of money to the Community Foundation. Same for Lawrence Hart. When they find and declare Jan dead, her money also goes for good causes. Now tell me what's so wrong with that?"

"Nothing. I guess I can take it as it is. We'd be in a perfect world if the good guys pitched no-hitters all the time. Just as long as we can say Karen's death is solved, I'm fine. I feel that she has finally spoken."

"We did solve the puzzle of her death. I always will suspect there is more. Things like this usually lead to more related things. The connections go on in ways we never imagine. But, I can stop. If you say so we can claim a victory. Maybe it isn't a no-hitter, just a shutout."

"So, what's still bothering you?"

"I hate being ignorant of my own ignorance. You taught me how to see that flaw in myself when you were a kid. So, I'll chew on it all. You know me."

The door swung open and Win Blaine appeared.

"Hey," interrupted Win, as he came in looking back over his shoulder. He reached toward Trabue and smiled from ear to ear.

"Here, I want you to have this." He handed an envelope to Trabue. Inside was a check made out to R.C. Trabue for $100,000.

"What's this?"

"My thanks. Forsythe had a company group life insurance policy. That's Karen's. I want you to have it."

"No can do. It's yours."

"I've put my share in a scholarship at her high school. I don't want to benefit in any way from what happened."

"Well, neither do I."

"It's your problem."

Trabue paused and looked to Albert. "Got a pen?"

Trabue grabbed the one offered and jotted a note on the check and then signed it.

"Here," he said, giving it back. "Give this to Reggie."

Win read the note above the signature: Pay to Blaine & Trabue Investments, R.E. Shavers, Inc.

"What's this mean?"

"You and I are partners."

"Partners? In what?"

"Tell Reggie that we're investing in his new transportation division. Sam is going to run it."

Before they could add anything else they were interrupted by Amelia.

"Out! Out now! All of you! If I'm going to become a practicing physician in a small town, I need to stop being an M.E. and become a nag. I expect total, and I mean total compliance with my directives! Win, get moving! Albert, good-bye! Trabue, rest! Now! All of you pack it in!"

Win scampered out, faking a whipped puppy look.

Albert waved as he headed for the door, and Trabue rolled over and assumed the fetal position in a mocking act of submission. Amelia smiled in appreciation of their efforts.

"You guys! Go!" she repeated. "My patient needs rest."

Albert offered a parting shot, "Before I exit, I want you to speed up the recovery, my lad. I've told the University of South Florida to be flexible for the remainder of this term. Trabue, you and I have a boat trip to take—a long, slow cruise to The Big Easy. You're needed at the hotel. Business is picking up at the loveable old dump you call home. Mrs. K. has been doing a great job running the place. But, she has instructed me to, 'get him cured, rested and home.' As soon as

Amelia gives you an all clear we pull anchor. The *Awfria* is headed home!"

Epilogue

Good-byes had been said. They were brief, sincere, and tear-laden.

The *Awfria*, sitting low in the water of the Cumberland River, was weighted with Albert's gourmet provisions and was headed home. The twin diesels purred. The weather was perfect.

Having volunteered for the dual role of deckhand and chef, Albert was in the galley making jazz-like noises and preparing the first of many memorable meals. He had temporarily abandoned all thoughts about recent events and looked forward to seeing New Orleans again.

Trabue was at the helm of his home on the water.

Ahead, a cluster of boats circled about a semi-submerged tree. The spot was familiar to Trabue. It was there that he had first seen Karen.

Trabue slowed his craft and brought it past the assembly without a wake. Cal Peters was at work, retrieving another bobber. Cal recognized Trabue and waved.

At the waterline of Cal's boat, tangled in an array of long black hair and tree branches, was Jan Hart Fellows. Her still-too-familiar face was discolored and her body bloated. She was a dead spider in a dark web.

"She's gone," Trabue assured himself.

He increased the throttles and the *Awfria* moved on.

Albert had been correct. The boat did bring adventures into life. Trabue focused his gaze ahead and proceeded on course. Much lay ahead.

★ ★ ★ ★ ★

Behind them, at the cluster of boats, Cal Peters secured Jan's body to his skiff.

"No doubt about the identity," he remarked. "You can't mistake that hair." Reaching over to his passenger, he said, "Here, Dr. Osbourne, you'd better make the call."

Over a thousand miles to the southwest, on a beach along the gulf coast of Mexico, a cell phone imbedded with a matching chip vibrated.

"Yes," was the curt greeting.

"We found her."

"Are you certain?"

"No mistake; it's her!"

As he spoke, Osbourne strained to get a view of the *Aufria* disappearing down river. "And our curious troublemakers seem to have departed. We won't be seeing them again."

"You'd better be certain!"

"We're finished here."

"Then clean up the mess. There will be no contact until I'm ready to return."

Osbourne attempted no response. He had his assignment and handed the phone back to his companion. Looking at the water he spoke. "Peters, tag her and let's get out of here!"

★ ★ ★ ★ ★

In Mexico, the man with a bruised and bandaged face headed off the beach with a distinctive pigeon-toed gait.

John Fellows murmured to himself. "*Yes, Mr Hart!* You can do anything you want, as long as no one knows about it." Grinning, he continued, "Still, I must be careful. The plastic surgeon warned that even the sun's angled morning rays could irritate my skin."

Coming Soon!

The exciting sequel to *The Muted Mermaid:*

Shaved Ice

There's been a shooting, and my friends were involved. The words ricocheted through Ledge Trabue's head as he read and re-read the shocking message sent from Nashville. How…and more importantly …why…had this tragedy happened? It simply made no sense.

Trabue and his close friend Albert are whisked away by military helicopter and soon find themselves back in Nashville, trying to separate good from evil while struggling to cope with their grief. Gradually, as they piece the puzzling bits of evidence together, they realize that the incredible evil of the Hart-Fellows empire has somehow found new life and is now, impossibly, hiding in plain sight.

Please check our website for updates on this and other news:
cablepublishing.com

TO ORDER ADDITIONAL COPIES OF

The Muted Mermaid

Fax orders: 715-372-8448

Telephone orders: 715-372-8499

E-mail orders: nan@cablepublishing.com

Postal orders: Cable Publishing, 14090 E Keinenen Rd, Brule, WI 54820

Name: _____

Address: _____

City: _____ State: _____ Zip: _____

Telephone: _____

E-mail address: _____

_____ Number of copies at $24.95 each $ _____

Sales tax: *Please add 5.5% for Wisconsin addresses* $ _____

Shipping: _____
($3.50 for the first book, $.50 for each additional book)

Total order: $ _____

Payment: ☐ Check or ☐ Visa ☐ MC ☐ AMEX ☐ Discover

Card number: _____

Name on card: _____ Exp. date: _____